DANGEROUS

Allies

Julie Verne

When murder comes knocking, Naomi hears it all

DANGEROUS
Allies

Julie Verne

PUBLISHER'S NOTE

About the Author

Julie Verne is a queer, disabled Australian author. She mostly writes romance fiction with some crime as a little treat. She enjoys hiking and being a lesbian stereotype. She lives with a millennial cockatoo, enjoys reading and is completely normal about a lot of things. Website: https://thejulieverne.com

CHAPTER ONE

It started with the shutters. Well, when asked, that was what she remembered.

What it actually started with, like most things for Diana, was murder.

* * *

Detective Diana Stapleton sighed as she pulled up to the crime scene: lights and sirens, the crackle of radios as officers coordinated around the property, floodlights on to chase out the darkness. She checked her face in the rearview mirror and tied her hair into a ponytail. She wasn't sure why she still took night calls. Still, they'd asked specifically for her. Suspected murder, and an uncooperative witness. She shrugged on her heavy coat, shivering a little in the fall air, and fastened her scarf a little closer around her neck to keep the cold from creeping in.

The house was large and set well back from the road. She made her way to the tape and announced herself to the officer maintaining the perimeter, eyeing the house disdainfully. Ostentatious. Probably murdered by a relative who thought they were due to inherit. Most of these people tried to take as much as they could with them, though, rather than upkeep their investments. She nodded to the detectives on scene and took a more careful look at the house: crumbling facade, gutters falling away from the roof, moss clinging to downpipes. The little signs of disrepair—overgrown garden, window frames gaping away from the stone, unkempt garden beds.

Detective Frank Busco was at the front door, and Diana gloved up, slipping disposable booties from the box by the door over her boots. It was cold inside as well, with the doors open. The houses in this neighborhood were old and had been renovated in the '70s and '80s, when people had that kind of money. There were a lot of lime greens and patterned linoleum. The garish wallpaper grated as she peered through the door.

She entered and took a cursory look at the body. The coroner, Daisy, was already hunched over it like a crow. The younger woman—too young for her morbid career, Diana had thought initially—was large and vaguely menacing. Diana liked her. She was quiet, and her reports were always thoughtful. She seemed to like Diana too, or at least hate her less than anyone else on the squad. She deigned to speak to Diana, at least. They weren't the kind of friends that would catch up outside of work, but they were friendly enough. Their silences were comfortable; they had nothing to prove to each other.

"We don't need you here, Detective," Detective Percy Hamilton said, walking over to stop her approaching his crime scene. The body lay at the bottom of a flight of stairs, a broken railing evident on the floor above.

"Trip and fall?" Diana asked, eyeing the neck. The angle looked unnatural. "No, thrown over—" Diana looked to the upstairs landing, calculating the angle. "From up there."

"We don't actually need your help with the body," Hamilton said, looking annoyed. He was young, newly promoted to the homicide team, and had been trying to grow a mustache for a while. It was his case, and he was right—she'd been called in because of something only she could do. She peeled off her disposable gloves in favor of the warmer leather ones she'd tucked into her pocket at the door, then leaned against the doorframe.

"Then why am I here?"

"Witness. Next door. No one's been able to interview her, but she called it in twice. Once early yesterday morning, and again a couple of hours ago. Uniforms came for the welfare check and found him like this. Coroner said it was suspicious, and here we are."

With a nod and another careful look at the decaying decor, Diana left.

Officer Andy Newton was still standing by the tape with the crime scene entry paperwork on his clipboard, maintaining the perimeter and signing people in and out.

"Witness?"

He pointed at the house next door. Tall fences, offset property. Set back from the road, lots of trees. Security cameras were evident on the stone wall, mounted high on the outside of the building and next to the gate. Almost a fortress. Diana could tell it was in much better repair than the neighboring building.

She approached and pressed a button next to the gate, looking through the wrought iron, aware she was probably being watched. She pushed her coat back so the badge on her belt was visible. Lights came on inside the gate, illuminating the path with an orange, lamplight glow. Overgrown trees lined the cobblestone path, and for a moment Diana was reminded of a book she'd been read as a child.

"Be there in a minute." The quiet, disembodied voice came from the speaker in the gatepost. Diana eyed it with a measure of distrust, then turned her attention back to the front door, partially obscured by trees. There was movement as the door opened and someone came down the walk, then paused out of eyeshot before stepping onto the path.

Diana glimpsed her then, from between the trees, like something from a fairy tale, dark-red hair caught in the breeze like a thick stain of blood, like the casting of a spell. Diana squinted through the mist curling around the strange witness. There was an old Irish myth about women who would portend the death of a loved one with a scream—it wasn't selkies, those were Scottish. And kelpies were those bog-horses as well as some kind of Australian dog. Banshees. That was what she reminded Diana of. A portent of death. All cloaked in black, with Doc Martens boots and a wariness to her face that made Diana force herself to relax.

She resisted the urge to chuckle. It was fall. It was night. It was, all things being equal, quite a spooky situation. The heavy Gothic overlook of the house must be getting to her. She was just tired, only half-awake from another poor night's sleep.

The woman didn't come any closer, and Diana watched her curiously, the way she would watch a deer in the woods. Camouflaged against the night and the red and gold of the falling leaves, Diana might not have known she was there, save for her pale face looming in the shadows. Diana tilted her head back in acknowledgment, waiting for her to approach.

Hamilton had called her in because she knew American Sign Language. From this distance, sign would carry in a way spoken words would not.

She moved her hand into a wave to signal *hello*, then removed her gloves so she could finger spell her name, leading with the sign for *police*.

A look of relief came over the other woman's face, and she took a step forward. She was dressed for the cold, with thick gloves that would muffle the way she used them to speak. Headphones covered her head under the hood, and she eyed Diana dubiously as she finally approached. A heavy coat and scarf engulfed her, breath huffing out into a thin mist that she moved through as she came closer. Despite her own coat, Diana shivered in sympathy. There was something eldritch about all this—the predawn air, the chill, the dew on the plants that brushed the woman's coat, leaving shimmering patches on the thick wool that caught the eerie light.

Prepared, the woman took a piece of paper from her pocket and shoved it through the gate, waiting anxiously with her hand outstretched until Diana took it.

Diana scanned it quickly, aware of the other woman's eyes on her. Some kind of disability, hearing sensitivity and a migraine—she could look up the details later. She digested the woman's statement, nodding. She went to speak, but the woman—Naomi Happleburn, according to the note—drew away. Diana held the paper out as a question. When Naomi shrugged, she slid it into a pocket. Diana pulled a business card from her pocket and handed it over. Naomi took it, looked it over in the dim light, and tucked it away.

More window noise than usual? Diana signed, careful not to let her doubt show in her face as she gauged the distance between the houses.

More, Naomi agreed, making the gesture bigger, more emphatic.

Diana looked again at the neighboring property before signaling Naomi to wait as she walked back to the road to use her car radio. She signed a quick *sorry*, then lifted the radio to her mouth.

"Sometime in the next, say, thirty seconds, someone close a shutter?"

"She actually spoke to you?" Hamilton said, and Diana saw Naomi flinch, then held down the transmission button so no more noise would come from the set. She lifted her other hand so she could see the hands on her watch move, counting seconds. Naomi flinched again, although Diana heard nothing. She counted off another ten seconds, then cupped the speaker of the radio to muffle it.

"Ten seconds ago?"

"'Bout that."

"She's legit. I'll question her, find out what else she heard." Diana turned off the radio. She looked over at the bustle of the crime scene with a sense of detachment, then locked the car and went back to the gate where Naomi waited.

More? Different? Diana asked, and Naomi nodded. *How?* Diana continued, putting her fists together, thumbs up, moving her right hand forward.

Naomi took a deep breath in, then reached for the gate. Diana expected it to squeak from disuse, but obviously Naomi wouldn't have a squeaky gate if she could hear a shutter closing twenty yards away.

Edging away from the open gate, Naomi indicated that Diana should come in.

Looking back at the road, Diana felt very isolated. She waved an arm at Andy, then pointed at the house, waiting until he nodded that he understood she was going inside. He'd be the last one off the scene, so he would at least buzz Naomi's gate if Diana's car was still there when everyone else left.

She let her hand brush her service pistol, the cool metal reassuring to her bare, cold fingers before she slid them back into the warmth of her coat pockets. Giving the glowing lights of the squad cars a last longing glance, she stepped through the open gate, watching as Naomi closed it behind them.

The path to the house was slippery, and Diana was careful placing her feet to reduce the crunch of freshly fallen leaves as well as to keep her footing. She followed Naomi closely, wondering what she needed to say that she couldn't say outside. Although, with the temperature in the high twenties, Diana couldn't blame her for wanting to go in.

A wave of warmth exuded from the building when Naomi opened the front door. Diana followed her lead and sat on a wooden bench in the foyer to pull off her wet boots. She took off her coat and hung it beside Naomi's, then waited patiently for Naomi to indicate what she needed. Naomi looked nervous as she beckoned Diana to follow her down the hall.

The inside of this house was vastly different from the neighboring property: walls limned in soft downlights; the wood a deep, luxurious mahogany with brass fixtures; deep carpeting with underfloor heating, deliciously warm and soft against the soles of Diana's socked feet. She could understand why Naomi preferred to do the interview inside her own comfortable home. She couldn't hear any of the crime scene chatter—the windows were clearly double glazed at least, and Diana doubted she would be able to hear even a car door slam outside.

She followed Naomi to the kitchen, careful of her footfalls as the hallway carpeting gave way to tile. Naomi held up a box of instant coffee sachets that jarred against the surrounding opulence. Diana considered the noise of a coffee machine, the sound of beans grinding, the hiss of a milk steamer. She nodded, and Naomi poured two mugs, adding water that steamed straight from the tap, stirring with an unusual-looking spoon that made no noise against the side of the mug.

Diana examined her mug when it was handed over; there was a silicone ring on the base to muffle any noise it might make when it descended on a surface. When she sipped, the coffee was richer than she'd expected—dark and warming with a light hazelnut aftertaste. Sitting down in the offered chair at the kitchen table, she faced her witness.

The headphones remained on, but without the scarf covering part of her face Diana could see the other woman better. She was short—shorter than Diana, in fact—with the kind of thin frame someone frail typically had. Diana had presumed her to be elderly, but she was probably a few years younger than Diana's own fifty-one years. She had deep-brown eyes that were startlingly dark against her pale skin. Her teeth were straight at the front when she smiled, which she did once, hesitantly, ducking her head before her eyes could quite meet Diana's.

Her hair was a dark red, almost russet, and it was tucked out of the way for the headphones, which had rainbow tape on the stems. Diana pulled out her notepad and pen, but Naomi shook her head, getting up from her chair and disappearing deeper into the house, leaving Diana with nothing but her coffee for company.

It was good company.

Naomi came back with an electronic tablet, drawing on it for a minute before she handed it over. Diana took it with interest. On the screen was a blueprint, the address matching Allie's house next door. It looked modern, like it had been created digitally rather than drafted manually, and there was a real estate logo in the corner. Naomi had circled the windows on the main floor.

"It doesn't match," Naomi said finally, her voice lower than a whisper as she sat beside Diana. "I'm sorry—my batteries—I had a migraine yesterday and ran down my hearing aids. They provide more sound isolation, but I had to charge them."

Diana nodded. *Tomorrow?* she gestured, but Naomi shook her head, spelling the name of the man who had lived next door, letter by letter with her fingers. *David.* Using a stylus, she indicated the windows she had circled. There were eight.

"I heard nine. There was a long gap between the fifth and the sixth. There usually isn't. I assume he used to go...based on the amount of time it would take to walk between..." Naomi marked out a route on the blueprint as she spoke. "I can see him start from here," Naomi added, marking a window that faced west, toward her house. Diana suspected she'd need binoculars to cover that kind of distance, but the woman was earnest. "And he always closed this one last. We used to joke that we would send an SOS if anything happened to one of us, since our windows looked in on each other—he was deaf and alone and I'm..." Naomi sighed, and then shrugged.

Diana breathed slowly, and almost under her breath on the exhale asked, "And why do you think the windows are important?"

Diana had tried to keep level with the volume Naomi was using, and Naomi met her eyes with something akin to gratitude. She hadn't flinched, and Diana found herself feeling strangely proud of that.

"He does the same thing at dawn and dusk every day. Same routine. Last night was different. I was the one who called the police when he wasn't up at dawn this morning, and I called again at dusk. I thought he might have had an accident."

Suspicious, but not unreasonable. She wasn't lying about the noise sensitivity thing; her house had too many accommodations that were obviously long-term for it to be a ruse. But someone who could hear their neighbor close their shutters from that kind of a distance, someone with that kind of sound intolerance could easily be the kind of person to kill said neighbor over making those kinds of noises, especially if the neighbor had been deaf and unaware of how loud he was. Regardless, Diana nodded. She'd been in the force too long to simply discount witness observations, no matter how strangely they were presented. Diana thought she'd seen it all; this was new.

Naomi hesitated, then drew another circle on the blueprint. Diana raised her eyebrows.

"Was he—was he here when you found him?" Naomi asked. She'd come closer, somehow, her voice still low.

Diana shook her head and took the stylus, her bare fingers brushing Naomi's. She circled the base of the stairs—not far from where Naomi had circled, but a floor below. Diana shouldn't be giving out this sort of information to a potential suspect, but Naomi had been right about where the old man had been killed, and she wanted to see where this was going. Naomi concentrated, her eyes running over the blueprint again, the fingers of one hand tapping the table to mark time between when the index finger of her other hand paused at a window. She stopped again where she'd drawn the circle.

Diana watched, drawing her lips over her teeth so they wouldn't clink against the mug as she took another sip, the coffee warming her from the inside. She pitied the detectives at the cold, open property next door. Witness homes were always an unpredictable facet of murder investigations. To be warm and inside on a night like this with a coffee that didn't taste like sink water more than made up for the eerie silence of the house.

"He stopped here. I don't know why. And he was in a rush for the rest. He went faster, I think, after he stopped."

"And the shutters stayed closed all day yesterday?"

Naomi nodded.

"And that was unusual?"

Naomi nodded again as Diana jotted down the details in her notepad, careful that the tip of her pen didn't scrape the paper. "And you didn't see or hear anyone come onto the property?"

"Not from the road. No cars. I would have heard a bike—I usually do. I might not have heard someone walk up on foot from the far side of the property, but I didn't hear his front door close at all yesterday or the day before."

"Back door?"

Naomi shook her head.

"And no one came while he was out?"

"He was home every day this week. He goes for groceries today—yesterday. He should have gone out yesterday, and he didn't. I'm not—I'm not obsessed with him or anything. I just hear him. He has a predictable routine, which makes living next to him bearable."

"What about when you were asleep?"

Naomi gave her a look that she couldn't interpret. "I didn't sleep. Migraine."

"Could someone have come from the back of the property? Or the other end of the road?"

Naomi shook her head, dropping her eyes back to the tablet. "I know the cops out there think I'm a freak. But I didn't hear anyone. I know what his doors and windows sound like, and none of them closed. I heard the police break down the front door when they came."

"And you don't think this was an accident?"

Naomi laughed noiselessly. "You don't call out this many police at this time of night for an accident."

Diana sighed. She had nothing solid to go on, but she had the feeling her witness was telling the truth. Naomi was too earnest to do otherwise. However, nothing she'd said had been particularly helpful. And Naomi could also be wrong. She could have been mistaken about what she'd heard, or whatever she'd heard could be unrelated to the death of the man next door.

But if Naomi was right and the old man did have a habit which was suddenly interrupted, then this cryptic series of taps she made between windows might be significant.

Diana pulled out her phone.

"Mind if I record you doing the—" Diana indicated the tablet, and Naomi shook her head, waiting for her to start recording then repeating the pattern.

Diana finished her coffee, swallowing as quietly as she could, then lifted her chair to pull it back from the table as she stood so the legs didn't scrape against the floor.

"Can I have your number? I won't call. I'm guessing it's easier for us to text?"

Naomi nodded and pulled Diana's card from her pocket, sending a text a moment later. She flinched at the ding from Diana's phone, and Diana grimaced in sympathy. It had been loud, in the silent house, but she hadn't thought to mute her notifications. She rubbed her fist over her chest in apology, but Naomi shook her head, pointing at herself. She'd sent the text, not asking if Diana had alerts on.

"I can, um, if you give me an email, I can send through the camera footage I have of the road and that side of my house. Or I can make a guest account to my online archiver."

Diana stared at her in shock. She hadn't indicated—at all—that she had solid evidence. Although given the technology at the front gate, she shouldn't be surprised; someone with the kind of money this house would cost—as well the renovations it had clearly had—and who heard everything would have technology set up to monitor whatever made noise around her house.

"That—that would be very helpful. As have you been, also. Thank you."

Naomi shrugged diffidently and stood to lead Diana back to the front door. At any other time—when it wasn't the middle of the night, when she wasn't in the middle of a murder investigation—Diana would love a tour of the house. There was something so cozy about the lighting and the warmth of the furniture. Tempting bookshelves lined the hall, and Diana looked longingly at their overflowing shelves.

When they reached the door, Diana pulled her boots back on, and then her scarf and coat and gloves, watching Naomi watch her, careful of her movements, of her boots on the stone floor of the foyer. Naomi opened the door and looked up at her.

"It was surprisingly nice to meet you, Detective," Naomi said, her voice just above a whisper.

Diana nodded, feeling the cold night air already seeping into her bones. She'd come out here on what seemed like a wild goose chase. But despite the creepiness of the grounds, the locked gate behind her, and the dead body next door, she'd had at the very least an interesting night. It wasn't often she was surprised by people anymore, but Naomi had managed it.

"Likewise," she said, giving her most professional smile, and headed down the path. She paused and looked back when Naomi didn't follow, but Naomi signed *automatic* and pointed at the gate. Diana nodded and continued. The gate opened for her seemingly on its own and closed again behind her once she was clear of it.

She looked back at the woman silhouetted in the doorway and watched as the door closed off Naomi's inner sanctum. She drew her coat tighter around herself and shivered, then headed back to the crime scene.

CHAPTER TWO

Naomi left the headphones on, padding silently to the bedroom to check the charge on her medical-grade hearing aids. She'd had to manage the interview with just the in-ear protection and the noise-canceling headphones, and her head was filled with the dregs of phantom noises she could almost hear.

She'd been diagnosed with hyperacusis—a type of hearing damage that meant her hearing was more sensitive than most—following a migraine that had knocked her flat a few years ago, and as such the hearing aid was adjusted to reduce and muffle sound at the frequencies that bothered her eardrum. She had a number of backups from things she'd tried before the diagnosis, various noise-canceling earbuds and headphones. They helped a little, but not enough.

The pain was the worst of it. The condition hadn't magically given her super-hearing; it had just made her more aware of every noise everything in the entire world could make. It was frustrating and exhausting. Her little sanctuary was quiet enough on a good day, but the migraine the day before had knocked her around, made her cranky with residual pain and lack of sleep.

Naomi was surprised she'd managed to convey anything to the detective. She had no idea if any of it was useful. She assumed David was dead and felt a small wave of panic rise when the reality of that hit her. The house would either be inherited or sold—there would be new people next door. David had been tolerable because he'd been set in his ways, but someone new would likely have erratic noise patterns.

It had been a long day, and she'd just fallen asleep when the police had arrived. Her nerves were raw. Even the sound of her own blood pounding in her ears was intolerable. She couldn't take sleeping tablets in case the police needed something else, so she sat at her desk in her home office, setting up a guest account for her perimeter cameras and sending the details to the detective she'd met, along with the pertinent footage for the last two days.

She moved the timestamp to the detective's arrival and watched again as she approached the gate, a bored, disinterested look on her face. The critical appraisal of the property, the apprehension as Naomi approached, the relief when she'd seen it was a woman.

She'd still taken steps for her personal safety, signaling to the officers next door where she was going so they would know where she was last seen if she went missing. It was a good call, a wise move. Naomi herself posed no threat, but for all the detective knew, she could have murdered her neighbor or had an enormous boyfriend waiting behind the door to clobber her.

Not that Naomi had ever had boyfriends. She'd had girlfriends in the past, before her hearing had changed, but not for years now. She pushed away a memory of Rose, knowing she would have insisted they shouldn't get involved even if Naomi had told her that something was wrong next door. She looked at the live footage from the gate camera. The detective's car was still there; she was probably next door contributing to the case, or telling the rest of her team that Naomi was a crackpot.

Naomi ran the footage again. In a world of mostly silence, she could read the way people presented resentment at not having their primary form of communication available. There was none of that in the detective's body language. She rewound again to the flinch, the closed fist rubbing the sternum of the detective's coat when the radio crackled. Detective Stapleton had apologized, even though she had been testing Naomi for her ability to react to noise.

Most people didn't apologize. Most people didn't know how to apologize, and especially not in sign language. Naomi knew the other detective who had tried to talk to her had called Stapleton specifically, and she was glad he had. It was the nicest thing he'd done. It was about the nicest thing anyone had ever done for her.

In Naomi's limited experience, most ASL interpreters came independently of other occupations. They weren't usually the person providing a service; they merely translated. But the woman had the badge and the gun on her belt. She wasn't a bureaucrat or a social worker; she was a detective who happened to know ASL.

And not just ASL. She'd had a kind of empathetic awareness that very few people had. She'd been bearable, even with the remnants of a migraine still playing merry hell with Naomi's skull, even with her makeshift hearing protection. While she was thinking about it, Naomi put in an order for a second set of hearing aids to the same specifications so she wouldn't be caught out next time.

She didn't know how well she'd managed to convey her concerns about the neighboring property. No one had come or gone for at least a week, and even before the police had come, she had heard unfamiliar noises from the property. Nothing she could pinpoint. Like rats in a barn wall, moving through straw. Something scurrying in the closed house.

She hoped it had been instant, that whatever happened had killed him immediately. She feared it hadn't, that the little noises she'd heard had been him feebly trying to get to his feet, to a phone, falling down the stairs and landing where they'd found him.

No. She'd heard him fall, hadn't she? She had; it had been after the shutters had closed, quicker than David usually closed them, after the first pause, the extra shutter noise. She just needed to remember. The shutter that was out of place, and then a thud.

Or was she just imagining it to absolve herself from not calling in sooner?

She glanced at her computer and was surprised to see an email back already. The detective must be working from her phone. She said she'd review the footage in the morning with the forensic data team and asked to review the preceding week as well.

They'd probably be looking for times Naomi left the house, as well as David, or evidence she'd doctored the footage. Probably making sure Naomi hadn't popped next door and done a quick murder, then called it in herself. Naomi knew she was probably high on the list of suspects; she'd called it in, she lived next door, she seemed obsessed with his shutters. She knew how she presented to the outside world—a world she herself had once lived in without questioning why it might be seen as too loud.

That had been before the migraines. She'd been at work one day, and she'd become aware of a bright line in her vision, then the overwhelming sensation of sound.

It hadn't lessened. She'd used up her sick leave, and then worked from home, waiting for it to get better. It never had. She'd been fortunate that her former company had understood, and that she'd still been able to work at all. She'd had to swap her mechanical keyboard for a membrane one and adjust her meetings to add subtitles in real time, which came with a degree of error, but she'd been productive enough to keep her job, for a while at least. She used filters on her screens to prevent migraines, but they still flared up, making the world even louder and less bearable than usual.

Naomi worked freelance now, which was helpful because she could work nights. The world was typically a little quieter, and it allowed her to make appointments with specialists during business hours.

Not that specialists had been able to help, other than providing the hearing aids, which at least diluted the noise of the world a little better than her commercial-grade noise-canceling headphones.

She'd gone into graphic design because she'd wanted to do something with her art degree that would at least let her pay off her student loans. Currently she had enough clients to keep her busy. She did most of her business online, which meant she worked across time zones—there was a game in Australia she'd built some flora models for, and she was consulting on webpage design for a number of small businesses.

Global clients meant that if she couldn't sleep, at least she had some work to keep her afloat, and usually someone online to respond to her queries. She'd lost her health insurance when she'd had to leave her job at the animation studio, but after the initial diagnosis, there was very little health professionals could do for her anyway. She had to pay hefty fees to get insured now that she was classified as disabled, but they covered the cost of her hearing aids.

Aunt Isobel had inherited the house and left it to Naomi, so there was no mortgage or rent to worry about. Some of her technical equipment was getting a little dated, but she had money put aside to replace things as they reached their end of life.

She wished she had a singular, physical representation of what she did. A painting, some kind of masterpiece she could hang on the wall and look at with pride. She knew she was fortunate—her work provided enough to pay her medical bills and maintain the property, which she'd imaged sharing one day with the woman who had been her partner.

Rose had known her before her hyperacusis, and Naomi was aware she wasn't the same person afterward. She'd become quieter, smaller. She stayed at home, in bed, when she wasn't working. She had stopped taking Rose on dates, the idea of live theater or a train ride to NYC intolerable now, rather than the fun jaunts they used to be. She hadn't loved Rose any less, but she'd been fighting for a diagnosis and spending the rest of her time cocooned from a world that hurt so much to engage with.

Rose hadn't lasted long. She hadn't been able to modulate her tone, or her volume. She hadn't been able to deal with someone who could no longer leave the house whenever she wanted. She hadn't had the patience to deal with Naomi now that she was disabled. So Rose had left, and Naomi had been holed up in her fortress ever since.

It wasn't so bad—Naomi wasn't a fool. Rose would have left her anyway, at the slightest inconvenience. If she'd left because of Naomi's inability to tolerate noise, she wouldn't have stuck around long-term. The timing had been fortunate, since they hadn't been cohabiting long enough for Rose to have any claim on Naomi's home.

The property itself had turned out to be perfect—Naomi had planned to build her own studio, so she'd already sorted out the insulation, which had significantly improved the sound dampening of the house. David had been understanding, too, when she'd explained why she'd retreated. He didn't know sign language, but he had painstakingly written notes with his shaking hands in order to talk to her, and never seemed to mind reading hers with his big, thick glasses perched expectantly on his nose. He had heard too little, and Naomi had heard too much. They had both been alone, and now it was just Naomi.

Naomi checked the time. She could get started on the animation one of her clients wanted for their next television advertisement. It would keep her busy, at least, until she had an update about poor David.

She looked again at the live footage of the front gate and found Detective Stapleton looking into the property, curious but serious. The lamplight made her hair glow like honey, her eyes bronze. Her clothes were nice but practical—tight jeans that wouldn't get in the way if she had to chase someone, a green blouse that was vaguely feminine, a cream blazer and a forest-green wool coat. Her scarf was a mix of peacock colors, versatile and flattering to the ensemble. She wore boots that gave her at least an extra inch of height. She'd been shorter inside the house, more real, her face softer in the glow of the migraine-safe LED downlights. Her hands were in her coat pockets, and the quality of the camera showed her breath huff out of her in the crisp night air. Giving the gate one last look, she raised her hand to the camera and then got into her unmarked vehicle, the glow of her phone highlighting her face as the car warmed up.

There was no question about it. Detective Diana Stapleton was gorgeous. She'd smiled at Naomi once on her way out, revealing a cute little dimple in her left cheek, and Naomi found herself wanting to see that smile aimed at her again.

She sent another email to the detective, confirming that she'd backed up the footage from the week before and given the guest account access. It felt a lot easier to deal with her in written words than it had been in person.

When the detective had warmed up a little in the house, she'd smelled like something Naomi hadn't been able to trace. Something festive, like a holiday; something sweet like nutmeg or cloves. It had been distracting yet comforting somehow. That, teamed with the way the woman spoke, her voice low and soft, her consonants rounded for safety, had instilled a sense of ease in Naomi that she hadn't encountered much; no one else spoke to her that way, and usually a spoken conversation was uncomfortable. It had been bearable tonight.

It would have been harder in ASL, Naomi had to admit, and they both would have been a little frustrated. A new email arrived, another expression of thanks for supplying access and an assurance that someone would touch base via email in the morning, and that Detective Stapleton would make herself available should there be any further questioning needed.

Naomi went back to her animation, feeling an odd mixture of anxiety about her neighbor's break-in and wistful anticipation of perhaps seeing the gorgeous detective again.

CHAPTER THREE

Diana had reviewed the footage, then passed along the guest account credentials to the Technology Investigation Unit, who were quickly able to confirm it hadn't been tampered with. Naomi hadn't left the property during the window for the time of death, and that was a small measure of relief.

Diana tried not to be biased with her cases. She'd learned that anyone could be a criminal. But the tiny, anxious woman she'd met last night had been so genuine, and Diana had felt her urgent desire to be helpful. Naomi had called it in, provided access to footage, and despite what must be a difficult disability to live with, conveyed everything she'd seen and heard and established a pattern of behavior for the deceased.

Naomi hadn't seemed sad, but perhaps she hadn't been told that David was dead yet. Perhaps Diana should have told her, but the lead detective on the case hadn't given her the all-clear. She'd have to check in with the team in the morning, get a full brief.

Her own partner, Raymond Sloan, was on leave after being injured in their last case. Diana had as well, but she'd managed to walk away with just a few bruises and sprained joints. Raymond had broken his leg when the perp had driven at them, pulling off the road as they'd been about to leave the scene, no lights on the approaching car, just a roar in the darkness.

Diana shuddered, remembering the sound Ray's femur had made when it had snapped. She'd seen the car's reverse lights come on, grabbed Ray, and rolled them both over between the trees that lined the street so he couldn't run them over again. Their suspect had driven off into the darkness. Ray had brushed her off, clutching his leg as she tried to stabilize it while calling an ambulance out to the backwoods they'd found themselves in. She'd had to tourniquet Ray's leg while the paramedics on the call walked her through it. She'd got the plate and called that in, and their suspect had been apprehended at the Canadian border.

Their perp had killed three women before they'd caught him, and the captain gave her yet another medal for her part in stopping his killing spree. If Diana had been a man, her arrest report and high marks in the Lieutenant's exams would have her ranked higher than Sergeant by now.

Instead Ray was stuck at home, probably annoyed at having no work to do and Diana was stuck working cold cases until he returned to duty or they assigned her a temporary partner. It almost felt like a punishment. Apparently translating for people who couldn't communicate verbally had been added to her caseload. She didn't mind; it suited her fine, for the moment.

Her kids had given her the speech again, about how she needed to get out of her role as detective and rise through the ranks if she wanted to stay in the force, how she wasn't getting any younger and she had grandkids to think of and should get the kind of job where people didn't try to shoot her or run her over.

She felt that last case in her bones; her sprained joints had ached fiercely in the cold night air of the crime scene tonight. Perhaps it was time to take both her children and her bones seriously.

She loved the job for the freedom and independence it gave her. Her father had been on the force, and she'd been accepted into the academy right after college. Dad had been so proud. Her ex-husband, Andrew, hadn't minded at first. But he'd expected her to quit when she had Jake. FMLA had kicked in, and as much as she loved being a parent, she'd needed something to do outside the house. Andrew had tried to push her into resigning or taking a year off, but she'd known, even then, that if she left the Montpelier Police Department, she'd never return to any kind of job.

When Kate came along, Andrew doubled down. Diana's father had stepped in; he'd seen through Andrew, even back then. Andrew had reluctantly backed down after being confronted by someone stronger than him.

He'd always been upset that Diana earned more than him. As a contractor, his income wasn't steady enough to justify the resignation he'd demanded from Diana, especially not when Diana's mother—since passed—had watched the children until they'd been old enough for kindergarten.

Andrew had framed his demands as concern for Diana's personal safety, but she'd made detective fairly early in her career and was rarely in danger after her promotion. She knew she had her father to thank for that, as well as for the lack of comments about her gender and sleeping her way through the ranks. The promotion had meant fewer domestic violence calls, less crowd control, and fewer late nights.

It wasn't until she'd been assigned to homicide that the late nights had started again.

Diana shook her head and focused on the videos. In that whole week of footage, Naomi only appeared outside once, and that was to pick up packages from a parcel locker built into the gate. She'd collected the mail as well. No groceries, unless they were in one of the boxes she'd loaded into the hand cart she'd brought down the path with her. She looked pale in the daylight, and she struggled with the weight of the packages. Diana would have expected her to have a carer or some home help, but it was probably tricky trying to find someone who could accommodate her specific needs.

David had been a heavy man, and he'd been dragged across the landing, then lifted over the railing of the staircase barrier. From the footage, Naomi clearly lacked the upper body strength to have physically lifted him, even with the adrenaline that murder would provide. She could be wrong, but it was unlikely, especially given the rest of the evidence suggesting that Naomi hadn't killed the man next door. She could, of course, have hired someone, and turned over everything in the smug knowledge that they'd find nothing on her. But it would have made more sense, if she had killed him, to not call in a welfare check. David had no will; Busco was having a hell of a time tracking down his next of kin.

Her research into Naomi showed that she was a graphic designer, and that she donated a lot of time and money to LGBTQIA+ charities. For a long time, she'd been paired with another woman on social media. And then, right around when she must have been diagnosed, there were a few posts apologizing for being absent, an explanation of hyperacusis, and a complete disappearance of the other woman from Naomi's digital footprint.

Diana tapped her pen against her lips and replayed the clip. Naomi had gone out without a coat, and when she bent over the knobs of her spine were visible where her shirt lifted at the back. She lived in luxury; the quality of the cameras themselves told Diana that, not to mention the lush interior of her home. Something didn't add up. She didn't know if it was relevant to the case, but she kept it in mind in case it became relevant later. The official background check came back with nothing disturbing, not even a speeding ticket.

* * *

It rained the next afternoon. The crime scene techs had finished up at David's house, and Diana had convinced the lead on the case to let her check something. She showed up at the gate at the arranged time and sent a text. Naomi came out a few moments later, headphones on again under a hood to keep the rain off.

She looked less pale today, what little of her Diana could see; she wore an enormous coat and gloves, and her eyes were, as before, wide and scared. Her coat might have been waterproof, but it didn't look like a raincoat. Hearing her own raincoat squeak, Diana retreated to remove it, placing it on the hood of her car because closing the door would be loud. Given the strangeness of what they were asking Naomi to do and that she was their only witness, Diana didn't want to put her off.

Diana opened her umbrella and let her hood fall back on her shoulders, giving Naomi a smile and a wave, then walked in stride with her over to the neighboring house, close enough that they were both under the shelter of her umbrella.

"Thank you for agreeing to do this," Diana said quietly, since her hands were busy.

"I have my hearing aids in today. I have much better attenuation. You can talk a little louder, if you'd like."

"Oh. This is fine for me."

"It's a relief. I can finally eat again."

Diana had read up on Naomi's condition, but there had been no mention of it interfering with appetite. She must be talking about the migraine. Even covered in her thick coat, she looked so frail. As though feeling Diana's pity, Naomi turned her face away. Not knowing what to say, Diana said nothing.

"What do you need me to do?" Naomi asked as they entered the house.

"The shutters. It'll be a lot louder up close. But we want to know if you'd be able to tell us which ones made which of the sounds you heard in order, and see if you can identify the sound you heard when you think he was attacked. We want to know where he was interrupted."

"You must not have much to go on."

Diana bit her lip. They'd seen a face at one of the windows before the shutters had closed on the footage Naomi had sent. It hadn't been David. They hadn't been able to identify him, or how he'd entered the house. The techs had spent two days on the footage, and they hadn't been able to see how the building had been entered.

The cameras didn't cover the other side of the house, but they did cover the front and back doors, as well as the garage, and there had been no signs of forced entry anywhere.

They really *didn't* have much to go on—except some case files from another neighborhood where a few similar break-ins had happened months ago. No one had been murdered then, but houses had been broken into, and no one had seen anyone go in or out. Footage of entry points hadn't found anyone coming or going from the properties, no suspicious cars were identified entering or leaving the neighborhood. Of course, cameras always had blind spots and people often didn't notice strange cars on their street, but there had been no signs of forced entry in those cases either. If it had escalated to murder, that would have been Diana's wheelhouse. That was something she could do something about. People deserved to feel safe in their own homes.

"We're testing a theory," Diana said. Naomi looked over at her with curiosity, and Diana smiled. Naomi's cheeks were flushed from the cold air, and she returned the smile with a shy bemusement that made Diana wonder how long it had been since anyone had smiled at her.

Naomi closed the shutter facing her house, the one David started with every morning and evening. Her eyes were closed. She opened them, looked at Diana seriously, and nodded.

"I'm shorter than him," Naomi said. "But he moved slower than I do." That said, she walked down the hall to the next room and closed the shutter there. She flinched at the noise but nodded. She continued to the next two shutters, then the next two. She paused after the sixth, looking toward the seventh.

"He wasn't alone, was he?" Naomi asked. "There was someone else here, wasn't there?"

"There might have been," Diana said noncommittally, half-lifting her hand toward Hamilton before he could answer.

"The noise I heard between didn't sound like any of these shutters, but it had the same kind of cadence." Naomi's brow was drawn up in concentration. "Maybe it wasn't a shutter."

"Okay. But you thought it was when you first heard it?" The sound technicians hadn't been able to enhance the audio enough to hear anything other than the noise the police had made breaking down the front door, and then the sirens that followed.

It had been an odd experience for Diana to see herself in action, on the screen, assessing Naomi's home. Diana thought she looked shorter on camera. She'd seen herself squint and then relax as she'd identified Naomi as unlikely to be a threat. She wondered if Naomi had noticed, if she'd been relying on appearing nonthreatening to police, if this was just an elaborate ruse.

But no, looking down, the bloodstain was too far from the stairs; she'd never have been able to lift him over the barrier. He'd been lying on the landing below for a day, though, and maybe she could have used a pulley system if she'd managed to get in and out without being seen on her own cameras.

The body had been moved quickly after it had fallen to the floor, though; the bloodstain didn't support the pulley theory. There had been a thick trail of blood on the floor from the hall through to the staircase. Diana had asked the crime scene techs to check for anything that would indicate such and returned a negative. No unusual bruising on the body. No ligature marks, no damage to his clothing that couldn't be put down to wear and tear. But Diana was still wary. They had no other suspects and no motive, nothing but the noise of the shutters.

"I thought it had to be. Whatever happened must have happened when he was between his bedroom and the bathroom. Which you already knew." Naomi deflated, looking down at the dried blood on the floorboards underfoot.

Diana had let her know gently that David's death had been quick—he'd bled out in minutes, according to Daisy.

"We can close the shutters on the top floor and the basement if that's going to help," Hamilton offered.

Naomi flinched, and Diana grimaced, even though he'd kept his voice low. She let her hand rest on Naomi's back in apology, feeling her body relax a little when he finished speaking.

"The microphones on my cameras didn't pick it up—I don't think—" Naomi looked at the wall in front of her, then walked into the primary bedroom. She came back out and went into the next room, staring at the wall facing David's room. The bed had a tartan bedspread, but other than the bed the room was empty. "It wasn't one of the doors he used. But it could have been a door? No, it sounded like slats. Like a shutter, multiple pieces of wood moving at the same time. The camera didn't catch it. The microphones aren't very sensitive."

Naomi was paler now, and Diana gestured to Hamilton when he looked like he might speak. He looked annoyed, unable to hear more than half the conversation, but his annoyance was merely an inconvenience in comparison to the physical pain his voice appeared to cause Naomi.

"Okay. Do you want us to close all the doors and windows on the other levels? You can stay here or go home and listen and text me if you hear it."

"I'll go outside. They're too loud in here."

Diana walked her down, retrieving her umbrella and unfolding it as quietly as she could, not expecting the grateful little smile Naomi gave her. Diana held it up over them both, and Naomi brushed against her when they stood facing the house. She moved away briefly, then moved closer again, pressing against Diana's side to use her as a windbreak, shivering slightly against Diana where their bodies touched. Diana was warm beneath the coat she had wisely decided to keep wearing inside the cold house. She wanted to put an arm over Naomi's shoulders and bring her closer to share that warmth, but forced herself to remain professional.

They watched her colleagues through the windows as they went room by room, closing any kind of door or window they found. When they'd cleared the floor David had been killed on again, Diana looked over at Naomi to check in. Naomi looked back at her, brown eyes huge and sad. She was paler still; they were running out of usable time.

Diana tilted her head. Hamilton and Busco repeated the process for the floor below, where they'd found the body. Naomi shook her head. The detectives went to the top floor next, while Diana watched Naomi carefully. She was flinching at each noise now but showed no signs that she recognized any of the noises as the one she'd heard that night. She shook her closed fist instead of her head when they finished on that floor, her jaw set with pain. Diana felt guilty for asking too much of her. She'd said the hearing aids helped, but Diana saw no sign of that.

Diana shook her head when Hamilton leaned out an open window, then pointed toward the neighboring property. Naomi was already turned toward home, and Diana matched her stride, staying close to keep the umbrella over them both, hovering in case Naomi needed support. The other woman didn't pull away or move closer, just kept walking, her head down, the back of her neck bare and goose-pimpling in the cold air. The bones there were very round and exposed; Diana averted her eyes.

The weather report claimed it was going to snow soon, and the empty house next door to Naomi's was likely to attract the unhoused with the promise of shelter. The outside walls were stone, but the interior had a lot of wood to burn, and people set fires when they were cold. They still hadn't found a successor for the property, but Diana was thinking it might be worthwhile to set someone to watch the house, just to make sure it didn't catch fire. It was so close to Naomi's home, she would probably know before anyone else did if someone illegally moved in.

It felt mean-spirited to bring it up. Depriving homeless people of shelter in what was shaping up to be a very cold winter sounded cruel, but too often they became victims of the house fires they started, and the smell of burnt humans had haunted Diana since her first immolation case.

Naomi stumbled, and Diana remembered her initial impression of frailty. She slid her hand into Naomi's elbow and pulled her close so the umbrella would remain overhead, using it as an excuse to hold on to Naomi in case she stumbled again. Naomi didn't look up at her, but she didn't pull away either. She accepted the assistance with no qualms, and Diana's hand warmed in the space between Naomi's arm and her body, the slightest hint of softness against her thumb where it rested against Naomi's side.

"I should have brought an umbrella with me, but I can't stand the noise they make when I open them."

Diana nodded. She'd never thought about the noise an umbrella might make before, but she could see why it would be unpleasant; the whiffle of nylon and the clank of metal.

"Thank you," Naomi said, so quiet Diana almost didn't hear her. "For the umbrella. And for...understanding."

"Any time," Diana told her. She meant for the case, but she knew that if Naomi ever asked for any kind of help once this was over, she wouldn't turn her down. She did understand, and it felt like Naomi didn't have many people in her life that did.

Naomi stumbled again, and Diana adjusted her grip on the shorter woman, putting an arm around her waist so they were pressed together. The ground was slick and wet underfoot, but Diana wore boots year-round, ones with a good all-weather grip for when she photographed birds in the woods upstate in the fall, where the maple leaves were slippery and stacked together like pages of a story. With Naomi snug against her, layers of wool and cotton and maybe even lace between them, Diana slowed down a little, tucking her thumb into the belt of Naomi's coat to keep her close and safe on the unsteady terrain.

At the gate, Naomi pulled out her phone, shivering as she removed her gloves to use the screen. Diana moved her hand over Naomi's ribs to warm her just as her own hood flew back, and with no hands free, hair whipped around her face unchecked. Naomi half-raised her free hand, her index and middle fingers extended. She paused, suddenly wary of something she saw in Diana's face. Her jaw tightened, and she pulled her hand away. Diana didn't loosen her grip.

"You'd be doing me a favor, my hands are full," she admitted, and Naomi reached out again, not for Diana's loosened hair but for her hood, sliding it back up. She hesitated, but eventually tucked the loose curls still flying in the wind back under the hood as well. Her fingers were tentative and gentle, and Diana found herself savoring the reverent touch.

Diana wasn't used to people being gentle with her. Her colleagues were more likely to jostle her in congratulations at the bar when she closed a hard case; her children and grandchildren gave her firm hugs. Andrew had never been this gentle with her in their entire relationship.

Naomi's fingers moved from behind Diana's ear and trailed down her jaw, and Diana felt her eyes close. She was working, even if it was just a human relations role; she didn't have time for this. She'd never had time for this because nothing like this had ever happened before. One day she should make time, because it was one of the nicest things that had ever happened to her.

When Diana opened her eyes, she noticed how close Naomi's face was, so close she could feel Naomi's breath on her lips, tasting vaguely of peppermint; she must have brushed her teeth before she'd met Diana at the gate. Diana didn't draw away; she'd pulled Naomi this close because she wanted her this close. When their eyes met, Naomi tucked her bottom lip under her teeth and swallowed anxiously, uncertainty in those deep-brown eyes.

Naomi's bare hand trembled as it withdrew from Diana's face. Her fingers hadn't been cold against Diana's cheek or ear. It had been so intimate, that moment, and somehow it hadn't been enough. The fear had gone from Naomi's face, replaced with something Diana couldn't read. Diana was used to being able to read people; she'd never seen such an intense look aimed at her. Diana exhaled, realizing she'd been holding her breath, and whatever spell had befallen them dissipated.

Suddenly hyperaware of the detectives at the neighboring property, Diana looked at the gate. She adjusted her grip on the umbrella's handle, her nose brushing Naomi's cheek as she turned to look. When she turned back, Naomi was blushing, her face slightly turned away.

There was no room for Diana's hand to meet her chin to gesture her thanks, and both of her hands were full anyway. One with an umbrella, the other with Naomi.

"Thank you," Diana breathed, and the air was so crisp and chill that it formed a mist between them, one that was inhaled by Naomi almost immediately, like she was absorbing the words. Naomi's eyes closed, and she leaned in closer.

"I don't find the volume you've been using for me particularly painful," Naomi said, and Diana found her breath catching, her hand tightening on Naomi's waist above the belt of her coat. "If your hands are busy, I don't mind if you talk."

"I don't want to hurt you," Diana whispered, aware of something tight in her chest clenching tighter, wondering why this was so important to her. She'd been called out because she was the kidskin gloves the situation had required. She hadn't meant to get involved in the case at all, and especially not with the only witness.

"You haven't," Naomi insisted, her eyes now fixed on Diana's face. "And I feel like I can tell you if I need you to be quieter. So many people take it as a criticism, or a personal failing."

"It's just an accommodation," Diana said, aware she wasn't telling Naomi anything new.

Naomi caught a few more flyaway strands of hair and tucked them away with the others, her fingers grazing Diana's cheek again, but Diana's eyes stayed open this time, unable to look away.

"One most people find too hard to make. So thank you. I was dreading calling this in, but you made it as easy as it could be."

Naomi's hand dropped to Diana's coat, to the little flap on the shoulder. It should have felt strange, too intimate, but they'd been exchanging emails, and Diana liked what little she knew about Naomi.

"The crime scene techs are packing up this afternoon. You should get less street traffic, after today, but they'll send out a patrol car tonight to make sure whoever broke in doesn't come back. They'll leave the shutters open before they go, to see any light inside if someone breaks in again. If anything happens, we'll have the footage from your cameras as well. Thanks for being so cooperative."

"Thank you for taking me seriously."

Diana was aware of the warmth of Naomi's body from where they were pressed together at the thigh, and from the collar of Naomi's coat, a sweet scent drifting out between them, not overpowering. Probably soap rather than perfume, since her face was bare, and she didn't seem the type to use makeup. Probably because of the sound, Diana realized. The scraping on skin. She didn't need makeup anyway. Those dark-brown eyes were so soulful that she could draw in anyone she wanted without further effort.

Diana wasn't immune; she knew that. She'd seen Hamilton eyeing Naomi and felt Naomi shrink from that gaze. But she met Diana's eyes with such ease that it felt like nothing else existed, nothing outside the soft warmth of Naomi's body pressed close to hers, the sound of rain bouncing off the umbrella above. The peppermint of Naomi's breath, the sweetness of her smile. There was a wholesome gratitude seeping from her, a sag of relief to her shoulders. Her lips curved into a smile, her expressive eyes echoing it.

"If you need anything, you know how to reach me," Diana said reluctantly. She didn't want to pull away, and she knew they likely wouldn't need Naomi for the case anymore. The wind picked up then, damp leaves gaining momentum in the air around their feet, and Naomi shivered.

It made Diana aware that she'd just spent far too long intimately sheltered under the umbrella with this woman, and that they were right outside Naomi's home and she hadn't attempted to get inside to shelter from the upcoming storm, too caught up in the moment as well.

"Let me walk you to the door."

"You've done more than enough." Diana took it to be a terse complaint until Naomi looked up at her with shining eyes. Naomi's gaze darted away from hers, back to her phone, and the gate unlocked itself, the keypad flashing green as she reached out to push it open. "Thank you," she said, moving as though she intended to slip through unaccompanied.

But Diana didn't let go, instead following her through. She'd seen the crease in Naomi's forehead, the haunting pain in her eyes. Diana had done that to her, subjecting her to the weird theory MPD had conjured. She could at least make sure Naomi made it inside safely.

Naomi slumped at her side, leaning heavily into her, and Diana took the weight of her easily, still holding her close.

"For what it's worth, I'm sorry."

Naomi signed *okay*, so Diana pursed her lips and shook her head. Her hands were both occupied so she spoke under her breath, hoping she wouldn't be too loud.

"Don't let us—or anyone else—push you into something that hurts you. You could have gone home after we checked the floor he was found on."

Naomi paused, then spelled out David's name emphatically.

"I know, but we'll find who did this to him some other way if we have to."

Help, Naomi signaled, then pointed to herself.

Diana interpreted it as a statement that she wanted to help rather than a request. "You did. You have. You did everything you could. It's up to us now."

Naomi smiled sadly, and the light on the door keypad flashed green as they approached. Diana found it strange and wonderful how Naomi had used technology to make her life safer and more convenient. Naomi shivered still, her jaw trembling from trying to stop her teeth chattering. Diana let go of her at the door and signed her thanks. Naomi's resigned smile made another appearance. She didn't look upset, just exhausted. Diana nodded and turned to go, recentering the umbrella over herself and feeling a chill against her side where Naomi's warm body had rested.

When she looked back, Naomi remained huddled in the open doorway, watching her leave, even though she had cameras set up so she could remotely open the gate without exposing herself to the cold fall air.

Naomi looked good against the gray sky and the gray stone of her home, the dark russet of her hair spilling out as she tilted back her hood and removed her beanie, eyes emphatically dark in her pale face. She'd reminded Diana of a deer the first time they'd met, with her big doe eyes and flinching wariness that made Diana slow her movements deliberately. Now she reminded Diana of something else—something that camouflaged itself in fallen leaves, waiting for the sound of prey to come into range, nothing but dark, watchful eyes.

Diana didn't know which of the two Naomi would categorize her as. If she were to photograph Naomi, she would do it in the woods, in shades of green and brown, setting her up in dappled light so the first thing anyone saw would be those expressive eyes before realizing there was a person in the photo.

Diana shivered, even in her coat. Every instinct she had was telling her to protect Naomi, but she'd been wrong before. Or rather, she'd been fooled before. Naomi's trust could be manufactured. Her footage could have been doctored. She could have murdered her neighbor, although she had seemed fond enough of him.

Diana had joined the force to help people, usually turning up too late to do any good. All she could do was help the survivors seek justice and catch criminals to deter reoffending.

Helping Naomi—the gratitude Naomi gave her for accommodating her necessities—felt good. It felt warm, not just where Naomi had been pressed against her, but also within her chest, like something soft had nestled in there.

She'd felt like this before, but not to this extent. Perhaps it was because Naomi trusted her so much. She had let Diana in so close that any noise Diana made could have hurt her. She'd let Diana into her home, a veritable fortress of solitude.

Diana turned back to David's house; at the end of the drive, she turned her head, and upon seeing Naomi still standing in the doorway, waved with two fingers and a thumb before she left the view of Naomi's cameras.

Feeling as though she'd missed something monumental, Diana shifted her grasp on her umbrella and went back to David's house. The techs hadn't been able to amplify the sound from the recording, and they were going off a memory of a sound that might not be accurate. They didn't have anything else to work with, so Diana joined her colleagues opening and closing doors, looking and listening for anything out of place.

CHAPTER FOUR

Diana was shaken when she got home. She was always professional at work, and with Naomi she hadn't been. She'd let someone under her guard, and for a moment, a *brief* moment, she'd found herself looking at Naomi's lips. Thinking about how soft they looked and how close they were to her own, how easy it would be to close the gap between them.

Was it because Diana was sure Naomi was gay? Did that make a difference? Diana knew lots of lesbians and bisexual women, and she'd never found herself staring at their mouths like that, wondering what it would feel like to kiss them. She'd never found herself looking at a straight woman like that either. Perhaps it was simply Diana's urge to protect Naomi.

She wouldn't have let a man come that close to her. She wouldn't have helped him walk back to his home, not like that, and she wouldn't have invited him to brush her unruly, windswept hair away from her face.

If the others had seen them there would be rumors already flying around the precinct, but Diana didn't care about rumors;

she cared about results. And Naomi had supplied several answers to questions they hadn't even had the sense to ask.

If anyone asked, not that it was anyone else's business, Diana could just pass it off as accommodations, though she felt bad using Naomi's disability to justify her own uneasiness.

It didn't matter, since Diana would probably never see her again. That thought shouldn't be so annoyingly persistent, but it was. It felt like she'd missed something important. Like an opportunity had passed her by. She sighed and rolled over in bed, avoiding looking at her alarm clock. She'd be useless in the morning once again, and this time she didn't have the excuse of being at a crime scene all night. Her phone rang and Diana sat up, groaning.

Here came an excuse, after all.

Diana answered the phone without looking at the screen, eyeing the clock with resentment. "Stapleton."

"Detective?"

A whispered voice.

Diana had been expecting Operations. She sat up, blinking rapidly, checking her screen to make sure. "Naomi?"

"Someone is in my house. Oh God, someone is in my house."

Diana got to her feet, cringing at the slapping of her bare feet on the floorboards as she made her way to her study, pulling open her laptop. She waited impatiently for the computer to boot, then for the webpage to load. She'd cached the credentials, so when the live feed from Naomi's cameras came up, she checked the footage from the gate, looking for an intruder.

"Where are you? Are you safe?"

"Hidden."

"Okay, good. Do you know where they came in? You only gave me access to the gate and the east side walls."

"No. I haven't heard that sound before. It wasn't my front or back doors, or the garage entry."

"Okay, I'm sending a squad to come check on you now. Naomi? I believe you. I'm coming out too. I couldn't see anyone on the cameras. Can you stay on the call with me while I call this in? Turn your volume down."

Diana grabbed her house phone and called it in, getting confirmation of a cruiser headed that way. David's house was now empty; Diana had requested monitoring for the property until a will or heir was found, but that would take a few more days to get set up, and even so it would only be drive-bys to check for lights in the building.

"Naomi? Okay, we have some officers headed your way. It's going to be loud when they get there. Are you sure you're safe?"

"I'm in my safe room."

Diana let out a relieved sigh as she put the phone on speaker in case Naomi said anything while she dressed, cursing under her breath since her hands hadn't caught up with her brain yet. Two nights this week now she'd been called out late at night, and the rain hadn't stopped. Perhaps these were just burglaries that had escalated—the properties were isolated and had reclusive owners. The houses looked like good targets, yet David hadn't had much in the way of material goods. His money was mostly tied up in investments. He'd inherited the house and land and lived off dividends, only heating a few small rooms on a single floor of the house. He'd opened the shutters every day since he'd been told—and had told Naomi, who emailed Diana whenever she remembered anything about David that might be important—that it extended the life of the mechanisms.

Diana grabbed her gun, sliding it into the holster, hoping she wouldn't have to use it. She'd been quiet too long; Naomi must be frantic with anxiety, must need some reassurance. But, given it was Naomi, perhaps this silence was more welcome than Diana babbling at her over the phone. Diana grabbed her bag and headed for the garage, even her socks sounding too loud on the stairs.

"I'm about to get in the car—do you want to mute me while I drive?"

"No!"

It was the loudest and most adamant Naomi had ever been, and Diana had to quash the instinct to hush her, not wanting her to attract any attention. But the emphasis had been nice, had let Diana know that her voice or presence or existence or whatever was comforting or reassuring somehow for Naomi. Naomi trusted her. Naomi had called Diana instead of making an emergency call to 911.

She spoke as evenly as she could, moving through the house to the garage. "It's going to get really loud, so please turn the volume down on your end. I'm going to open the garage, and then I'm going to start the car. You're on speaker, and I'll put you through Bluetooth when I'm driving. If it's too loud, I can switch it back to speaker, just let me know."

"Okay."

Taking a deep breath, Diana started the car as the garage opened, hitting the button to close it behind her as she drove what was becoming a familiar route.

"How many people?"

"One, I think. I heard one set of footsteps, and I hid. There might be more, this room is insulated, and they were trying to be quiet. They shouldn't be able to hear me. Or find me."

"Good. That's really good, Naomi. Can you hear any sirens?"

"Not yet."

"Okay, that's less good. I'm at least ten minutes away. Are you trapped in there? Can anyone else get in? Do you have another way out?"

"It's hidden. Behind a bookshelf, and the door is locked."

"Is there any other way in?"

"Not unless they start breaking down walls. There's a trapdoor, but that's locked too."

"Can you get out that way if you have to?"

Naomi's breathing filled the car, fast and scared. She didn't answer, and Diana assumed that meant the intruder was close. Naomi's anxiety was palpable, and Diana felt, for the first time since she'd been a rookie, a very real sense of worry about the situation she might be walking into.

"Okay," Diana said reassuringly, trying to calm Naomi. "Okay, honey, you've done really well. You did a really good job. You're okay. I've got my beacons on. Can you handle me putting the siren on as well? I'm in my unmarked and there's some lights up ahead."

"Just get here, please."

Diana flipped the sirens on, hoping they wouldn't be too loud through Naomi's phone speaker. She sped up and proceeded through the red light, checking cross traffic as she went, flipping the sirens off once she was clear of the intersection. She did it twice more, watching confused cars slowly change into the right lane to let her through.

"I'm turning onto your street. I'm nearly there. Are they still in the house? Can you still hear them?"

"I'll take my headphones off."

There was silence for a few moments.

"I hear sirens. Is that you?"

"I'm pretty close. I can see a patrol pulling up ahead of me. Is the intruder still inside?"

"I'll open the gate for the police once I see them on the camera. And the front door. Hold on."

"Stay where you are, I'm headed your way."

Diana barely pulled over, grabbing her bulletproof vest from under the passenger seat and tugging it on over whatever clothes she'd pulled on in the dark. She grabbed her flashlight as well, feeling her holster and pulling her service pistol once she locked her car. Two officers were walking toward the gate, which opened as they approached. Diana hailed them, joining as they entered. The officers eyed the gate with mistrust as it swung shut behind them, effectively trapping them with whatever awaited them inside. Diana flashed her badge at them, but they'd already recognized her. She'd met them before—Officer Antonio Gilberta and Officer Robert Akins.

"I'm on the phone with the homeowner. She'll unlock the door for us. Not sure if anyone else is still in there—she's quite upset."

"Guy next door just got murdered, didn't he? That'd make me jumpy too." Tony was casual, only just pulling his gun as they approached the door despite the looming shadows of the yard.

"She's holed up in a safe room. Lives alone, as far as I know." Diana watched the officers prepare to enter. "Stay where you are, we're coming in," Diana said into the phone, sliding it into the front pocket of her jeans without hanging up. She shivered; she'd left her coat behind, and the hard Kevlar of her bulletproof vest wasn't exactly a suitable replacement for the warm wool.

The house wasn't completely dark. Light filtered in the windows as they entered, and floodlights from panels on the skirting boards shone upward. It was enough to make all three of them jump at every shadow, mistaking furniture for a huddled burglar. Diana turned her flashlight on and heard a muffled sound of surprise from a dimly lit room to her left. She inclined her head that way and let the uniformed officers take the lead, flinching a moment later when they announced themselves, aiming their flashlights into the room at shoulder height, guns drawn. Diana peered around the doorframe, trying to ensure she didn't present enough of herself to be a target.

There was a man in the room. He had a sack in one hand and a gun in the other. The gun had been at his side, but he raised it, blinking as the sudden light blinded him.

"Drop your weapon!" Tony yelled.

His words didn't have the desired effect. The man dropped the sack and fumbled with the slide on his weapon. A moment later Tony took the shot. He was fresh and Diana was nervous; he'd probably never shot at a real person before. His aim was good, though; the bullet struck the man's shoulder. The gun fell from his hand as he staggered and dropped to the floor. Tony closed in, holstering his weapon and pulling his cuffs as the man started screaming, clutching his shoulder. Rob stepped in and kicked the gun away from the man's outstretched hand, pulling the radio from his shoulder to his mouth to call for an ambulance.

Tony tried to help the man apply pressure to the wound, but he screamed louder and jerked away. Diana holstered her gun and retrieved her phone from her pocket. Naomi was silent on the other end.

"You heard one shot. Officer Gilberta has disarmed an intruder. We need to check the rest of the house. Stay where you are until I confirm the house is clear."

"Okay." Naomi's voice was the barest whisper. Diana wanted to find her, to pull her from wherever she was holed up and make sure for herself that Naomi was okay. But she had a job to do, and a criminal bleeding on Naomi's living room carpet. Akins found the switch and turned on the light. He disappeared for a moment and came back with a clean tea towel.

"Bus on the way. I'll take it from here, kid." Akins took over, pressing the towel to the wound despite the man's weakened attempts to resist.

Tony staggered away, and Diana heard him being sick in the kitchen. A moment later she heard the tap, and then Tony joined her, wiping his wet mouth and unwrapping a strip of gum, offering the packet to her. She took one to make him feel better.

Diana felt sorry for the kid; it was a clean shot, but it was probably his first. Still, she always felt better when the rookies took it to heart; the kind of recruits that laughed after shooting someone always chilled her, and she refused to work with anyone with that kind of reputation. She'd make sure Tony went into the employment assistance program after this.

"Nothing else you could have done, Tony," Diana said, her voice low and sympathetic. "He was going to shoot you. I saw. I'll add my report to the mix. You announced yourself and told him to disarm. You did everything by the book."

Tony just nodded, wiping sweat from his upper lip, swallowing hard. His eyes shone in the low light, and Diana looked away, letting him have a moment to compose himself.

Methodically, room by room, they searched the rest of the house. No one else was evident in any of the rooms, not even Naomi. The back door, when they found it, was locked, along with the pantry door that led to the garage. Naomi had unlocked the gate and front door for them, but even they were locked again now. Naomi's equipment would have logs; she had sensors on all the doors and windows for insurance purposes.

They could confirm the entry point later, and the tech team would be able to collate all the timestamps. Diana trusted Naomi's hearing, but they had to have gained entry from somewhere. People didn't just teleport directly into a house; this wasn't a science fiction movie. Having cleared the house, Diana dismissed Tony and told him to wait out front for the ambulance.

"We've searched the house and found no one else. We're just getting an ambulance for the guy we found. I'd prefer if you let us remove him from the property before you come out, if you could wait a little longer."

"Can I let you in instead? I heard—his screams, I heard—"

"Oh no." Diana's heart dropped. The gunshot. "Oh, I'm sorry. Shoulder wound. He's in custody. He can't hurt you. I'll come to you. Where do I need to go?"

"Where are you?"

"Looks like a laundry." Diana studiously avoided looking at Naomi's clothes basket, where something made from lace lay enticingly on top of the hamper.

"You'll have to go down the hall, to the left. The bookshelf in the study. I'll open it when you close the study door."

Diana went back to the living room to tell Akins where she was going, then followed Naomi's directions to the study. There was a projector pointing to one wall, and a series of serious-looking laptops, all open and turned on, the kind with colorfully glowing keyboards. There were bookshelves on one wall, and a small model of the solar system suspended from the ceiling. Pluto was glowing, the red heart exposed. Diana closed the door behind her, and there was a little noise, and then one of the bookshelves swung open like a door.

It was surreal—the doorway glowed, a little hollow in the world. Diana stepped forward, wondering which fantasy novel Naomi had designed this room from—the garden was obvious with its streetlamps, but this wasn't a wardrobe filled with fur coats. This was something else. Not a spaceship like the Tardis, larger on the inside. Not futuristic, not rustic, but it was something familiar, nonetheless. Naomi tugged the door closed behind Diana, sliding a bolt into place, then shook her head, smiling sheepishly as she slipped the lock open again.

The space was lined with soundproofing panels and there was a desk set up with a complicated-looking microphone and a few sets of headphones. The desktop computer case was made of glass and glowed through the colors of the rainbow, and there was an array of colorful LED lights lining the walls.

Diana didn't have time to look around any further, because Naomi released a sudden, harsh breath and her arms wrapped around Diana, hands gripping tightly, head finding the slope of Diana's chest and resting against it as she clung to her. Diana's arms folded around her out of instinct; as the only woman on her team, she was often stuck with the task of consoling victims and widows, who often needed this kind of physical reassurance. They found something about her comforting, and she didn't usually mind.

"I was so scared."

Diana let herself hold Naomi for a moment, let herself stroke Naomi's back before closing her eyes and pulling her tighter. Diana had been scared, too—scared for Naomi, scared she would lose her only witness, scared she would have a second murder to investigate. She was glad Naomi was safe, that she'd built herself this little nest. She wouldn't let herself imagine what could have happened.

Naomi trembled in her arms. Her home was warm, but the insulation kept the safe room cooler, and her thin T-shirt wasn't sufficient for the temperature of the room. Some of the shaking was probably from the cold, the rest from fear and adrenaline.

Naomi pulled away a little, but Diana wasn't ready to let go yet. She pulled back just far enough to look Naomi over, checking for injuries, moving her hands to Naomi's shoulders. When Naomi didn't meet her eyes, Diana reached up to tilt back her chin. Naomi's lips trembled when their eyes met, but there were no tears.

"Are you okay?"

Naomi nodded, her eyes glassy.

"Hey. You're okay. You're okay. I've got you."

Naomi sank deeper into Diana's arms like she'd been worried about imposing or being unwelcome and Diana's words had eased her fears. Diana stroked her back, feeling the harsh knobs of Naomi's spine protruding through the thin fabric. She wondered how long it would take for the ambulance to arrive; she couldn't hear much in this room.

Naomi was still shaking, but she slowly relaxed as Diana held her. She let her head rest on Diana's shoulder, her ear near Diana's mouth, showing a remarkable amount of trust Diana didn't think she'd earned. She'd just been doing her job. Naomi's hands clutched Diana's bulletproof vest, which suddenly felt stiff and bulky between them. Diana wanted to remove it, to bundle Naomi even tighter against her.

Naomi hadn't stopped trembling, but she had calmed down. Her breathing slowed to match Diana's. Diana wished she'd remembered her coat so she could drape it around Naomi.

"Thank you for believing me. Thank you for coming."

"Of course," Diana said soothingly as Naomi tucked herself in closer. "I'm so glad you called me." Naomi didn't seem inclined to release her, so Diana rubbed her back, feeling all the sharp bones of her through the thin shirt, which stirred something she couldn't name. Naomi melted against her, her trust little more than instinct; they barely knew each other. Diana's chest ached as she waited for Naomi to be ready to let go of her.

She knew Hamilton and Busco were heading out to investigate, since this home invasion was likely related to their existing case next door. Diana would have to trust them to take care of the case, because she planned on taking Naomi to a safe house until they could confirm the man who'd broken in had been working alone, that this hadn't been targeted, that Naomi was safe in her own home.

"I'm still calling you," Naomi said, pulling away and trying to breathe normally. She hadn't cried, and Diana wondered if she ever did. Naomi pulled her phone from her pocket and ended the call, clearly trying to compose herself.

"You don't have to be okay right now. You can…"

"I am okay." Naomi turned those deep-brown eyes on Diana. "I'm okay. Later, I might not be. But right now, I need to check the footage and see—"

"Just add the guest account to the rest of the cameras. We have people who can do that for you. I don't think you should stay here. We don't know that he was alone."

Naomi nodded. Of course she'd heard it too, that quiet scuffle of feet to the right of the kitchen. The doors had all been locked, but locked doors didn't mean much to Diana right now. Not when it came to Naomi's safety.

"I'd like to take you to a safe house until we can find out how he got in. You'll need to call your insurance and let them know you've had a home invasion—they should put you up in a hotel if I can't swing the safe house for longer than tonight. And your carpet might be ruined. I don't want to scare you, but this might be targeted. Oh, shit." Diana turned the volume down on her phone. "I'm not on call but I have to leave the volume on. I'll call in while you pack. I can take you to your bedroom if it's not near the living room. I don't want him to see you."

Naomi nodded, looking overwhelmed.

"This is a pretty good safe room," Diana said, looking around. The cameras were up on the computer, showing the ambulance arriving outside the gate.

"When I used to record things, I did it in here. I wouldn't call it soundproof but most people would."

"Record?"

"Oh, for the games. Video games. I work in graphic design, but I used to do some sound effects as well for independent game companies. I was going to make this my studio, and now it's…the only quiet place in the world. The room was already here. I just installed a bookshelf over the door. Aunt Isobel said this house was a waypoint on the underground railroad. There's a tunnel underneath us."

"A tunnel?"

Naomi nodded and pulled away.

Diana followed her to an unremarkable spot on the floor. Naomi pointed down and Diana saw the faint outline of what could generously be called a hatch. "I figured I might as well have a safe room with an exit. There's a gate on the other end, in the yard."

"So he didn't come in this way?"

Naomi shook her hand and touched the side of her head. Her face was screwed tight, like even that touch was painful.

"Let me make a few calls, sort out where we're staying tonight. I can call from the car, if you'll be okay to pack on your own. Not sure if…" Someone might still be in the house. Someone might have bugged it. Naomi herself might have sound equipment that someone could hack. This one felt personal, like he'd come for her not because he could, but because he'd wanted something. And with the gun, Diana didn't want to speculate about exactly what that something was. Naomi nodded. "You'll need to get—you don't—anything you'll need for the next week. Clothes, food, chargers for your headset—whatever you need."

"I work from home, I can't just—"

"Your safety is more important than any job."

"I'm freelance. I can't afford to lose any clients."

Diana eyed her. "What do you need for work?"

Naomi chewed her lip. "At least three of my laptops for the work I have this week. The portable gaming consoles for the beta of the game I'm working on, the e-reader to check the book covers, and the drawing tablet to work on. It's all in the study."

"Okay, pack it up. Then grab some clothes, whatever else you need. I want to get you out of here in the next half hour. I'm going to make some calls. I'll have an officer follow you through the house, to make sure you're safe until I come back."

Naomi nodded and opened the door. Sound burst into the room, making Diana flinch as well as Naomi. Diana opened the study door and grabbed Tony to keep Naomi company. He was still shaken, the poor kid. The first shooting was always the hardest, but he'd acted admirably. He smiled weakly at Naomi while Diana whispered instructions to him, and then Diana went out front to call in some favors.

CHAPTER FIVE

Naomi looked around. She'd shoved a bunch of clothes into a backpack, grabbed all her chargers and spare headsets—all the hearing protection she had. Her ears still rang with the gunshot and screams from earlier, along with the single "honey" that had spilled from Diana's lips over the phone. She looked over her bedroom with a critical eye; there were things she would miss but could live without, but she wanted to make sure she had everything she'd need to be away from home for a few days.

She'd lived alone long enough that she felt slightly embarrassed about someone else seeing her bedroom. The pride flag over the bed, the selection of books on the bedside table, the rumpled sheets. The room had obviously been rifled through, but it hadn't looked much neater before. She grabbed an inhaler she rarely needed but would prefer to have on hand and, glancing at the officer, two of the books she hadn't read yet from her bedside table.

Diana came back in, and Naomi blushed again, seeing her keen eyes dart around the room and land on the rainbow flag.

Naomi wasn't ashamed of being gay, it just hadn't been relevant, and now she felt like she'd been caught out pretending to be someone she wasn't. Diana's face was impassive as she quickly assessed the room.

"We've got somewhere to stay. That all you have?"

"Bag in the hallway," the officer chimed in. He'd thrown up; Naomi could smell it on him when he spoke, even under the cinnamon gum he'd been chewing before Diana had made him spit it out. She'd seen how his chewing grated on Naomi. He even talked quieter now that Diana had spoken to him, and Naomi was kind of glad he'd thrown up. She'd been left alone with someone who had just shot someone. At least it weighed on him. He wasn't a heartless killer, even if the man he'd shot had probably killed David. Even if that man had been coming to get her. She shivered.

"Coat?" Diana asked, eyeing her with concern. She came into the room and rifled through the wardrobe. "Better be prepared to dress warm." She pulled out some of Naomi's sweaters and jackets, along with a robe and a coat. Naomi hadn't expected to be away from home long enough to need that many clothes, and now she was worried. "We'll have someone stationed here, out front, while they work the crime scene. You have homeowner's insurance?"

Naomi nodded.

"Good. Get the carpet replaced. They're going to insist that a good cleaning will do the job. Trust me, it won't. Not on carpet that thick. You paid for insurance, you get new carpet." Jaw set, Diana folded the extra clothes into Naomi's bag. "What else do we need to pack?"

Naomi didn't feel overly disabled in her daily life anymore—most of her accommodations were habit to her now and she didn't notice them as long as she stayed in her house. But the food supplement always stuck in her craw.

"I need my food," Naomi admitted, going to the kitchen. Diana followed but hovered in the doorway, uncertain for the first time since they'd met. Naomi handed her a tin of hospital-grade food replacement powder with a shrug. It was better to get it over with. Diana took it without reading it, without reacting.

"Can you bring that coffee too, since we're here?"

"You like it?" Naomi was surprised; she knew the police ran on coffee, and hers was just shelf-stable sachets.

"It'll be better than anything they keep stocked in the safe house. Do you need anything else?"

"I'm good."

Diana chuckled softly. "Yeah. Yeah, you are. Okay, let's go."

Even in the car, Diana was quiet. Naomi liked that about her. Diana obviously thought a lot; there was so much going on under the surface. But she rarely spoke unnecessary words. At least, not around Naomi; she might be completely different when she wasn't working or accommodating someone's disability. Diana might be the most verbose person in the world and Naomi would never know.

Diana drove with confidence, and the silence wasn't uncomfortable. It was just there, the way it was when Naomi was alone. The car was noisy: the tires against the asphalt—one of them a little flat, sounding different than the others—the combustion of the engine. But Naomi could envision a bubble within the car, one large enough for herself and Diana, and she folded them within it, letting the background noise become a distant hum. She closed her eyes.

"I said it had to be standalone," Diana said, pulling into a driveway. She left the car running and pulled the garage door open, parking the car inside and shutting it behind her once she turned the engine off. "I just hope the bedrooms will be far enough back that the street noise won't bother you."

No house in this neighborhood would be quiet enough for her to sleep in, but she didn't want to hurt Diana's feelings, so she grabbed her electronics bag and headed for the door without replying. She didn't like to sleep with headphones on, but she could if she had to. Diana grabbed the other bag—the one with clothes and less important things. She used a code on the door, letting Naomi see her enter it.

"You can leave whenever you want, but you won't be under MPD protection if you do," Diana warned as she set the alarm on the panel inside the door. She shed her boots, then put the duffel on the couch and took the canvas bag with the tin into the kitchen. Reading the instructions on the tin, she scooped some out, moving around the kitchen quietly.

The house was cold, even though Diana had adjusted the thermostat as they came in. Naomi shivered. It was just a normal house; one she wouldn't look at twice on any street. It was furnished like a hotel, and it smelled the way old houses did when they hadn't been aired for a while. The color scheme was bleak—all beige and gray—and Naomi hoped she wouldn't have to stay somewhere so depressing for too long. The couches sagged in the middle. The house had probably been built in the 1950s and the furniture looked original; the yellows and reds and greens were nauseating.

"Have a shower if you need to warm up—the house should be warmer when you get out, once the furnace kicks in." Diana eyed her.

Naomi nodded, digging in her bag for her waterproof noise-canceling earbuds and taking off her headphones, pulling out the hearing aids beneath them. Diana was studiously not watching her, but she also remained entirely still until Naomi had inserted the waterproof earbuds. Naomi took out the chargers and plugged both sets in, then pulled out a shirt and pants from her other bag.

Diana deserted the kitchen, moving through the house to check the rooms, Naomi trailing behind her.

"Take whichever bedroom is quieter. Bathroom is through here. Let me check that we have hot water before you get in." There was something nurturing about her tonight, as though Naomi's panic had brought it out in her.

Naomi waited as Diana checked the temperature and made sure there were clean towels. Satisfied, she headed back to the kitchen, running her hand down Naomi's bicep with a reassuring smile as she brushed past.

The water was warm and delightful, the only sound water on tile and muffled by the earbuds. It had been a long day. Although Diana had tried to stop her, she had seen where the man had laid on her floor, the wet, shiny stain of blood on her carpet, the thick, metallic smell of it in the air. She'd seen the devastation he'd carried out in her home, nothing in the right place. She'd heard the awful impact of bullet into flesh.

Alone now, she cried as quietly as she could, aware she'd already shown too much emotion to Diana in the last few days. David was dead, and his killer had come for her. Perhaps it had been an accident, but he'd known David's routine, known enough that he had continued the nightly shutter ritual with barely a pause, as though he'd known Naomi had known it like a heartbeat, the shock of wood against wood like a whip crack.

And now she was here with Diana, who more than once had dropped everything in the middle of the night for her. Diana, who had been so thoughtful, so kind, so strong when she'd held Naomi. Diana, who was quiet for her, who understood that it wasn't Naomi being demanding or high maintenance in her requests for silence but that there was an unrelenting tide of noise that poured out from everyone else and never let more than a trickle escape from her own soft mouth. She cried because she felt understood, because she finally felt safe with someone.

Diana knuckled the door a little later, her hand barely brushing the wood. Naomi hadn't even heard her walk down the hall to the bathroom.

"Okay?" Diana asked gently, her voice soft with concern. This was probably just another day for Diana, just another really long day at work, and Naomi cried a little more because David was dead, and she could have been dead too if it wasn't for Diana, and none of it made sense to her at all.

"Honey, I respect your privacy and all, but I need to know you're okay and if you don't tell me I'm going to have to open the door and make sure."

"I'm okay." Naomi managed to choke the words out, and she heard Diana's palm brush against the door, as though she wished she could reach through it and take the sorrow from her.

"Okay. I'm putting the kettle on, and I've put out a warm robe for you. It's still a little chilly."

Diana left again, and Naomi let the sobs pour out of her. Diana had called her honey again. Naomi had so little contact with other people that she'd forgotten they sometimes used terms of endearment for each other when they felt someone was especially emotionally fragile.

When Naomi came out, Diana was dressed in pajamas, reading a book as she stood by the stove waiting for the kettle to boil. There was a mug in her other hand, which she set on the counter when she saw Naomi.

Diana's sleepwear felt like protective camouflage. It wasn't sexy or revealing, just a practical matching flannel set with a gender-neutral T-shirt beneath. As if it was carefully chosen to be masculine, unflattering, unsuggestive. Yet Naomi found it cute; the other woman was too short for clothes from the men's section that fit her hips and chest. The pant legs were rolled up, and the sleeves as well, exposing her taut, tanned forearms. For a woman her age, Diana was incredibly fit; her tight jeans showed calves that flexed as she walked, and her arms had been firm and strong around Naomi.

Naomi looked away. The last few days had been hellish, but without Diana as a buffer they would have been a lot worse. She was more accommodating than anyone Naomi had ever met, and it wasn't her fault that Naomi had a little crush on her. The little swagger she had when she was walking, the way she touched her lips when she thought, the tight jeans that hugged her perfectly, so tight that her fingers wouldn't fit in the pockets, the thick belt drawing attention to her waist and hips. The flattering shirts beneath her thick coats, the colorful scarves she wore in deference to the cold, something that was clearly hers outside the job. She tended toward mostly neutral colors and clothes, but her scarves betrayed a sense of style that didn't come across in the rest of her professional wardrobe.

Aware she was staring and that Diana was watching her now with fingers pressed against lips that looked soft and plush, Naomi turned her attention to setting up her laptops. Hopefully this would all be over soon, and she could go back home knowing she'd done everything she possibly could to help the police catch David's killer. She felt Diana's eyes lingering on her and wished she had brought something a little more neutral than her flannel button-down and fluffy pajama pants with little rainbow unicorns on them. She felt immature in comparison to the other woman, and it made her a little insecure.

"Go bag in the trunk," Diana said in response to Naomi's questioning look. "Spare clothes, books, toiletries…"

Naomi eyed the book. It was one of hers. Diana looked down at it, then back up at Naomi with a sheepish grin.

"It's a murder mystery," Diana said. "Color me intrigued."

"It's a…it's a *lesbian* murder mystery."

"Still murder," Diana said with a shrug. "Plenty of good cops are gay. I'll swap you one of mine."

There was a small pile of books on the counter, well-thumbed. Naomi craned her head to read the spines.

"Agatha Christie? Really?"

"Never can remember all those British upper-class names when I reread them." Diana shrugged, then set the book down and took the kettle off the stove. "I hope you don't mind. I made some of the meal replacement up while you were in the shower, just to see what it's like. It's not great. But it's warm and sweet and better than it was without the hot chocolate in it."

Diana filled a mug and stirred it slowly with a spoon, staying away from the edges and bottom of the mug. "I read somewhere that a teaspoon against a mug is, something like eighty-seven decibels or some shit. I can pick up something tomorrow that's going to be less—less bullshit loud. Sorry. Tired." Diana yawned and held out the mug.

Naomi assumed Diana was close to her own age—there were the little smile lines around her mouth, and noticeable gray in her strawberry-blond hair, which was tied up and out of the way in a ponytail. It was endearing. But even tired and in pajamas, Diana was so good to look at—a little rumpled and soft around the edges, her guard down a little more than usual.

"Spoons are bullshit loud," Naomi agreed. She took the mug and sipped. It was still bland and unpalatable, still not as good as chewable food, but it was indeed sweet and warm and better than it was without the hot chocolate in it, and she kind of loved Diana for how much effort she'd put into making her meal more tolerable in a way Naomi hadn't even thought of. "Thank you."

Swallowing still hurt, still sounded loud in her ears, but the fact that someone cared enough to prepare a meal for her out of such limited options was louder still.

Diana shrugged and sipped at her own mug.

"I won't sleep," Naomi told her out of courtesy. "Not—not because of today. Tonight. Because the sound profile here isn't what I'm used to. You should go to bed. I'll stay up and work. I work nights when I can't sleep, and I'm a bit behind."

"It'll be noisier in daytime. You won't be able to sleep during the day," Diana said.

It took physical effort not to roll her eyes. Naomi knew a lot more about noise than Diana did, but she also knew the detective didn't mean to sound condescending. She resisted the urge to be sarcastic as Diana eyed her, a little smile on her lips, the dimple showing in her cheek for a moment.

"Your call. Choose a bedroom anyway. I'm not particular."

Naomi claimed a room and then set up at the ugly dining room table for the night, swapping between projects in order of priority by due date and work remaining. She sent out emails, not mentioning that a man had come for her in the night, not mentioning that she was in a safe house.

Diana stayed up with her for a while, reading, glancing over at Naomi now and then as though she was an unhatched egg that had reached incubation date. Waiting for her to fall apart, to be overwhelmed. But she wasn't. It was quiet enough here—louder than home, but everywhere was. Diana had done the best she could, and until Naomi was able to figure out the audio blueprint of the house, she wouldn't be able to tune it out.

"I like being able to see your ears." Naomi looked up, startled even though Diana's voice had been quiet, and lifted a hand to her head. She'd left the waterproof earbuds in so her hearing aids and headphones could fully charge. "They're kind of cute."

Naomi blushed. The detective had complimented her ears. While reading one of her lesbian books. While holed up in a safe house alone together. They were spending the night—oh Lord, they were spending the night together.

"Not that it's a judgment on what you usually wear, or the functionality of your adaptive equipment," Diana added, looking a little flustered.

"Who?" Naomi asked. Diana was too good, too well-versed at accommodating someone who couldn't stand sound not to be directly related to someone like her.

"Who what?"

"Who in your family has hyperacusis? Or are they deaf?"

"Oh. No one. But my brother's son's kid is autistic, and he gets overstimulated to the point he can't talk. Sensory processing disorder. Can't talk, but he can sign. He likes things quiet too. Been meaning to grab some recommendations from you, actually, but I was going to wait until the case was over. Just brands to look into for some of the sound softening. Might make things easier for him. He has other sensory issues too, so nothing we've tried has worked for him yet."

"Yeah, let me know what he needs. I can hook you up."

"Thanks." Diana turned back to her book.

"Wait, so you learned sign language for your nephew's kid?"

"Well, when he got the diagnosis, not that many people in his life bothered because he can talk when he's not overwhelmed, and that felt kind of shitty. He's a good kid. He's worth it."

Naomi found herself blinking back tears, and Diana got to her feet and came to stand beside Naomi, lifting her to her feet. She looked into Naomi's eyes like she was considering the available information. Naomi tilted her head away from the scrutiny in that gaze, but Diana gently rested her fingers against her jaw and adjusted the angle until Naomi's watery eyes met hers again. Diana nodded, having formed a conclusion.

"People didn't bother to learn for you either, huh?" Diana asked, and Naomi shook her head. It took some effort to keep her bottom lip from trembling, and tears started to well in her eyes. She was ashamed of her own self-pity, her jealousy of a kid she didn't even know.

Diana sighed and released Naomi's chin, her arms fitting over Naomi's shoulders to hold her close as the cascade of tears truly started. Naomi felt the soft flannel of Diana's shirt against her face.

Having anyone else this close would be unbearable, but Diana made sure not to touch Naomi's head and remained still when Naomi adjusted to rest her head on Diana's shoulder, keeping her ear away from the warmth of Diana's chest and the sound of the heartbeat within.

"Yeah, well, you were worth it too. You are worth it." Diana's hands were strong and sure, not hesitating even though between the pride flag and the lesbian books, she had to know Naomi was gay. She didn't seem bothered by it, didn't act like it mattered to her. She just held Naomi close and rubbed her back, even though Naomi was clinging to her and whimpering at the shock of being told she was worth learning a language for. Rose hadn't even bothered to lower her voice in Naomi's own house. Rose hadn't thought Naomi was worth sticking around for. Her own parents had abandoned her. She'd ended up alone, with only her work for company.

She let herself return the hug for a moment, her hands sliding around Diana's waist.

Diana, who had seen this coming. She couldn't have known the form it would take or what would trigger it, but she'd known Naomi would need the space to fall apart, and she'd made herself available to help put her back together again.

Diana, who kept her tone low and usually spoke only if her hands were full or her questions too complicated. She had the words but not all the fine syntax and grammar of ASL; it was obvious she primarily used it in emergencies rather than in conversation.

Still, it was better than nothing, which was the amount of effort Rose had put into learning how to sign or speak to Naomi. It wasn't that Rose hadn't understood or believed her; it was that she didn't want to change any of her habits or learn anything new. Not when she could go out and find herself an undamaged, able-bodied girlfriend instead. Much easier for her; Rose was pretty and funny. Whereas Naomi was just—she was laden with hearing protection for one, and being a marginalized part of an already marginalized community meant her dating pool was nonexistent. Hell, even the number of people who could reliably accommodate her was nonexistent. There was only Diana, who had been kind beyond measure.

A little ashamed, Naomi drew away, wiping her face. Diana caught her chin again, brushing Naomi's cheeks with her thumbs before removing her hands.

Bed now? she signed.

Naomi laughed, the noise sounding foreign to her own ears. She pointed at Diana and nodded, then to herself and the computer behind her. Then, tentatively, lifted her open hand to her chin and took it away in a gesture of thanks.

Diana's smile was tired but pleased; she shrugged the thanks off and picked up her book as she headed off to bed.

Naomi paused in the doorway of Diana's room, unable to resist looking in. Diana was still awake and reading. At some point she had retrieved reading glasses from somewhere; a tortoiseshell frame that brought out the highlights of her hair. Now she looked over the rims of her glasses at Naomi as she paused. She looked concerned. She put her book down in her lap.

Okay? Diana signed.

Naomi nodded, swallowing. Diana's strawberry-blond hair was down, flowing over her shoulders in loose curls, and her smile was softened with sleepiness, her dimple flashing.

Think walk. Naomi signed back. *Sorry.*

No problem, no sorry.

Naomi nodded again, shifting her weight in the doorway. Diana looked so warm and cozy, and she'd left the door open which felt like an invitation of sorts, although it was probably to monitor movement in the house, which Naomi was currently doing a lot of.

Sleep well, Naomi signed finally, walking back down the hall. She'd been pacing, trying to break out of her creative funk, and the image of Diana's smile remained lodged in her brain. She sketched the smile on her computer, conveying the relaxed interest the other woman had shown her.

Naomi continued pacing through the night. It was how she got ideas. She went from the hall to the laundry and back around to the front of the house where the kitchen was. She looked out the windows when someone drove past. She continued to peek in at Diana, still reading in the bedroom she'd chosen. It was reassuring to know she wasn't alone.

Diana looked up and smiled every time Naomi walked past, but she didn't say anything or close the door. She looked relaxed and unbothered by the change in her own routine, by the inconvenience Naomi had caused her. At some point during the night, she fell asleep with the door still open, the book slipping from her slackened hand, the bedside lamp giving her hair highlights in the gold range. Naomi paused. Diana had helped her so much, she owed it to her to make sure she didn't sleep with her neck at that awkward angle, to take her glasses off so she didn't break them, to rescue her own book from being slept on.

Naomi retrieved the book first, using the bookmark she'd left in it to hold Diana's place instead of hers. She put the book on the bedside table, then carefully took the glasses from Diana's face and folded them, placing them on top of the book. Diana's face had little freckles, this close, dotting her cheeks and nose. They were cute. Diana was cute. Naomi looked away.

She slid a hand under Diana's torso and shifted her to lie down. Diana went willingly, grabbing a pillow and pulling it to her chest as she settled herself with a little huff. Naomi brought the blanket up over her, and it was then that she noticed the wedding ring.

Of course Diana was married. Naomi was a fool. There had been a moment earlier tonight that Naomi had wondered if it was really all just Diana's job, or if there was something else between them. And now she had her answer. Diana was married. Probably to a man. Probably had children with him, and that was why she'd been so good at comforting someone distraught. Naomi hadn't expected it to feel quite this bad, though, finding out that Diana wasn't single. It made sense that someone like her was married. Of course she had someone at home waiting for her, someone that loved her. It had already been a loud, awful, long day, and this latest blow completely numbed her. She turned out the light.

Anyone else would have missed the almost silent "'night," Diana mumbled, but Naomi didn't let it break her stride.

CHAPTER SIX

When morning came, Diana walked past Naomi to the kitchen, yawning and adorable, bare toes poking out below her manly pajama pants, fingers barely protruding past the cuffs of the sleeves. Naomi enjoyed looking at Diana in the morning light; she was so unguarded and casual, so comfortable with Naomi's presence. Her hair was rumpled and loose around her shoulders, her eyes soft and warm behind the glasses she now wore openly, as though this was just a sleepover or a breakfast date.

She made herself a coffee and brought one over for Naomi, placing it gently on a coaster on her left side so she could still work her mouse. Diana's hand brushed Naomi's shoulder on the way past, the small gesture grounding. She sat down with her book and drank her coffee slowly, savoring it. Her lips were pink, and she glowed with warmth.

After a while, she rose and set down her book, a little smile on her face. "You're not much of a conversationalist, but you're good company."

Naomi agreed with the sentiment. It should have been awkward. They were relative strangers, forced into sharing a space. But the vibe in the house was good—calm and relaxed.

Diana disappeared and came back out a few minutes later in the same kind of tight jeans she wore to work, but black and slightly distressed in a way that seemed fashionable. Naomi had to drag her eyes away from how well they fit. She ran her hand through her hair, creating soft golden highlights where the light caught it. Her hazel eyes were lit through as well, highlighting the green and gold in them. Diana had put some basic makeup on and brushed her hair, and she looked closed off and professional again. No more freckles.

"You said there was a tunnel," Diana said, all business now. "Where does it go?"

Naomi brought up the blueprint to her house and showed Diana the screen. Ground floor, then subfloor. A short tunnel, one that might be mistaken for a service tunnel or cabling conduit. Aunt Isobel hadn't been too interested in it, but Naomi had thought it was cool. She used to play down there when she was a kid, before she knew the harrowing history that had made the tunnel necessary. "See? Not much. It comes out in the yard. I had that gate installed." She pulled up the camera.

Diana slid her hand onto Naomi's back and peered over her. She pointed at the gate when she spotted it, leaning over. Her hair spilled over Naomi's shoulders, chest brushing Naomi's back. Diana turned to Naomi, her face very close. If Naomi pulled back, she'd press against Diana's chest. Heart pounding, she looked back at the screen, trying to focus on what Diana was saying.

"Do you have a sensor on that entrance? Did you record that camera last night?"

"There was nothing." Naomi flicked to the application page of her home security system and hovered the mouse over the gate sensor. "See?"

She went back to the cameras and played back the footage from the night before at high speed. She hadn't seen anything, and she only kept a day's worth of footage on the local drive.

Diana pulled back, apparently satisfied. "You had David's blueprints. Do you know if there's anything like that in his house? He wasn't high-tech like you, was he?"

David. Poor David. Swallowing, Naomi brought up his blueprint, which she'd downloaded from the real estate website the other night. Diana leaned in again to examine it, then pulled away with a frustrated huff. There was nothing there.

"It's a different type of diagram, isn't it?" Diana said.

Naomi flicked back to hers. "Mine is older. From some kind of county record, I think. This would have been when they were trying to sell it."

"Can you please send them both through to my work email? I'll have someone look into them. You're positive no one touched your doors?"

Naomi looked at the diagram of her house again. She nodded, then yawned. Diana's hand rubbed her back.

"You can sleep whenever you like," Diana said softly. "I have to go into the office later, and I'll swing by for food on the way back here. Would you drink soup if I bought some? Just soup, no noodles, no croutons."

Naomi nodded.

"Will you be okay on your own? Should I get someone to cover me?"

Naomi shook her head. "I'd rather be alone."

"I know, but we need you to be able to testify, and I'm not sure your house is secure, and I don't want you in a hotel alone. You'll just have to put up with me a little longer, okay?"

Naomi hadn't meant it to sound like she resented the care Diana had shown her. She'd just wanted to clarify that she'd rather have Diana than anyone else with her.

"Your presence isn't a hardship," Naomi said.

Diana's phone rang and her hand withdrew from Naomi's back as she left to take the call.

* * *

When Diana came back into the kitchen, Naomi was absorbed in her work and didn't look up. Diana poured another two cups of coffee, even though it was late morning. She could drink it all day, and Naomi's shoulders had a sag to them after her week of broken sleep. There was no milk in the house, but the stuff Naomi drank was almost like creamer. She raised an eyebrow as she opened the tin. Naomi processed the question and nodded, her eyes raising no higher than Diana's collarbone.

Diana read the ingredients as she sipped from her mug, careful not to let her teeth come into contact with the ceramic. She sat across from Naomi at the table, picking up her book again.

When Diana put her mug down, her wedding ring struck the ceramic, echoing loudly through the quiet house. She didn't know why she still wore it. Well, she did. She just didn't know why she hadn't bought herself one she actually liked. She reached to pull it off, surprised to find Naomi's hands reaching out to still her fingers.

"Your…*husband*…must miss you."

"He can miss me all he likes, the miserable bastard." Diana pulled the ring off and set it disdainfully on the table, resting her hand over it.

Naomi's hand settled on top of hers.

"Ex-husband. Divorced, but unfortunately sometimes it's better to look…unapproachable. Easier, I mean. People see the ring and assume I'm someone else's property."

"So I'm not keeping you from your family?" Naomi sounded relieved, and Diana turned her hand so her palm met Naomi's.

"If I wasn't here, I'd be at the precinct. This is my job. My captain's agreed that I should continue protection detail. Usually there would be a relief shift to cover me, but he doesn't have anyone on the squad who can accommodate your disability and ADA would need to be part of that discussion. I'm raking in the overtime in the lead-up to Christmas, so my grandkids will thank you."

Diana had intended it to sound lighthearted, but Naomi's hand lifted off hers and onto her mug. She hadn't drunk much.

"How long?"

"I don't know." Diana sighed and brushed her fingers over the ring, the solid metal comforting. She'd been divorced longer than she'd been married, and the ring didn't really remind her of Andrew anymore; it just kept men at bay. "Until we know if he was acting alone, or can pinpoint how he broke in. I haven't had an update today. It could be a few days. If we're out before insurance replaces your carpet, insist on being put up in a hotel. I don't want you in there before it's cleaned up." Diana sighed and left the ring where it was. "Like I said, you need anything, let me know."

Naomi's mouth twisted, like there was something she wanted to say. "You're a cop, and federally it's a gray area but…"

"What do you need?"

"Just some CBD gummies. 10:1 THC. I can eat and sleep if you get me some."

"Yeah, done."

"I mean, I try not to, but I don't want to be on sleeping tablets while I'm here. I won't wake up if someone…"

"It's not a problem. I'm not a Fed, and you have more than enough justification for medical use."

Naomi looked relieved and Diana wondered how much of her life was lived in misunderstanding. She'd lowered her voice without noticing, the entire conversation carried out in low tones rather than whispers, and Naomi hadn't flinched or asked for Diana to sign instead. Perhaps, now that Naomi was used to her, they could speak as though there wasn't a sleeping baby in the room.

Diana made a few more calls. When she came back out, she was pleased to find that Naomi had finished her meal replacement.

Reveling in the small win, she reached out to gather Naomi's mug. Her fingers didn't quite close around it and it crashed to the ground, smashing on impact, the noise unbearably loud in the quiet house even to Diana.

Diana flinched before it hit the ground, and Naomi cringed a moment later. She stood to help clean it up, and Diana swerved away from the movement automatically, one arm flinging up to keep Naomi away from her, to protect herself from a blow that wasn't coming.

"No, it's sharp." Diana's voice was low and quiet, but it took effort to maintain when she was worried about Naomi's safety; she was only wearing socks, and the shards were sharp. She could pretend that was why she still had her hand outstretched to keep Naomi away. "I've got this. It's my mess to clean up."

"I'd like to help."

"I don't need help." When Diana looked up, Naomi was pale and drawn again, and Diana cursed herself for the lapse in attention that had made such a loud, unpredictable noise.

"I'm not mad," Naomi said gently, her tone very soft, and Diana looked up again. The look on her face was so sad, so full of sympathy that Diana immediately returned her attention to the shattered remains.

Naomi knew, somehow. She'd picked up on something—the way Diana had flinched before Naomi had when she'd dropped the mug. Diana dropped her eyes from Naomi's knowing gaze and looked at the mess of ceramic and the dregs of brown liquid spreading across the tiles of the kitchen floor. At least it would be easily cleaned up. She took a paper towel from the counter and dropped it over the spill, scooping up fragments of pottery.

Naomi watched with wide eyes, then carefully stepped forward. "That's why you're so quiet, isn't it? Someone hurt you when you weren't."

Diana leaned back on her heels, grabbing more towels to bundle the rest of the sharp bits away into the trash. "That's not really any of your business," she said, louder and more sharply than she'd intended.

Naomi met her eyes without flinching. "It is, because I remind you enough of whoever used to hurt you for you to be scared of me."

Diana dropped the trash in the kitchen bin and washed her hands, examining a small cut from where she'd been careless. She turned, resting her hands on the kitchen sink behind her as she looked Naomi over.

"I'm not scared of you. I'm worried about hurting you, and loud, sudden noises hurt you. This wasn't covered in any of my training. I don't really know what to make of you, or what to do with you. All I can do is make your time here as quiet and comfortable as possible."

"And you have. I do appreciate it—I don't think I said so, but you're one of the only people who has understood." She fidgeted as she spoke. "If I have to be holed up in a safe house, then I'm glad it's with you. I'm sorry it's so stressful for you but thank you for drawing the short straw on this."

Diana exhaled. Naomi clearly felt like a burden, and Diana never wanted her to feel that way. "It's not exactly a hardship for me. I mean, you might be right. Being quiet is a habit for me, now."

"That's kind of sad. You have a nice voice. I know you soften it a lot for me but, um, yeah. No one should make you—not even me."

"You never asked it of me. You never demanded that I be quieter because you'd rather I didn't remind you that I exist." Diana breathed in again, aware of the physical response her body was having to a perceived threat. It was the same panic she used to feel when she drew attention to the fact that she was home. She'd hated the way his attention focused on her, snide comments from a man who had never actually bothered to get to know her as a person. She still felt dirty where he'd touched her. She forced herself to relax. "And you deserve to be given the accommodations that your disability requires."

"I like being reminded—how could anyone mind that you—" Naomi's voice was high and squeaky, like it had been when she'd cried the night before.

Diana clenched her jaw, trying not to let it get to her. "So that's clear now, isn't it? I don't mind being quiet, and you aren't mad when I'm not. It'll only be for a few more days at most." Diana turned away and put the kettle back on the stove. She watched it, aware that Naomi was still watching her. She took down a fresh mug and discreetly wiped her eye, which had leaked a little. She made the coffee quickly, efficiently, feeling tired down to her bones.

Her kids had been telling her to think about a career that let her sleep at night, but she never slept well knowing there were killers out there. If she'd been on leave, if she hadn't been working for MPD, Naomi would have had to deal with someone else. It was worth it—between the overtime and the sense of satisfaction she would get when this job was over.

"Like I said. Overtime before Christmas. Grandkids are going to be spoiled this year."

"You said you had grandchildren, but I thought you were joking."

Diana's shoulders dropped. Naomi was trying to defuse the tension with a compliment—a little manipulative, perhaps, and Diana didn't usually share details of her family with anyone involved in an open murder investigation, but the relief was enough to make her turn with her coffee, removing the kettle from the heat.

Naomi came closer when she saw Diana relax, and she reached for the first aid kit in the cupboard. She stilled Diana's hand once she was done pouring and held it under the running tap for a moment, then wiped it with a cotton bud loaded with antiseptic before carefully putting a Band-Aid over the cut. Diana bent the knuckle to test the flexion. Naomi's hand cradled hers. Diana had planned to tend to it later, but Naomi had seen it as a priority.

Naomi squeezed Diana's hand gently then released it to retrieve her coffee. Diana tried to remember what they'd been talking about. She'd been distracted by Naomi's proximity, the heady, clean smell of her, the warmth of her so close. The focus she'd put into taking care of an incredibly minor injury.

Diana was used to taking care of other people. She wasn't used to anyone taking care of her.

"My son and daughter both have kids now," Diana said, filling in the awkward silence.

Naomi smiled up at her over her mug, taking a sip, closing her eyes as she did to savor the taste. Her eyes opened again and took Diana in, assessing her. "You must have married young."

Diana had. She'd been too young to know any better. The world had been different then. She'd been expected to marry and have children, even though she'd wanted a career. She loved her children fiercely, but she'd wanted more from life than being a wife and mother. That was when Andrew had turned, had started the snide remarks about her body not bouncing back after the baby. When he'd realized she wasn't reliant on him, things got worse.

These days everyone knew the signs of emotional abuse in a marriage, and that sex wasn't rightfully owed to a husband. Back then it hadn't been as clear cut. She'd tried to make herself smaller, so he wouldn't notice her. It had devolved into what Naomi had somehow picked up on—being yelled at for any perceived imperfection.

"I did," Diana admitted. She thought over the way things were now—she was here with a woman who read lesbian books and slept under a pride flag, and it was the most comfortable she'd felt in her life. She had to be quiet, but that was an accommodation, not a demand.

When she looked up, Naomi didn't look disconcerted by the amount of time it had taken her to answer a simple question.

"We were too young. We didn't really know who we were when we got married, let alone each other. And then we grew up a bit and found out we didn't fit anymore. But I got my children out of it, and I have three grandchildren too now. It's not all bad. I think getting a divorce saved my family, to be honest."

Diana was very careful to use neutral language, to not blame Andrew for the failure of the marriage, to not expose him as the reason she'd flinched when she'd dropped a mug, waiting for him to come all the way across the city to call her a stupid bitch. She'd been too careful, and Naomi had been putting things together. She'd have made a good detective.

Diana tapped the sink with her index fingers, still leaning against it, aware they were both standing awkwardly in a house with plentiful chairs. "You never married?"

"Wasn't legal, and then she left me anyway. I don't blame her. I wouldn't want to live with this, and Rose had a choice." There was no bitterness in her voice, no tells to suggest she was lying.

Diana eyed her. There it was, the confirmation she'd been looking for, evidence that Naomi had been involved with women in the past, that she was some flavor of homosexual. "You don't— you've never thought about—"

"I'm not into men, no." Naomi was polite enough not to roll her eyes but amused enough that it was obvious she wanted to.

"How did you know?"

"It was kind of obvious. How did you know?"

"That I like men? I didn't, not really. Everyone else did, and I kind of assumed everyone felt the same way as I did."

"Which was?"

Diana shrugged. She couldn't turn back now; she'd started this incredibly personal line of questioning. "I don't know. I never really hung around waiting for one to show up. I was always kind of relieved when Andrew didn't come home. It was just kind of expected that I'd marry him, and I didn't hate him, not at first. But now I'm wondering if a relationship should be based on more than just not hating someone."

"That's bleak," Naomi said, her eyebrows lifted, and Diana wondered what it would be like to be in a relationship that wasn't like that. She hadn't dated seriously after the divorce because her children deserved better than the men she'd dated, but also because she'd hated being married.

"My kids more than make up for him, and their kids too. They both did better for themselves than I did. Jake married a teacher, and Kate married someone who joined the military to get his medical degree without a crippling loan. And their kids? My heart melts every time I see them."

"But there was never anyone you actually enjoyed being with?"

"The kids were too young when I found myself single. I couldn't trust my judgment back then, not after that mess of a marriage. I couldn't do that to them, and now they're all grown up, and I guess I don't have any excuses anymore. I think I'm too set in my ways now, and life without a man is better than life with a man like Andrew. I make all my own choices, and I don't flinch when I drop something anymore." Diana looked up and sighed, meeting Naomi's eyes. "Most of the time, anyway. I mean it. I'm not scared of you. I'm worried about hurting you."

Naomi looked uncertain. Diana gathered that people didn't usually worry about hurting her. She could relate only too well. It was too close to home, Naomi's vulnerability. Her whole life was in Diana's hands; was she protecting her, or keeping her hostage?

"I have to head into the office. You know the code for the door if you need some fresh air. I'll pop over to the dispensary and pick up a pizza on the way home. You want one?"

Naomi shook her head, then appeared to reconsider. "If you can get to the dispensary, then I'd like one with mushrooms, peppers, and spinach."

"You're really easy to take care of, you know that?" Diana asked. She pushed away from the sink and grabbed her keys, chuckling to herself at Naomi's blush as she brushed past, even though there was room to walk around her. She liked the way Naomi blushed too much to make any detours.

CHAPTER SEVEN

Naomi looked up when Diana came home with two fresh pizzas. She watched intently as Diana set them down, her eyes a little anxious.

Diana moved closer and pulled out a little jar and a tube from her coat pockets. "I didn't know which flavor you'd like, so I got mixed berries and a peach pearl thing. They sounded nice."

Naomi opened the tube and dumped one of the pearls onto the palm of her hand, examining it briefly. A light orange, crystallized sugar coated it. Diana wondered what they tasted like; they looked like normal candy. Naomi deliberated for a while. She read the packet carefully as though it was new to her, then slipped the pearl between lips that looked soft, letting it dissolve in her mouth without chewing at all. She waited half an hour before eating a second gummy, which seemed responsible, and shortly afterward she sighed loudly, her shoulders slumping.

"That pizza?"

"Want me to reheat it?"

"Nope."

Naomi moved as though she was going to stand, but Diana got up first, pulling the cold pizza from the fridge. She'd eaten a few slices from both because she hadn't expected Naomi to want any.

"Sure you don't want me to reheat it?" The cheese was congealed, and it didn't look appetizing at all to Diana. Naomi stared at the boxes hungrily, and Diana shrugged and brought them both over, watching with a kind of fascinated wonder as Naomi annihilated a single slice with unexpected fervor. She immediately started another, jaws working even as she flinched, practically inhaling the food, faster than Jake ever had, even in the midst of his growth spurts. She reached for a third slice, then looked up at Diana, squinting as she chewed rapidly.

"Did you want some?" Naomi said, sounding guilty.

"I've eaten my share. They're all yours." Diana had eaten her pizza in the car so Naomi wouldn't have to listen to her chew. It was amazing how loud everything sounded when she really listened.

Naomi paused after the third slice. "You can reheat them now, if you want."

"You'll have more?"

Naomi nodded, swallowing before speaking. "It's so much more tolerable now."

"I've never seen anything like that. You looked sick at the smell of them when I brought them in." Diana took both pizzas and turned the oven on, loading slices onto a tray. "I got two to be polite, not because I thought you'd actually eat anything."

"I know. I let it go on too long this time, but the dispensary I use ran out of the one I like, and the other one doesn't deliver."

"So you've just been suffering this whole time when there's something that helps?"

"Not—it doesn't—it doesn't exactly muffle noises, but it does affect the way my brain responds to them. Chewing is bearable. It makes me hungry enough to put up with how loud chewing is. Does that make sense?"

Diana ran her hand over her face. "So you're telling me you've just been putting up with it because—what—your dispensary stopped stocking the flavor you like? You didn't even tell me a flavor to pick up, just a ratio."

"That's what they ran out of. I was looking for another place that does delivery. If I have too much THC it ramps up all the sensitivity and anxiety. Not enough doesn't get me hungry enough to eat."

"Okay." Diana took a deep breath. "Okay."

"You looked angry when I told you it helps." Naomi's voice was timid, but she didn't look away.

"I thought you were suffering in silence when there was an easy fix. I thought you were—I see people who don't take care of themselves, and they look a lot like you. If I'd known that was the only reason you didn't have something that actually helps you, I would have picked it up for you. Before now. Do you know how worried I've been? I could see all the bones of your spine. I was trying to make that stuff you drink at least taste nice enough for you to finish one."

"I appreciate that. I do. When did you see my spine?"

"On the footage, your camera. You got a package and you weren't in a coat. And when you lean forward, your neck is all bones."

"It's not your problem," Naomi said stiffly, her gaze turned back to the oven.

"No, it's not my problem. You're not my problem. But you are my responsibility. I'm responsible for you while you stay here. And I was—I was worried."

"About the break-in?"

"No, about you not being strong enough to get on the witness stand."

"That's ridiculous."

"In grade school, my daughter started losing weight when I was working nights. I was worried something was going on with her, but she was—"

"It's not an eating disorder, and I'm not your daughter."

That sentence stopped Diana in her tracks. Naomi was right. It was her life, and she was allowed to live it however she wanted. Naomi wasn't—thank God—Diana's daughter. She was a woman close to Diana's own age, and Diana had been fantasizing about nurturing her. She was infantilizing someone with a disability. She'd thought she was better than that.

And there had been a visceral sense of revulsion at Naomi even suggesting that they could be related. She didn't want to examine that, so she checked on the pizza. She could see the cheese bubbling through the window in the oven door, so she pulled it out and brought it over to Naomi. She sat next to her and ate a slice as well, watching Naomi chew with something like relief on her face, her eyes closing with bliss as she moaned, the first involuntary noise Diana had heard from her. Even her sneezes, adorable as they were, were silent.

"I didn't mean to be rude. The crack about your daughter." Naomi swallowed and reached for another slice.

"And I didn't mean to project. I guess I have some unresolved food issues."

"No, you're right. It's your job, for the moment, to make sure I'm safe. And that's awkward for you, and it's awkward for me."

"Does it still hurt? When you eat?"

"It's just—it distracts me enough."

Fascinated, Diana watched as Naomi ate another two slices. Following that, Naomi stretched, then packed the few remaining slices away. On her way past the table, she grabbed what looked like a controller with a screen in it and curled up on the couch with it. It was almost silent, with only very quiet music coming from it. Curious, Diana joined her on the couch under the pretense of reading her book, but instead she watched as Naomi made her way through what was clearly a town in a video game. She remembered that Naomi had said she did some game development.

Naomi got up after a while to eat more pizza, then came back, her hands still damp from washing the grease off them. She'd left the controller on the couch, and she clocked Diana's interest.

"You wanna play?" Naomi asked, holding it out to her.

"Oh, I've never..." Diana had played some of Jake's games with him back in the '90s, but they'd always made her anxious. There had been no way to save between sections, and she had never been any good at fighting with the little pixel sword.

"It's easy." Naomi handed it over. "It's still in development. I designed some of the 3D models for the game and they asked if I could do some beta testing before they release it."

"What am I supposed to do? I haven't played a game since the kids were little."

"Do you need your glasses?" Naomi got up again and came back with them, handing them over with her fingers on the legs rather than the lens.

Diana took them and slid them on.

"So. Left, right." Naomi reached over and pressed the directions on the left joystick. "Up, down. The other joystick changes the camera angle. Jump, run, action, and menu. Just go for a walk through the town."

"What if I ruin it? Can you save your game and start a new one for me?"

Naomi laughed, a sweet, delighted, honest laugh. She seemed lighter, happier. She wasn't louder, and her headphones were still firmly wedged over her ears, but she leaned into Diana's side to see the screen without any hesitation. Diana wondered if this was what Naomi was like when she was a little buzzed.

"We're trying to break it, to make sure the people who buy the game when it's released can't. We're looking for anything that might impact someone's ability to play the game. Just walk around and talk to people. You have to solve the case from the clues the villagers give you."

Diana focused, which was surprisingly hard to do with the pleasant warmth of Naomi pressing against her, with Naomi's head nudging its way onto Diana's shoulder so she could see the screen. Diana got used to it faster than she'd expected, feeling a little silly as her character slammed into a wall at full speed when she turned using the wrong joystick.

"No, you're good," Naomi said encouragingly when Diana tried to hand it back. "Keep going. It'll be good to get feedback from a detective on this, actually. Since it's kind of your job."

"My job is not this annoying." Diana snorted, and Naomi reached over to take the controller back. "No, I'm not—it's fine."

"You're not enjoying it."

"I'm frustrated," Diana admitted, "but it is interesting. Just show me what you made."

Now she was the one crowding Naomi, who curled up again, her shoulder pressing against Diana's chest, making her lean over Naomi's shoulder to watch the screen. Naomi leaned back into Diana a little more as she got further into the game; it was easier to follow when someone else was playing, and the characters were pretty cute.

"Wait, go back," Diana said. "It's that guy, right?"

"No, I made someone else. They're in the next building."

"I mean, the guy who stole all the potatoes. It's this guy." Diana pointed to the giggling gremlin in the basement.

"How did you—Of course you figured it out from one clue. Yeah, it's him."

Diana chuckled smugly.

"It's a game made for kids, Detective. It's not especially difficult."

Diana deflated a little.

"See? This one's mine." Naomi zoomed in and walked around the character.

"It looks like the other ones."

"Yeah, I made the base models. I did this one as a demo and they liked her enough to buy her as a character too."

It was cute, and the game was cuter still now that Diana knew Naomi had designed not just one but the basis for all the little people.

"I don't know how you do it," Diana said in wonder. "I wouldn't even know where to start with something like that."

"I don't solve murders, and I didn't have kids. I had plenty of time to learn."

"When you said 'graphic designer,' I didn't picture anything like this. But does this mean you're technically working right now?"

"Aren't you?" Naomi shot back, nestling deeper against Diana's chest.

Diana's breath caught as she realized how close Naomi had crept, how soft she was against her. She knew she should pull away now that she was aware of their proximity and how inappropriate it was; if a male witness had tried this, he wouldn't have gotten close. It was just that Naomi was so small and harmless and cute and excited and warm and soft and… And high. Just a little bit high, which meant Diana was technically taking advantage of her. She stiffened, uncomfortable at the thought, and Naomi noticed and pulled away, a confused look on her face as she registered the lack of distance between their bodies.

"Oh." Naomi handed the controller over again, swallowing. She went to the kitchen and drank some water, then checked the cupboards. They'd been here the whole day and night and Naomi had shown no interest in the kitchen prior to this awkward moment.

Diana turned her attention to the game, wandering around the little town and interrogating more people. Naomi had been right; this was kind of like her job, now that she was less nervous about using the controls. Naomi came back with some chocolate.

"You're going to make yourself sick," Diana commented. "And I won't hold your hair back for you when you are."

Naomi pouted, halfway through a mouthful of chocolate. "You're supposed to take care of me," Naomi pointed out, looking over at the screen again.

"I have a vomit clause in my employment contract," Diana said seriously, then looked over at Naomi's surprised face with a chuckle. "Kidding. I'll take care of you, even if you throw up on me. Just slow down and chew before you swallow, okay? You want your game back?"

"You can keep playing if you want." With that Naomi tucked herself against Diana's side again, bringing up her knee so she could rest her chin on it. "You're getting the hang of it," she noted, and Diana felt inexplicably proud of herself. The game had seemed so daunting, and she'd never found them interesting. But Jake was thinking about buying a console for his son, Ollie, for Christmas this year. She might as well get some of the basics down so she could be a cool grandma and play with him.

Naomi gave a little "yay" when Diana found a golden egg. Diana tried to get the character to pick it up, but she couldn't.

"Oh, let me." Naomi took the console, and Diana watched as she tried the same thing, which resulted in the game freezing and throwing up strange symbols before abruptly closing.

"Damn, two in one," Naomi said, sounding impressed. She exited back to some sort of interface that looked like a computer desktop, and from there she ran the type of program the tech guys used, all flashing lines of text. "I'll send off a bug report to the developers. Good work, Detective."

Naomi clicked some more buttons and looked up at Diana, almost glowing with contentedness. She smiled, her eyes half-lidded. "You're gold," Naomi said firmly. "Solid gold." She handed the controller back and Diana resumed her game, heart pounding in her chest.

Naomi's cheek rested against Diana's shoulder as she watched her make her way through the rest of the town, her head growing heavier as she relaxed, yawning. Naomi's hand found Diana's forearm, slid down to circle her wrist, then slid over Diana's hand. Diana had to suppress a shiver. It was so sensual, but when she looked up, Naomi was entirely focused on the console, where she'd brought up the menu and selected a shovel.

Diana didn't particularly notice when someone touched her. She did when it was Naomi. There was something so deliberate, so intense about it. It made Diana aware that Naomi was there. Which was ridiculous; of course Naomi was there. Where else would she go? But it reminded her that Naomi was a woman and Diana was a woman and that they were alone in a house with multiple bedrooms and not much to do. It made Diana wonder what two women might do. It made her remember Naomi's book, made her wonder what it would be like to want a woman like that.

Naomi's fingers trailed back up to Diana's wrist then moved away, tucking into Diana's elbow. It surprised Diana how much she didn't mind. It surprised her even more how much she enjoyed it. There was no pressure or intent behind it; Diana was certain Naomi was just high and comfortable—and that if she'd wanted to seduce Diana, she'd have had her by now. Diana wouldn't have even put up a token resistance, so entirely was she fascinated by this woman.

Naomi trusted her so much. Her head rested on Diana's shoulder, her ear so close to Diana's mouth, but she didn't flinch when Diana spoke. Diana felt like she was melting. There was a liquid warmth starting where Naomi touched her and spreading through her.

She'd never felt like this, not even on one of Andrew's good days. It was something uniquely Naomi. The vulnerability of her, the bravery she'd displayed. Her unwavering trust that Diana would provide the accommodations she required. It made Diana feel like a better person than she usually thought she was. Softer, kinder. Trustworthy. It felt like being warmed from the inside after being out in the cold for hours. Years. Like the wildflowers in spring, slowing unfurling each petal to luxuriate in the sun's warm rays. Diana could feel herself opening up to Naomi, and it hurt.

Diana wasn't attracted to women. She hadn't been, not before now, not like this with her chest on fire and her hands aching to hold the woman who was already so close to her. She'd never looked forward to coming home to Andrew the way she'd anticipated Naomi's muted delight at her return earlier today.

Then Naomi looked up at her again with that smile that made Diana's chest ache, and she felt like an asshole. Naomi was here to be protected, not objectified. Not that Diana had been staring down her shirt or anything—she'd just been wondering what it would be like to be with someone this gentle and emotionally intelligent.

Diana smiled back, and Naomi's smile grew shy and pleased before she tucked her face back into Diana's shoulder, like she'd confirmed something she suspected, like she realized she was welcome where she'd nestled in. Naomi was relaxed and soft against her, and it surprised Diana to realize she was relaxed as well. Naomi posed no threat, and Diana didn't particularly want to pull away.

She watched a cut scene and felt Naomi's head grow heavier on her shoulder. Naomi's head slipped, her forehead resting against Diana cheek; she made a tiny noise of protest and huddled closer.

Diana had never had this kind of female friendship before. Not that they were friends. Diana liked Naomi; that was part of the problem. But she'd never had someone to just exist with like this. No justification, no excuses. No coercion or attempts at seduction. Just comfortable silence.

She'd never been this comfortable with someone she wasn't related to. Yet she was acutely aware they weren't related, that Naomi was attracted to people like her, or had been in the past.

Diana hadn't thought much about dating, although Kate had hinted at it. Kate was always hinting at something. Usually that Diana was too old for her job, or that she needed someone in her life.

Could Diana come home to something like this? Naomi obviously wouldn't be waiting at the door with dinner on the stove; she was a working woman with her own busy life, and cooking was noisy.

But to come home to the lights turned on and a friendly, warm body to snuggle up with on the couch? Why had she only realized she wanted this now, when Naomi was the one snuggled up to her?

It wasn't like it was new information, that there were women who lived like this. Coming home to each other, taking care of each other, listening to each other. She just hadn't imagined it would feel so...

Safe.

Diana felt safe. She hadn't even looked up when a car had parked outside, which wasn't great since she was supposed to be protecting the woman beside her.

And then Naomi's thumb gently stroked the inside of Diana's elbow and suddenly Diana couldn't breathe, couldn't think. She was just a series of nerve clusters sending signals to places that had never before received them, awakening as Diana shivered with anticipation and trepidation. Naomi's breath was close to her throat, brushing the skin there, turning Diana into little more than a dull ache of want she barely understood. She could feel all her little mammalian hairs standing on end, goose bumps breaking out on her skin as she choked in a breath.

The noise startled Naomi awake, and she pulled away and looked up at Diana.

"I think I need to go to bed." Naomi's voice was thick, and she blinked slowly.

"Do you need help?" Diana asked, then blushed at the implication.

Naomi smiled, raising a single finger to trace the dimple in Diana's cheek. "Thank you. I feel safe now."

"You are. Trust me."

"I do," Naomi whispered, her face close, taking in Diana's expression. Her eyes shone and her mouth pulled up into a smile as she reacted to whatever she'd seen. Her finger followed the line of Diana's jaw and Diana felt her mouth open in anticipation before Naomi's hand slid away from her face. She leveraged herself against Diana's arm as she got clumsily to her feet.

Diana quickly stood, steadying her as she swayed a little. She walked with Naomi to the bedroom she'd chosen and turned down the sheets, watching as Naomi tucked herself in. She took the cup from the bedside table and filled it with fresh water from the kitchen, giving herself a moment before she went back in.

Naomi was almost asleep already, the slits of her eyes shining in the hallway lights. Diana set down the cup.

Naomi caught her hand. "I do feel safe," she reiterated, and Diana squeezed her hand.

"I'm going to hop in the shower. You know where I am if you need me."

"I do," Naomi said seriously, her dark eyes fixed on Diana's face until she blushed and turned away, more than ready to wash away whatever had just happened to her.

CHAPTER EIGHT

Diana showered and went to bed. She picked up the novel she'd been reading. It was getting interesting—she couldn't tell who the killer was, but the detective had an obvious crush on one of the female teachers that was intriguing to watch develop. Plus, the detective was kind of a badass—she'd taken down one bad guy already, and she hadn't backed down under pressure.

At the sound of footsteps, she looked up to see Naomi shuffle into the room and slump onto the bed next to her.

Your room. There. Diana pointed to the hallway.

Naomi signed, *cold* and *lonely.* Her eyes were half open and a little red when they focused on Diana. *Stay. Warm,* she signed, then followed it up with a heartbreaking *safe.* Her eyes closed and her breathing became slower.

Diana couldn't turn her away. Not if she felt safe enough to finally sleep.

However, closing her eyes after expressing her intentions was the most manipulative thing anyone had ever done to stay in Diana's bed, and she had an abusive ex-husband, two kids, and three grandkids. The audacity—the cheekiness of Naomi to sign that and then fall asleep to end any further discussion.

But Diana supposed it was better than hearing her wander the house all night, bouncing from room to room like a ping-pong ball. She read a while longer, turning the pages with a little more confidence when Naomi didn't stir, careful of the brush of her fingers against the paper. Naomi was on top of the covers, despite her claim of being cold. The room was warm enough, so Diana simply draped the spare blanket over Naomi's legs. She was sure it would be fine if they slept under different blankets.

Naomi had curled up a little and seemed almost peaceful for the first time since Diana had met her. She hadn't expected that, or how relieved she was to see her finally eat and sleep. Normally protection detail wore on Diana; being away from home, being with a stranger, the possibility of someone dangerous finding them.

Naomi's presence wasn't intrusive at all. Even the fact that she'd claimed half of Diana's bed wasn't off-putting. Naomi was probably still scared, and she seemed to find Diana's company reassuring.

It didn't mean anything. Just because Naomi was gay didn't mean that Naomi was attracted to her. And Diana didn't get the sense that she was in the presence of a predator. Then again, they learned to disguise themselves well.

No, Naomi had already had the opportunity the night before, and she'd pressed no advantages.

And Diana wasn't—she hadn't particularly been attracted to Andrew, especially not once he'd stopped putting any effort into the relationship, always leaving a mess for her to clean up. The resentment had built over time until she couldn't even stand him touching her shoulder. But she'd know by now, surely, if she was attracted to women.

She looked over at the woman sleeping beside her, her small hands curled up against her chest, headphones over her ears, a little smile on her soft-looking lips.

Uncomfortable with her own thoughts, Diana turned back to her book only to find the detective engaged in what would be called unethical practices in MPD; the female teacher had not been cleared as a suspect, and what they were doing was both very obscene and somehow thrilling. Blushing, she put the book down and took her glasses off, placing both on the bedside table and turning the lamp off. She tucked an arm under her head, staring at the line on the ceiling from the streetlight outside, cutting into the room where the curtain didn't entirely close. When cars drove by outside, the light changed, but Naomi didn't flinch at any sounds, her breathing steady and soothing in the dim light.

Diana must have fallen asleep, because she startled awake at a sudden noise. There was a weight on her chest, and late evening had shifted into the darkest part of the night. There were fewer cars going past more infrequently, the world outside seeming far away. There was another noise, a little sigh, then a hand at Diana's waist, grasping her. Diana tensed, but Naomi pulled closer, her body warm and soft where it nestled against Diana's.

Naomi was used to sleeping with women—with that Rose woman. Diana was used to sleeping with toddlers sprawled across her bed. She hadn't had a sleepover with someone her own age since the '80s, and they hadn't shared a mattress. Maybe if they had, maybe if she was used to this, it wouldn't feel so overwhelming.

The weight on her chest—what she recognized now as Naomi's head—wasn't what was making it hard to breathe. She really should wake Naomi and send her off to her own bed. Instead, she pulled her arm out from under her head and let her hand settle on Naomi's back; if it woke her, it wouldn't be deliberate. But Naomi just sighed again, some of the tension in her back easing away as Diana's hand brushed across her ribs.

"I've got you," Diana breathed into the dark room, too quiet for even Naomi to hear. Naomi shifted anyway, nuzzling her face into Diana's chest, the hard shell of her headphones digging in for a moment before sliding away so Naomi's ear rested over Diana's heart. She gave a contented little hum, and Diana felt a tension in her chest ease. It was lovely to be blanketed in the warmth of her.

If Diana was honest, when she was younger, she'd wondered for a while if she might like women. She'd had a bit of a crush on her history teacher, a tall, elegant European woman who'd dressed mostly in black and spent her holidays in Canada. Any praise from her pink lips had Diana blushing, and she'd kept all the papers that teacher had marked with her little compliments and criticisms. But all she'd wanted from the older woman had been the support she'd offered. Or at least that had been what she'd told herself.

There hadn't been anyone since then—man or woman—who'd taken her fancy. She'd married Andrew because he'd asked, because he'd won her parents over, because it meant she could leave home. None of those, she realized now, were particularly good reasons to get married. She'd thought she loved him. She'd tried to love him. But as he'd soured, she'd believed it was her fault, that he could tell she didn't feel the same way about him. She'd blamed herself for too long.

After Jacob was born, she almost forgave Andrew for everything. Jacob had been so small and perfect, so incredibly present. It had hurt to leave him with her mother so she could go to work, but she knew if she stayed home, she'd never leave again, and they weren't getting by on Andrew's meager wage. She'd had to do what was best for Jake, and being able to afford formula when her milk dried up from stress outweighed placating Andrew's ego.

She could see now that she'd been very passive in her life. She'd applied to the academy because her father had wanted her to, made detective because he'd wanted her to, married Andrew because he'd wanted her to. And now her father was dead and her children were grown, and Diana had to figure out what she actually wanted when no one else wanted anything from her.

Naomi roused a little, rearranging herself to fit more comfortably against Diana.

If Diana wanted to, she could get up and leave Naomi here. She could wake Naomi and make her go to her own bed.

She didn't want to do either of those things. She wanted to lie here with someone who trusted her.

And it was nice. She didn't want to move Naomi because sleeping with her was nice. Naomi was soft and smelled good and had been nothing but polite to Diana even with frayed nerves from lack of sleep and constant noise.

Diana hadn't enjoyed any part of sleeping with Andrew. He'd snored, flailed, woken her up when the baby cried, expected sex upon waking.

Naomi expected nothing. And there was no harm in letting someone this worn down and exhausted sleep against her like this, Diana rationalized. She wanted to figure out what she needed to do to make her life more like this. Less nights out in the cold looking at dead bodies. More nights feeling like she was still worth something to someone.

She should get up. She could pretend she needed the restroom, then go sleep in Naomi's room instead of coming back in here. Getting back into bed with the woman she was protecting would be inappropriate.

There was a difference between knowing all of that intellectually and feeling Naomi snug against her chest.

There was another sweet, contented sigh, and Diana realized she'd been running her hand over Naomi's back, and the action was comforting herself as well as Naomi.

Naomi, who was brave and reliable and… Impossibly pretty. She didn't wear makeup or expensive clothes—she lived in T-shirts and hoodies and jeans, cartoon characters on most of them—but she had those deep-brown eyes and soft dark hair. The headphones were cute, too. But it was her freckles and her lips that drew the rest of Diana's attention. She couldn't remember ever looking at someone's mouth and wondering what it would be like to kiss them.

She wanted to know what it would be like to kiss Naomi. And that wasn't the worst of it. Diana wanted to know everything about her. She wanted to take care of her. She wanted to hold her close and trail her fingers over her skin. She wanted to sit out in the woods with her and watch the sun set.

Diana didn't usually sleep well, or with women. She found herself drifting off anyway, the guilty pleasure weighing heavier on her mind than Naomi's body did on hers.

CHAPTER NINE

Diana woke to the morning light and the usual suburban noises from outside: car doors slamming, dogs on their morning walks. There was a weight on her chest that was compressing one of her breasts. She'd worn a DARE shirt to bed, her breasts loose beneath the cotton, and one of them was cushioning Naomi's head. She couldn't speak to how comfortable they were as a pillow, but Naomi was only just now waking up despite the noise outside.

Naomi lifted her head, leaning on one arm to look at Diana. She was clearly aware of and comfortable with the unlikely intimacy of their position, but it was just as clear that the drugs she'd had the night before had worn off. Diana, used to reading facial expressions, was unable to read Naomi's. It wasn't hard or calculating, wasn't challenging or uncomfortable. There was an awareness that they were too close, but it didn't make either of them draw away. Naomi's eyes moved when cars went past, and her jaw tightened. In the night, her headphones had slid back on her head, away from the ear that had been resting on Diana's chest.

Diana grasped the earpiece that had migrated and carefully pulled the cushioning away from Naomi's scalp. She moved it forward, lifting it further away so it didn't brush the cartilage of Naomi's ear, so focused on replacing it that she almost didn't notice the intense look on Naomi's face. Diana glanced to check in with her and lost her breath in a sudden rush, overwhelmed by the implications of what she was doing and the way she hadn't even considered the vulnerable position she'd put Naomi in before reaching for the headphones. Diana's breath caught and her eyes remained fixed on Naomi's.

Naomi's lips were slightly parted, her eyes wide and filled with anticipation. Diana inhaled shakily, turning her attention back to the journey her hand had begun. She let her tongue wet her suddenly dry lips and was distracted by the way Naomi's eyes flicked down to follow the movement, her breath shortening. Slowly Diana lowered the cushioning back over the exposed ear, making sure it was firm against Naomi's skull before releasing it so there would be no pressure when her hand moved away.

Naomi signed a thank-you, and Diana had a moment of regret when she realized she'd firmly removed the possibility of Naomi lying back down on her chest. Naomi was still propped on one arm, and now she used the other to pull away, stretching her torso as she went. Diana hadn't noticed much beyond the head on her chest when she woke, but she realized now the extent of Naomi's colonization of her sleeping body. Their legs were pressed together, and when Naomi rolled to the side, parts of her brushed against parts of Diana, who blushed again, remembering where she'd left off in the book last night.

"You slept," Diana commented, once she'd regained her composure.

Naomi had the grace to blush and look away, which was only more endearing. "I had a surprisingly comfortable sleep. Your heart—it's nice. I like how steady and reliable it sounds."

"Thanks. I might keep it."

Naomi nodded, looking worried rather than amused by Diana's attempt at levity.

"Does she always sleep with her suspects?" Diana asked, nodding at the book on the bedside table. "It seems like a pretty bad call, on her part."

"Am I a suspect?" Naomi's voice was cool and amused.

"It's an open investigation. She shouldn't be sleeping with anyone involved in the case," Diana said, dodging the question. "Anyway, we're not sleeping together."

Naomi gestured to where their legs were still entangled atop the covers.

"Not—not the way she is." Diana was flustered. "In case you were getting any ideas."

"Why would I, Detective?" Naomi yawned, then blinked sleepily over at Diana, a little smile on her face. "It's not like we just slept together or anything."

The grin turned cheeky, and Naomi got up and left the room before Diana could think of anything to come back with. She decided that the sleep-deprived, depressed, quiet, hungry version of Naomi she'd known before last night was much, much easier to deal with than this well-rested, fed, cheerful, flirtatious one.

Naomi came into the living room after her shower, wearing a shirt that Diana glanced at, then read in full.

I might not go down in history, but I will go down on your mom.

"You cannot wear that around my kids," Diana said, rolling her eyes and chuckling.

Naomi looked down as though she'd forgotten what she'd decided to wear. She froze and met Diana's eyes with that deer-in-headlights look Diana was learning to appreciate. She turned around as though she was about to go back upstairs.

"No, it's fine, I'm just saying they won't be impressed and they'll definitely be suspicious. Where did you even get that?"

"I was at an event—a comic convention. I worked on a graphic novel a while ago and we were there to promote it. And these men half my age kept coming up and asking if I was single. It was a line from the book, so I got someone at the con to print it, and they still didn't get the hint. I'm pretty sure—give me a moment."

Naomi came over and sat next to Diana on the couch as she looked through her phone, then handed it over, leaning in so they could both see the screen. It took Diana too long to find Naomi in the picture, even though she'd seen other photos of her before the headphones. She was in the middle of a small crowd posing for the camera, with everyone's arms around each other, and she was smiling. Her ears were bare and her hair was in an asymmetrical bob with one side shaved, the longer side shining under the harsh fluorescent light, curling over her shoulder. She was wearing the same shirt under a blazer, and the other people wore similar shirts with other snappy catch phrases. Naomi had a rainbow lanyard and wristband, and Diana wondered about the density of the men who'd tried to hit on her.

The picture was part of an article which was very flattering to both the graphic novel and the artists, including Naomi. There were other pictures, of the group signing copies of the book with excited fans crowded around the booth. And there was one with just Naomi, peaceful and pleased in a moment of calm, her chin resting on her cupped hand, the sleeves of her blazer rolled up to expose her forearms.

"You look great," Diana said without thinking. "I mean, you look happy." She scrolled back through the article. "Do you miss it?"

"Miss what? I still do most of the same jobs I used to."

"The conventions."

"Oh. I only did a couple. The ones for the games are pretty rough—a lot of the guys don't bother if you're with an indie publisher. They don't respect women gamers or developers. The comic conventions were fun, but they were exhausting, and I'm too old for all that now."

"If you don't mind me asking, how old are you?" Diana held her hands out when Naomi shot her a look. "I can't tell. You're better at technology than my kids are, and you wear shirts like that. You're proudly gay and that wasn't a thing back when I was younger, but you had to have gone through the same eras I did."

"I'm forty-eight," Naomi said reluctantly. Only a few years difference between them, after all. Diana couldn't define why that mattered. "You look surprised."

"But how did you know?"

"That I wanted to be a graphic designer?" Naomi's smile was gently challenging, and Diana rolled her eyes.

"That you liked women. I know I asked before, but it didn't make sense to me. You grew up the same time as me, you saw the whole AIDS thing play out. It can't have been easy for you."

"I don't know how to explain it. I saw a woman once and I've been hooked ever since." Naomi's face was deadpan, then the smile from the photo broke through. "I mean, kind of. I was twelve and one of the cheerleaders was—she was something else, you know? I was all sweaty palms and stammering when she spoke to me, the way my friends were with boys, the way boys were with my friends. I figured one day I'd feel like that about a boy, but I never did. And then I grew up and found out it was normal for some people to love like that, and it wasn't a problem. I mean, my family disinherited me. All except Aunt Isobel, who left me the house. I think she was like me too but couldn't be. Not back then."

"Wait, disinherited?"

"Disowned. Whatever." Naomi shrugged. "We didn't get along before I came out, anyway. No big loss."

Diana thought back to her own teenage years. Disappointing her parents might have meant they'd leave her alone, but they'd have never disowned her. She didn't think they would have. It was too late now to know for sure.

"Hell of a thing," Diana said, aware she was still staring at a Naomi that no longer existed, at the smile captured on her face. She handed Naomi back her phone. Their fingers brushed, and Diana blushed.

Naomi must have been sure before telling her parents. She must have weighed all her options and decided a life of conforming to someone else's expectations wasn't worth it for her. It would have been terrifying. Naomi was incredibly brave.

"Your turn."

Diana shook her head, distracted.

"Show me a memory," Naomi continued. "Since we're memory-ing and all today."

Diana pulled out her phone. She handed it to Naomi after pulling up a photo of herself at an award ceremony, where she'd been honored for saving the life of a fellow detective and an officer while gravely injured.

"This isn't what I meant—wait, you got stabbed?" Naomi looked up, incredulous.

Diana chuckled softly, nodding. "Perks of the job."

"Damn. I meant—you said I looked happy. I wanted to see some time you were happy."

Diana took her phone back and scrolled. The same event, but with her two children and their spouses, and the two grandchildren she'd had at the time, Ollie nearly waist high and Violet propped on Kate's hip.

"Wow, they must be so proud of you."

"They want me to find a less dangerous line of work." Diana felt for her holster, which was preventing her from getting comfortable on the couch. "I'm starting to agree with them."

* * *

Naomi filed a claim with her insurance company via email, sending photos of the crime scene along with the testimony she'd given Diana. Despite both her file and her email explicitly requesting written communication, the insurance company called her back. Diana noticed her flinch and offered to take the call. Naomi watched as Diana reiterated that they were violating the ADA, that the carpet needed to be replaced, and that the point of entry still hadn't been ascertained.

When Naomi's phone buzzed again later, Diana took that call too, pacing tigerlike through the house as she explained to the insurance company the liabilities their policy had left open, and that they were, in fact, required to replace blood-stained carpet.

When she got off the phone, Diana joined Naomi at the table to catch up on paperwork on her laptop, cursing under her breath when it needed to update for nearly a full hour before she could log on properly.

They settled into an easy rhythm. Naomi had already become used to the way Diana would touch her whenever she walked past, to make sure Naomi was aware of her. It was probably habit, from her kids or something. It was as unnecessary as it was welcome. She also kept the kettle just below a boil, and whenever Naomi found her mug empty, it was refilled within moments.

"I can feed myself, you know," Naomi blurted out. "I appreciate you bringing me food and coffee whenever you make some, but you don't have to."

"I'm making coffee all day anyway, and you're working. I'd rather you stay busy and kept your mind off everything that's happened."

Naomi ducked her head. Diana had layer after layer of considerateness.

"Sorry," Diana said.

"No, you're right. I should keep busy."

"And I'm sorry. It's none of my business."

"I know I'm difficult—"

Diana gave a low scoff of disbelief. "You're not. You're a goddamn delight, compared to the people I usually deal with."

"Oh."

"You just can't tolerate loud noises. That's not hard to mitigate. For the rest of it, you stay put when I tell you to, and despite everything going on, it's been fun."

Naomi looked down at her hands on the keyboard. No one had ever said anything like that to her before. It had all been well-meaning advice about immersion therapy and pushing through, with the implication that her disability wasn't that bad. And she'd learned that people found her inconvenient, and that catering to her needs made *them* mildly inconvenienced, which was inexcusable in their eyes. The only clients she took on were people who could accommodate her, people who knew to email or text rather than call.

As though she knew what Naomi was thinking, Diana looked up. "You deserve better," she said firmly.

Naomi tried to regather the thread of the conversation, unreasonably flustered. "And you're the first person who hasn't made me feel like I'm asking too much."

"Oh, honey," Diana said. She paused as though realizing the endearment might not be appropriate, but then she shrugged, worrying her lower lip with her teeth.

"Legally, you're just complying with the ADA," Naomi mumbled.

"Please. You ever had an ADA accommodation before?"

Naomi nodded. "You're better than ADA," she admitted. "I don't know if I thanked you, so thank you for coming when I called."

"Of course," Diana said, as though there had been no other option. Her phone buzzed and she excused herself to take the call, her hand resting on Naomi's shoulder a moment before she was gone. She came back a few minutes later with news. "Insurance company has finished up, and crime scene techs have given us the all-clear. I can take you home."

"What about the man who broke in?" Naomi didn't want to ask. She didn't want to think about it. It was childish, but she'd rather pretend she wasn't in danger.

"He's in custody. In the hospital. Expected to recover. The team working the case says he was working alone."

Naomi nodded, trying to shake her disappointment. It had only been two days, but they had been the nicest days she'd had in a while.

"I thought you said the insurance company had finished up?" Naomi said, looking around as they walked into her home. Diana touched her back and signed to her to keep still while she searched the house.

The carpet was still bloodstained and now stank of cleaning chemicals and something rotten. On top of that, Naomi's belongings were strewn throughout the space. Diana was sure there had been a television in the living room the last time she'd been there. Now there were just cables sticking out from the console table.

After ensuring there was no one lurking in the house, she called the crime scene analysts that had left a few hours earlier. When she hung up, she took some photos and sent them through. Naomi was already on one of her laptops in the kitchen, flicking through footage from her home security system.

"I really thought it was just the one guy. Looks like he had an accomplice. Can you tell how he got in?" Diana was disappointed in herself; what if she'd let Naomi come home alone? How had she almost put Naomi at so much risk?

"No, there's only the timestamp on the front door from your team and the insurance company contractor, as far as I can tell. No one else came in, at least not through any of the doors."

"Same as last time. Damn. Okay, get together a list of what's missing, then let's get you out of here."

Naomi nodded dully.

"I'm sorry. I really thought—"

"It's not your fault, Detective. I'm insured."

Her words did nothing to assuage Diana's guilt. She should have prevented this somehow. It had looked targeted before; it looked more so now. She followed Naomi from room to room, watching as she checked for what was no longer there.

In the study, Naomi's safe room remained closed, the bookcase undisturbed. Her projector and smart screen were both gone.

"It's just things. You weren't here when they came back. You're safe."

"Am I?" Naomi wouldn't look at her.

Naomi's bedroom was a mess, her rainbow flag torn down and wet with urine. Naomi gagged and ran from the room to throw up. Half-expecting it, Diana was quick on her heels, holding Naomi's hair back as promised. She held Naomi as the heaves turned into sobs.

"I'm sorry. I should have had someone check. I never imagined they'd come back."

"It's not your fault. You didn't do this," Naomi said once she'd recovered.

"But I could have shielded you from seeing—that." Even as she said it, she was thinking about the DNA they'd be able to collect. She'd make sure Naomi got new sheets, a new mattress, new everything. She was already going to give the insurance company hell for not replacing the carpet.

Naomi still huddled in the circle of Diana's arms. She rested her head against Diana's, her forehead against Diana's cheek. "I just want this to be over," she breathed.

"Come on," Diana said gently, looping her arm around Naomi's waist.

They gathered Naomi's things and went to the garage, where she threw her bag on the backseat of an old beater and climbed in.

"Just follow me, nice and slow, okay?" Diana said.

Naomi nodded numbly.

"I have to call in and get your protection detail extended."

"Don't bother. Just let me get a hotel somewhere. Insurance will cover it."

Diana doubted that, given the terrible job they'd done so far. She thought for a moment. "I have a cabin. Not far out of town. You'll be safe there, and you won't be disturbed. It's more isolated."

"Cabin?"

"Upstate a little. Quiet, I promise."

Naomi sighed and looked away, and Diana took her resignation as consent.

CHAPTER TEN

The cabin was two stories, set well back from the road and equipped with an alarm system. It had a cedar smell to it, the air inside cold and stale from being closed up since late summer, but it was still cozy and inviting. Some of Diana's wildlife photos were framed on the walls, and the furniture was rustic but functional.

Diana had come up on her own a few weeks ago to photograph loons on the lake, still and silent in the woods as the wildlife scampered around her, her shotgun never far from her side. She hadn't seen any bears this year, but they inhabited her neck of the woods so it was important to be prepared.

Naomi followed Diana inside, looking exhausted. That one night of sleep and one good meal hadn't done her any good, long-term. Diana led her to the den and sat her down on the couch. She saw Naomi's eyes dart to the security screens on the windows and doors.

"We came up here one fall and Andrew had broken in. He'd been living here with a twenty-four-year-old. No matter how old he gets, they always seem to be twenty-four. Anyway, I kicked them out and threatened to have him arrested for trespassing. It was a bit awkward since I had the kids with me. That was the last time he saw them, and he didn't even say hi. They understood, by then. That he wasn't coming back, that I wasn't the bad guy who'd kicked him out. But that's why there's grills on the windows and deadbolts on the doors. We should be safe here. You should be safe here."

Naomi watched her warily and Diana wet her lips. "I'm going to go chop some wood, light the fire. You get comfortable, okay?" She reached for Naomi's chin, chucking it up a little so Naomi's eyes met hers. "There won't be any trouble out here. I'll chop some wood, turn on the water and power, then call the precinct."

* * *

Naomi watched Diana chop wood from the doorway, flinching at each blow but unable to look away, unable to move further away. Diana had removed her coat and jacket in the crisp fall air, and she'd rolled up the sleeves of her button-down over her wiry forearms. When she paused, she seemed unsatisfied with even that much clothing, since she unbuttoned and removed her shirt, leaving only a white tank top tucked into her ever-tight jeans. Her biceps rippled as she swung, a sheen of sweat on her skin struck golden in the afternoon sunlight.

She was gorgeous, glorious. Strong and beautiful and everything Naomi had ever wanted in a woman. Despite the sweat, Diana's nipples were hardened to peaks and straining against the thin cotton of her tank top. She brushed her golden-lit hair from her face with the back of her hand and looked back at the cabin.

Naomi drew away from the door and found herself filling a glass with water, which she brought out to Diana.

Diana took it, shucking off a thick deerskin glove to hold the glass. There was sweat above her upper lip. She looked fierce and powerful with the axe resting over her shoulder.

"I wish I could help," Naomi offered.

"This is helping," Diana said, tipping her head back to empty the glass. "Another, please?"

Naomi nodded and returned to the cabin, coming out with a fresh glass. The water must be from a well, out here.

Diana's fingers brushed hers over the glass, eyes meeting Naomi's with some kind of acknowledgment—as if she knew, on some level, the underlying attraction Naomi had to her. And she didn't mind. Naomi shivered, and Diana handed the empty glass back.

"Get inside. Stay warm."

She took Diana's discarded clothes inside with her. They were still warm from Diana's body, and they smelled like her.

* * *

When Diana brought the firewood in, she set it down as quietly as she could, then built and lit the fire, resting back on her heels at the hearth as she coaxed the flames to life.

"I've called in. Officially I'm off duty until tomorrow but I'll stay tonight. I'm not leaving you alone right now. Let me put the boiler on and you can have a shower, okay?"

Naomi nodded and kept her gaze the fire, not looking at Diana. Worried, Diana cupped her cheek, wanting Naomi to look her in the eye. Reluctantly Naomi's eyes met hers. Her lips trembled.

"Okay?" Diana kept her voice gentle.

Naomi's eyes filled with tears, but she blinked them back, smiled faintly and nodded. "Okay."

"I've got you, okay?"

"Okay." Naomi moved back—Diana hadn't noticed how close they'd been until she drew away—then swallowed and smiled. "I'm okay."

Diana sighed and stood from the crouch she'd been in to make eye contact, muscles complaining. She'd have to get back into the gym when she got cleared for field work again. This inactivity was weighing on her, making her nervous, leaving her with too much time to think about the way the evening sunlight caught Naomi's hair, making it shine as brightly as her eyes when she looked at Diana. It was too much.

"You can take my room. It's to the right at the top of the stairs."

"It's your cabin. I could…"

"You're safer upstairs."

"I'm safer with you." Naomi bit her lip. "I'm scared. The violence and malice in the destruction of my things…I'm used to getting hate for being what I am." It took Diana a moment to realize Naomi was talking about being gay rather than disabled. "But most of that's online, and they don't know anything about me. This was so personal, so deliberately destructive."

Diana thought back. The slashed couch cushions, the fridge door hanging from a single hinge, the books that stank of urine. If someone had done that to her home, she'd be angry—and she was angry. But she'd had decades to grow her thick skin, and Naomi was so fragile.

And her lips looked so soft.

"We can figure out the sleeping arrangement later. I need to make some calls."

Naomi nodded.

Shaken, Diana went back outside with the cordless landline.

There was something about the way Naomi smiled when she saw Diana. Like she'd seen something nice, something she liked, her lips curling up into the sweet smile Diana could never get enough of. Like she felt safe, like she'd come home at the end of a long day and found everything perfectly in place. Like Diana made sense to her somehow, like she understood.

It made Diana feel attractive in a way no man ever had. Naomi's eyes rarely slid down from hers, rarely assessed Diana's assets. But when they did, the wonder in Naomi's eyes was unmistakable. She didn't look at Diana like something to use, like an empty shell to be forged into an unwilling matrimony. She looked at Diana the way people looked at sunsets. She looked at her like she saw and understood all of Diana and she liked what she saw. She looked at Diana with wonder and hope in her eyes, and Diana wondered what she'd done to deserve it.

Diana never let her guard down this much. Somehow Naomi had slipped under it, like a piece of grit in an oyster shell, pearlescent.

Diana found that she didn't mind. Not when it was Naomi looking at her with such reverence. The attraction was there, but it wasn't simply desire for Diana's body. It couldn't be, because it felt like Naomi had been courting her, despite the circumstances. And when Naomi touched her, it was always somewhere appropriate, always forecast so Diana could reject Naomi if she wanted to.

Diana knew, intellectually, that meeting Naomi had made her question her sexuality. Not because Naomi was gay and affectionate and spending time with her; it was because of Diana's response to her, even before she'd gotten to know her, back in those brief early meetings. Naomi's hand brushing hers to retrieve the stylus, Diana pulling her close under the umbrella. She'd wanted to do that, even if it might have given the other woman the wrong idea. Or the right idea. She'd just wanted to touch her.

They still barely knew each other now. It was so soon, but Diana had spent a lifetime waiting—although she hadn't known it at the time—to feel like this about someone.

* * *

Naomi looked around. The room Diana had told her to use had a big hardwood bed and bedding in the blues and greens she knew Diana favored. Diana had slept in this bed, in this bedroom, probably with her husband. Before the kids came, they'd probably had romantic weekends up here. It made her skin crawl to even think about it.

She checked the next room, to see if she would feel less weird sleeping there. There were pine bunk beds and a cot in the corner. She noticed a framed photo on the dresser—a family photo. Diana was so young. So beautiful, even back then, but she hadn't fully grown into it the way she had now. The kids looked thrilled, the little girl smiling broadly enough to show a number of missing teeth, the little boy on his dad's back.

Andrew. The reason Diana flinched when she made noise. Naomi scrutinized his face.

He was attractive enough, if someone liked that sort of thing. But his smile looked forced, and he didn't hold his son's legs to keep him stable. One hand was on Diana's arm in a firm grip, and her smile was different than the one Naomi was used to seeing on her. She was looking at her daughter, but there was something deeply sad in her eyes. A melancholy sense of foreboding, perhaps, or the face of a woman planning an escape.

Diana came up the stairs then and saw her looking at the picture. Naomi put it down quickly.

"I forgot that was still up here. Ollie loves it—he looks just like his dad at that age." Diana picked the photo back up and smoothed her fingers over her son's face. "I think it's the only photo I have left with Andrew in it. I gave the rest to the kids, and they digitized them. I love seeing them when they were little, but I couldn't look at them until Jake cropped him out for me."

"He looks like a wet potato," Naomi blurted out.

Diana looked up from the photo, an amused smile flirting with her lips. "How so?"

"I don't know. I don't like the way he's touching you. I don't like the look on your face. You look scared."

"I'll swap it out." Diana pulled open a drawer and took out a different photo from an album in there, one with more people in it. The kids were grown up here, fifteen years gone in a flash, a spouse each, one of them heavily pregnant. Diana looked happier, immeasurably so. "God, I was so young."

"You're not old yet," Naomi said.

Diana chuckled. "I wish I'd trusted my gut back then." Diana looked at the first photo again. "I wasted years when I looked like that on someone who didn't appreciate me."

Naomi took the album from Diana.

"Did you take these?" she asked, looking through the photos. They looked like they'd been taken before digital photography had become popular and affordable. Naomi stopped on a photo of a fawn, perfectly camouflaged against leaf litter in the dappled sunlight of the woods—except for those startlingly calm deep-brown eyes.

"I know I'm not very good. But I enjoy it. Taking a memory and pinning it down."

"I think they're good, but I understand." Naomi nodded. "I used to draw. Back before there were cameras and computers everywhere. We've come so far, haven't we?" Naomi turned the page, and there Diana was, anxiety in her eyes, her hand resting on her pregnant belly, with people who were probably her parents.

"I think you look happier now," Naomi said, trying to sound casual. "Everyone was young once, but not everyone learns from it. You did the best for your kids, and look at them here." Naomi pointed again at the older photo. "See how happy they are? Not every family vacations together, and they definitely don't all enjoy it. If you're thinking about dating again, you know better this time. You know what men like him are like now, and you can trust your gut. You'll find someone who appreciates you."

Diana gave Naomi a strange look. "Why are you in here, anyway?"

"I didn't want to sleep—that's your room."

"You can sleep wherever you want. There are sheets in the cupboard. I just thought you'd be more comfortable in there." Diana walked back into the primary bedroom. Naomi followed. "I've always loved the view from here," Diana said, nostalgia touching her voice.

Naomi joined her at the window. The lake was visible, and the leaves on the trees were sunset colors, glowing in the evening light.

"It's lovely," Naomi agreed, but when she looked up, Diana was looking at her like she was something more worth looking at than the view. She tucked her lower lip into her mouth to keep from saying anything else, to keep from breaking the moment, but Diana's eyes followed the movement. Naomi took a step back, not sure what was happening.

Diana widened her eyes and shook her head, taking a step back too. "Do you mind if I cook something? It's going to be noisy, you might want to eat a gummy."

If she took the marijuana, she could relax a little, and maybe eat something. "I will. Thanks."

Naomi found a jigsaw puzzle in a cupboard and, still sucking on her second gummy, tipped it gently onto the table. It was a winter scene, a thousand pieces. She didn't expect to get much of it done. She just needed a distraction that wasn't work. She could feel the warm expansion in her chest that meant that the drugs were kicking in, loosening her limbs and blanketing her mind in a calming haze.

"I would feel better not taking your bed," Naomi said when Diana brought over dinner. She'd made a lasagna from dry stock and tins that had Naomi's mouth watering, her eyes closing as she chewed to savor the first bite.

When she opened them, Diana was watching her hungrily.

"God, that's good." Naomi dabbed at her mouth. "You've already given up your time off for me, and you've provided me somewhere safe to stay. I can't kick you out of your own bedroom in your own cabin. It wouldn't feel right. I'll be fine in one of the bunks."

"I don't mind. I just thought you'd be more comfortable."

It was fully dark outside now, but between the gently crackling fire and the company, the inside was cozy and warm. Diana made such a good lasagna that Naomi got a second helping. Diana watched her with smug satisfaction, took every compliment spilling from Naomi's lips until she almost glowed.

Last night, Diana's body had been so soft and welcoming, her heartbeat so soothing to Naomi's exhausted ears. But it was too much, too soon, too intimate.

Diana clearly wasn't trying to seduce her, but still Naomi was getting that vibe that straight women sometimes gave her—the need to be desired, wanting to be wanted without having to address their sexuality. Naomi had dated women like that before, straight women who'd flirted with her until she'd caved and given them what they wanted, only for them to immediately realize that they didn't want women after all—the attention just felt safer.

Naomi was probably just reading too much into this, projecting her own feelings onto the blank slate that was Diana.

* * *

Shortly after putting the lesbian detective book down and turning the bedside lamp off for the night, Diana heard quiet footsteps. Her bedroom had an en suite that she'd offered to let Naomi use, but she was choosing to go downstairs. The footsteps came back up a few minutes later, followed by the sounds of tossing and turning. Eventually, Naomi got up again and the footsteps made their way to Diana's room. Knuckles softly brushed the frame of the open door.

"Yes?" Diana turned over and switched on the lamp.

Naomi huddled in the doorway, wrapped in a blanket, shivering. "I'm cold."

Without hesitation Diana lifted the corner of her own blanket in invitation. Naomi only paused for a moment before she accepted, sliding in but keeping distance between them. Her teeth chattered loudly enough that Diana reached for her. Naomi's hand was cold.

"You're freezing."

"I get cold, when it's cold. I have a hard time warming up."

Diana ran her hand over Naomi's back, feeling the harsh bones of her spine. No body fat, no wonder she was cold.

"I'll need to put some meat on your bones," Diana said. "So you can control your body temperature better." It was something she'd read about, back when she'd been worried about Kate; that, and hair loss. Naomi relaxed as Diana's hand moved over her, so Diana kept going, trying to rub warmth into her.

"That'll take time. How long do you expect us to be here? How long will it be before my home is safe?" Naomi's voice was tight with tension.

"I don't know. It's not my case. I'm sorry. When this is over, when you're not obliged to hang out with me…I'd like to have you over for dinner. If you're not sick of me and my cooking by then."

"How could I be?"

Diana swallowed; it was so completely the opposite of anything Andrew would have said. Here she was, lying in the same bed she'd shared with Andrew, hating the smell of him, the sound of him. Naomi smelled like the orange soap Diana kept in the cabin, fresh and clean and familiar.

Naomi stiffened. "I didn't come here to get into bed with you. I mean, I'm not trying to seduce you."

Diana didn't think she'd mind if Naomi was trying to seduce her; she wouldn't have to do much, in all honesty.

"I just wanted to know where you kept the spare blankets. I'm warm now. Thank you. I'll go back to bed."

"Naomi." Diana was surprised at how soft the name sounded in her mouth. "If I'd minded, I'd have gotten you a blanket and a hot chocolate, put some more wood on the fire, and set up the couch for you downstairs. You can stay. If anyone comes, you'll hear them before me, won't you? Will you be my early warning system? I don't expect anyone to find us out here, but I wouldn't mind knowing if you heard anything out there tonight. I'd probably sleep through anyone coming up the drive."

Naomi relaxed again, still too far away for Diana to hold her.

"It's okay to be scared. Everything that's happened has been scary, and you've been really brave. But after what's happened, I understand if you would feel safer staying together." Diana reached out and Naomi came willingly, snuggling up against her. "Okay?"

Naomi nodded against her chin. Diana couldn't feel the headphones; Naomi must have taken them off.

Her body still felt cold but she no longer shivered. A cold hand pressed against Diana's back as Naomi's breathing slowed down. Diana could feel Naomi's breasts against her chest, could feel how soft she was. She reached over to turn the lamp off, and when she lay back down, Naomi nuzzled back into her and was asleep within minutes.

Diana's chest hurt with everything she'd wanted and never had. She'd been so lonely, and she hadn't even realized it until she'd met Naomi, who filled the space of what had been missing so effortlessly.

Naomi's nose brushed Diana's throat, her breath spilling out over Diana's skin as she sought a more comfortable position. Diana had a lot of practice at lying still, but never had it been because something this nice was happening. Naomi settled again with a deep sigh, her body pressed to Diana's, her arm tight around Diana, holding her close.

It wasn't real. Naomi was just scared, and high, and lonely. Naomi didn't even really know her.

Then Naomi's lips grazed the bare skin on Diana's neck. Diana shivered and Naomi's arm tightened around her as she hummed contentedly. It was possessive without making Diana feel like a possession. Instead she felt safe, cherished. She had no idea if this was how she'd have responded to anyone else, man or woman. All she knew was the foreign tightening in her chest when Naomi touched her.

Diana rubbed the Band-Aid on her finger. Such a small thing, to mean so much. Such a small act of concern to have Diana reconsidering her entire life.

* * *

Leaving the next morning was one of the hardest things Diana had ever had to do. First, she had to remove herself from Naomi's sleepy embrace, and then she had to try to sneak out without waking someone who could hear a literal pin drop. She was, of course, unsuccessful. Naomi woke with a disappointed huff and watched with hurt, confused eyes as Diana explained that she would be back that afternoon to take up her duties officially.

"You'll be safe here. No one knows you're here. It's secure."

She didn't know if Naomi believed her. Diana didn't know if she believed herself.

"I trust you," Naomi said softly.

Diana let her tongue wet her lips, noting the way Naomi watched her tongue. She swallowed hard. "I'll be back as soon as I can. Let me know if you need anything. Anything at all."

"I will." Naomi's smile was small and brave, like it had been when Diana had asked her to listen to David's house.

Hoping she wasn't making another mistake, Diana got dressed in the en suite. She ignored the urge to lean over and kiss Naomi's sleepy forehead on her way out of the bedroom. After gathering her keys, gun, and laptop, she shrugged her coat on and headed back to Montpelier.

CHAPTER ELEVEN

Diana went to the precinct first, where she met with Hamilton. He'd finally been able to interview their suspect, Gerald Hastings, who'd been making noise about police brutality since coming out of surgery. Gerald was one of three brothers who were known to the police, mostly for minor drug possession charges and pawning stolen property.

Hamilton suspected all three of the brothers had been in on the burglaries, especially since they'd all managed to stay out of trouble with the law this year. He and Busco were preparing to interview Lanceolin—the brother they'd been able to find—who was in holding, awaiting his lawyer. The third brother, Neville, had gone to ground.

Diana put forth the theory that the burglaries may have tied back to the insurance company. After what they'd tried to pull with Naomi, she'd done a deep dive into the company and found that they also covered some of the other houses that had been burgled. Hamilton had not been pleased with her interference, but he had been impressed with her theory and agreed to follow up on the lead.

That done, she drove over to Naomi's house.

"You said you heard someone off the pantry," one of the crime techs said when he found her staring at the walls in the kitchen. "Can you show me where?"

"Not sure. It was just a little scuffling noise. Could have been a rat." Diana stopped, looking at the pantry. She pulled up her phone, navigated to her emails, and opened the blueprint again. There was a space in there that wasn't quite the full thickness of the wall. Space enough for a small room? Maybe another tunnel? She opened the blueprint of David's house. Now that she was looking for what wasn't there, she could see it. Empty space between his bedroom and the bathroom. She grabbed her phone and winced as she pressed Naomi's number.

"Naomi? Sorry. Urgent. Trapdoor?" Diana whispered.

"Oh, the trapdoor in the safe room?" Naomi sounded fine, fortunately, her voice low but her sentences fully formed, which usually meant she could handle a quick conversation. "It would have cost too much to have the whole tunnel filled in, and an engineer verified that it's structurally safe. The gate should still be locked. I haven't had any alerts from it."

"Are there any other tunnels that connect to that one?"

"I don't remember seeing any, and I was an inquisitive child. Besides, the engineers would have blocked off anything they found, wouldn't they?"

"Did they look anywhere else?"

"Only the tunnel from the study. What's wrong?"

"I think—" Diana tried to keep her voice calm. "I think you were right about the noise you heard in David's house. I can see space for a hidden room. I think the killer might have been in it when you were there, and he might have come after you yesterday. There must be another tunnel. I think that's how they've been doing all these burglaries. They must have a master list, or some kind of map from—where? The historical society? This matches the MO of the other burglaries across the city. We never thought about way stations and tunnels. It explains why no one ever saw anything, and why only the older houses were targeted in each neighborhood."

"That…damn. That makes a lot of sense."

"Are you okay up there? No issues, no one prowling around?" Diana swallowed, trying to keep the anxiety out of her voice.

"I'm fine. The cabin is lovely, and I'm getting a lot of work done."

"Good. Just make sure all the doors and windows are locked and the alarm is set."

"Is something wrong?"

"We picked up the brother of the man who broke in. He was caught selling some of the stolen goods from the houses over in the east suburbs. There are three brothers. One is in the hospital and we have one in custody, but I don't like those odds. Not when you're alone out there."

"You said…"

"I know what I said. Hell of a thing. Look, I'm going to go check in with the team they had come in to check the house, and then I'm heading back to you. I won't call again unless it's an emergency. Thanks for answering."

"For you? Any time."

Diana smiled as she put her phone away, but shifted her face into a more neutral expression when the tech came back a moment later.

"We've been over to the other property." He held out his phone, a photo on the screen. "We found this space, right where you said it would be." There was a little room with bare boards and insulation. An unfinished area, long forgotten, or perhaps, given the history, deliberately obscured.

"What's that?" Diana zoomed in.

"Rope ladder. They must have come down through the ceiling. Poor guy wouldn't have even known they were there until too late. Hamilton said he was completely deaf."

Diana zoomed in on the photo a little more. Wooden slats. They'd sound like a shutter from a distance.

David hadn't heard anything, but Naomi certainly had.

If only she'd looked at the blueprints Naomi had sent. She'd lived in Vermont long enough to know that every other old house had an underground railroad story to boast about. Especially in a place that old, with thick stone walls that could hide a myriad of secrets. Especially when Naomi had looked suspiciously at the wall between David's bedroom and the next room. They should have measured the house. They should have seen it.

Diana left the dregs of the suburbs, the road familiar. Long shadows were cast on the road from the surrounding pine trees, the air crisp and clear. The last thing Diana needed was for it to start snowing, although it would muffle the world a little for Naomi. Her unmarked had all-season tires, but they were only just adequate for the city roads in winter. She wished she'd insisted on snow tires or chains from the department or headed out to Naomi's house in her own car, which she'd already switched to winter tires ahead of the weather report. She hadn't checked Naomi's tires either. She should have thought ahead, before leading Naomi directly into danger.

She was anxious, and she recognized that. She hated this part of the job, when they realized there were more people involved than they'd known about, or when someone was in danger because MPD hadn't seen something in time.

Diana should have seen it, but she'd overlooked evidence supplied by the very person she was supposed to protect. She'd let her down, and now Naomi was in danger. They could easily find out who Diana was. She'd worn her badge when she'd been at the property, and there weren't so many women in homicide that they wouldn't be able to find her. Since the title of the cabin was under Diana's name, they could easily look up the properties she owned; they'd proven themselves proficient with real estate. They could have found Naomi by now. Naomi was smart, but these brothers had proven themselves to be both intelligent and deadly. She didn't want to think about what could happen to Naomi if they found her.

She checked the rearview mirror, not seeing much traffic behind her. Although she knew Naomi hated calls, she called again. No answer. She called the landline. No dial tone. Swearing under her breath, she flipped her beacons on and sped on through the lengthening dark.

CHAPTER TWELVE

Naomi heard Diana's car make the turn into the driveway, distinguishable by the slightly flat patch on the left rear tire. She put down her cell phone, which had stopped receiving service once it started snowing outside.

She opened the door as Diana reached it, and Diana rushed through, shoving the door closed behind her, resetting the alarm and then throwing on the deadbolt for good measure. Then she turned and pulled Naomi into her, sagging back against the door in relief, hugging Naomi like she would never let go.

Naomi was startled, but willingly let herself be cordoned into the hug, returning it as she realized how worried the other woman had been about her. She let herself revel in the warmth and comfort, even if she didn't need it. It was so rarely offered that it was almost a luxury.

She knew she enjoyed Diana a little more than she should. It wasn't just that the woman was quiet and considerate; she also had a good sense of humor, and she was fun. And gorgeous. That didn't hurt at all. But the moments she was most gorgeous were the ones when she looked at Naomi with that soft little smile dimpling her face.

A lot of people mocked Naomi or didn't understand her. Diana had been kindness itself, and it was a problem. There was no indication that Diana had any kind of attraction to women in general, or Naomi in particular.

"Oh, you're okay. You're okay," Diana breathed, her hands grasping Naomi as though she was trying to make sure she was real.

Naomi relaxed. She couldn't pull away, because Diana held her so firmly, so she squeezed Diana to convey just how okay she was. "I'm fine. What's wrong?"

"I was worried—I was so worried they'd found you. You didn't answer the phone, and I know you hate phone calls, but I thought something had happened to you, I thought they'd found you."

"I'm okay." Naomi pulled back out of the hug so she could look Diana in the face. "I promise you, I am okay."

Diana inhaled shakily, nodding. She let her hands drop, eyes narrowing as Naomi stiffened.

"You were followed. There's a car down the trail. It's stopping. Someone's getting out."

"I have to hide you." Diana shoved Naomi as kindly as she could, pushing the shorter woman ahead of her up the stairs. She snagged the shotgun from the safe on the way past and shoved it into Naomi's hands. There was a hidden access panel in the bedroom that led to the crawl space. She swung it open and paused, laughing mirthlessly. "I know I don't have to tell you of all people this but—be quiet. I'm going to bluff him."

The area inside was dank and dusty and smelled faintly of mice. Diana peered inside and took a flashlight from the bracket inside the door panel, checking the batteries and handing it over to Naomi, urging her toward the yawning darkness within the walls.

"I can help," Naomi insisted.

"No. Just stay hidden up here. I'll say I'm here alone for the weekend. I didn't see your car when I drove in, so hopefully he won't think to look for it either."

"I don't want to leave you alone with him."

"I'm not alone. You're here." Diana's smile was small and pinched. "That's why I'm so worried."

Carefully Diana closed the panel, shutting Naomi in the dark. Naomi waited, feeling like a coward. Perhaps Diana could fool him, but if they had been following her then they had to know Naomi was here too. She didn't know why she was so pivotal to the case. She'd seen nothing, heard almost nothing when David had died. She'd handed over all her digital footage to the police, and she wouldn't be able to identify anyone.

Except, she realized, she could. These footsteps were familiar, even with the crunch of gravel underfoot adding a little more flavor. She'd heard them before. In her house, that night. Her grip tightened on the gun she didn't know how to use.

Diana was right; whoever this was, they were after her. With one of their accomplices in holding and the other in the hospital, they wanted something. They must have known about the routine of the old man next door, and they'd continued it deliberately after they'd killed him.

Why were they focused on her? Why had they used the shutters that night, and then skipped the next dawn and dusk? If they'd been trying not to draw attention, they hadn't succeeded, but they had come close. They could have fooled her; if they'd continued David's pattern she wouldn't have called in the welfare check. With a cool detachment, she realized she was shaking. She heard the feet move around the house.

He might not find Naomi behind the wall, but Diana was alone down there, and she might not be able to hear the man walking the whole way around the house. Naomi heard him pause at the windows on his way past, and she could feel herself sweating despite being in an unheated space while the temperature was in the high teens outside. She shone the flashlight through the space. Dust motes caught in the light, the ragged edges of spider webs between the wooden frames of the walls. She could go deeper, so he couldn't find her—but if he hurt Diana, he would have free roam of the cabin, and the supplies Diana had brought up. He could starve her out easily.

Besides which, Naomi very much didn't want him to hurt Diana.

* * *

Diana waited on the couch. Though her hearing wasn't as sensitive as Naomi's, she had heard him circle the house. She knew he had to have seen Naomi's car as well as her own. Her sidearm was in her hand. The safety was off. She was just waiting, now, to see which way he would come in. Even if he wasn't part of the gang—which she doubted—he was still trespassing on her property. Diana was glad she'd brought the axe back inside with her when she'd finished with the woodcutting the day before.

She caught a glimpse of him at one of the windows as he worked his way back to the door. Cell service was still down, and there'd been no dial tone when she'd lifted the house phone's receiver. It could have been a coincidence. It could have been, but she doubted it.

Diana breathed in again. He was at the door. She wondered briefly if spending time with Naomi had honed her ability to discern the location of sounds, or if part of it was her years as a detective, or if it was all due to having to keep track of Andrew so he didn't sneak up on her. He'd liked to lull her into a false sense of security, make nice when the kids got home. She'd had to be quiet, then, not set him off, and later too, in bed. It could be a combination of all three, working together to let her track the movement of the man who had followed them up into the woods.

He was having trouble with the deadbolt, and Diana had to resist the urge to get behind the door and relock each of the locks as he managed to unlock them. When he finally got it, Diana stood, using the kitchen wall to cover her as he came in.

"Please forgive me," Diana whispered, knowing there was no way even Naomi could hear her. Then she swung out of the alcove to announce herself.

"Montpelier Police; drop your weapon," she called.

The last Hastings brother, Neville—Diana recognized him from the mugshots she'd looked over that morning—raised his weapon. Diana swore. Against an armed man—hell, even an unarmed man—she wasn't much of a challenge. She'd hoped to take him in without violence, hoped the threat of the gun would be enough to subdue him; she hadn't counted on him having his own. She ducked back into the kitchen and looked around. The axe was leaning against the stove. Too sharp.

"Got you now, bitch. Did you shoot him? Or was it one of your friends? Doesn't matter, I'm here now and you're going to pay."

Diana had thought he'd followed her to get to Naomi, that they were after her the way they might have been after David. "Why did you kill him?"

"The old man? He got in the way. He never left that damn house, did he? We were up there for three days and he never left. He didn't even have anything good. Now, are you going to come over here like a good little girl, or am I going to have to come get you?"

Diana shivered, even though she still wore her coat. "I didn't shoot Gerald," she said, playing for time.

It was possible he didn't realize Naomi was here. She checked her phone. No signal. She was glad she'd called in before she came out here, gladder still that she'd given the chief the address of her destination. How long would it be before he sent anyone out? Two missed check-ins?

"Don't really care. He was too soft for the business anyway. He cried, you know, after I bashed that old guy. Doesn't matter, I'm here now. You've got Gerald and Lance. You're not getting me too."

"What's the plan here, Neville? You kill me, then what? Like you said, MPD has both of your brothers."

There was a long pause before he answered. "I'm not the one that makes the plans. I just follow through."

He sounded closer now. Diana's breath caught. She checked her safety was off and risked a quick check past the kitchen wall.

He'd been waiting, gun raised. He fired off a shot and she ducked back behind the kitchen wall, but not quick enough to protect her left shoulder.

"Drop your weapon," she managed to gasp out, the stinging pain in her shoulder taking most of her attention. She hoped that Naomi would also hear her, would know Diana was still alive, that the gunshot hadn't been deadly. She swung out from the kitchen with her gun raised.

He was right there. Too close to shoot her, he struck out instead, flooring her. She rolled as he lunged at her, her hip hitting the hard wooden floor with an aching thud that jarred her bones. He managed to pin her beneath him with his body, and Diana had seen that look of rage on a criminal's face before. She wondered if this was the last thing David had seen, right before Hastings slammed her head against the floorboards of the cabin, making her brain rattle in her skull. She reached for her pistol, knowing she was weaker physically than him, knowing the amount of danger she was in.

Her gun was jammed between them. She couldn't tell where the muzzle was, but it was pressed against him rather than her. She'd wanted to take him alive, so he'd have to answer her questions. But he was stronger than her, one of the most precious people she'd ever met was upstairs, and she was the only thing standing between him and her, and she didn't know where his gun was. Diana would die to keep Naomi safe if she had to, but she'd rather not because if she did he could go after her next, and Diana didn't want to fail her like that.

"You took my brothers," Hastings hissed. He shifted his grip, but before he could slam her to the floor again there was a loud metallic noise, then something softer, fleshier, and he fell away.

Naomi stood over her, a heavy monkey wrench in her hand. Diana slumped back on the floorboards, breathing heavily. She glanced at the still body on the floor next to her and awkwardly transferred her gun to her holster. Her shoulder still burned.

Naomi dropped to the ground next to her, feeling at Diana's belt until she found her cuffs and pulled them from the clip. She cuffed the unconscious man, rolling him onto his side in the recovery position. That done, she turned back to Diana, kneeling as she slipped her arms around her, pulling Diana to her knees, then to her feet. Diana stood shakily, leaning heavily on Naomi. Her head hurt.

"I guess that threw a wrench in his plans," Naomi said, her face completely deadpan. Diana wanted to laugh. "Are you okay?"

Diana pulled her closer, clinging to her with hands that shook. Naomi's arms closed around her, squeezing her tight, holding her closer, keeping her stable on unsteady feet.

"Are you okay?" Naomi asked again, her voice louder than Diana had ever heard it, strained with anxiety.

Diana let her temple rest against Naomi's, closed her eyes and felt her nose brush against Naomi's ear. She'd taken off her headphones. Diana drew back and gestured to Naomi to lift them back over her ears, then sank back into her arms.

"I'm okay." Diana didn't use her voice, just the exhale of her breath, and Naomi immediately softened beneath her hands, wrapping her arms tighter around Diana, holding her impossibly closer. One hand went into Diana's hair, fingers gentle against Diana's scalp, where pain blossomed from the sharp, sudden impact with the floor.

"You're okay," Naomi breathed. "Thank God."

Diana had never known Naomi to be religious, but it was her second time in a home invasion, and they tended to be a religious experience. The confidence, the complete commitment to her swing, the satisfaction as she'd connected—she'd thought of Naomi as small and frail, someone who needed to be protected. But she'd just saved them both. Diana went to touch her head, but her shoulder wouldn't move that way.

"It's okay," Naomi said reassuringly, and it was then that Diana noticed she was crying. "We're okay. I need to check your shoulder, and we need to get back to the city and turn him in, but I think we're okay."

"You've got to check on him."

"He doesn't matter. As long as you're okay."

With that, Diana started crying in earnest, turning her face into Naomi's neck to muffle her sobs. Naomi valued her. Naomi worried about her as much as she worried about Naomi. It was too much, too strong, too sweet. It made her weep, the feeling of finally being safe. Of having someone else take action to ensure her safety. The savagery, the sound of metal against bone, the look of fierce determination on Naomi's face. The comfort of her arms, the way she didn't flinch when Diana's sobs burst out in close proximity to her ears. The sound was unbearably loud even to Diana.

Diana had never cried after being shot. She'd never cried in front of a witness. Between the stress and tension and that fact that Diana cared—more than she should, more than her job required her to, more than she ever had—about the woman holding her was what made her weak.

Diana could see why victims liked it, being held when they processed something awful.

"I've got you," Naomi said, gently stroking Diana's skull. It was tender—her skull was tender, but so was Naomi's touch. It felt nice. Naomi felt nice. Her hands were soft. "Thank you," she added.

"You were the one who got him. You saved me. Thank you."

"I couldn't lose you. I couldn't let him hurt you." Naomi's hands were under Diana's coat now, gently checking for other wounds. Diana shivered at her touch. "I need to take you to a hospital. Still no cell service. What are we going to do?"

"I'm okay. I've had worse."

But even as she said it, Diana was aware that she'd never been violated like this, her own cabin broken into and someone threatening the safety of the one person she'd grown to treasure more than anyone outside her family. She liked the silences they made together. She liked the way Naomi fit in her arms. She liked the soft little noises Naomi made when she was comfortable, and she loved that Naomi made them when she was snuggled up next to her.

She loved that Naomi enjoyed being with her; why else had she sought Diana out that night in the safe house? It had felt like something unfurling in her chest, something she'd kept locked inside for far too long. It felt like walking through the woods and finding a fawn blinking sleepily up at her.

Diana had saved lives before. And it had always felt nice, to have them hug her when they said goodbye before they went on with the lives she had extended.

But this wasn't a goodbye hug. It was an "I'm so glad you're safe" hug, an "I'm okay and so are you" hug, an "I need to hold you because the thought of losing you is terrifying in ways I don't want to imagine" hug.

Naomi felt so good, and she smelled so good, and she hugged Diana like she couldn't get enough of her, like any kind of gap between their bodies was an insult.

It was hard to stop crying when met with such understanding and kindness, and she wanted to be held like this. By Naomi. More than she wanted to seek treatment for the bullet she could feel lodged somewhere in her shoulder.

But Diana was a detective. She was supposed to take charge of the scene. Secure the prisoner, ensure the threat had been eliminated and her witness was safe. She was bad at her job right now, and it was the only thing she'd ever felt like she was good at.

She composed herself, squeezed Naomi tight and then released her, stepping back. Naomi touched Diana's face, and when she pulled them away there were tears shimmering on her fingertips.

"Are you okay?" Diana asked. "The noise when you—you were so close, it must have been so loud."

Naomi gave her a strange look. "You got hurt, and you're asking me—Detective, I'm fine. I'm upset that you're hurt, and my ears are ringing, but I'm fine. Don't worry about me."

That broke Diana completely. A sob broke out of her unwittingly, one that must have been buried for decades. She'd learned very young that if she couldn't be loved, she could at least be useful. Naomi's face softened and she pulled Diana against her again, running such gentle hands over Diana's back that she didn't know how she was ever going to stop crying.

They should get back to the precinct and turn in their—Naomi's—prisoner. And Diana needed to check her shoulder, which was throbbing now, and the prisoner would need medical attention as well. Holding Naomi and crying wasn't useful.

"I've got you," Naomi said comfortingly, and Diana swallowed. "You're okay."

She didn't seem impatient, or in a hurry to get on her way, or sick of Diana crying on her. She wasn't rushing Diana into action; she was just letting her process. Even with victims, Diana was rarely this patient. That was just part of her job, though, and Naomi, she realized, wasn't just part of her job. It was how they'd met, but she'd been terrified as she'd driven to the cabin, terror beyond any she'd known, and she'd been hunted in the dark winter woods by a serial killer before. She couldn't fathom losing Naomi. She was more than just protective of her.

She took care of Naomi, but Naomi took care of her, too.

Taking a deep, shaky breath in, Diana reluctantly pulled away. "I'm okay. Thank you."

"I couldn't let him hurt you," Naomi said, her face screwed up as if the very idea pained her. Her hands moved from Diana's back to her arms, careful of her shoulder. "I'll drive us back."

Diana nodded, trying not to flinch as Naomi's gentle fingers prodded her shoulder.

"First aid kit?"

Diana pointed to the kitchen and tried to quell her panic when Naomi moved out of sight. She was back a moment later.

"That must hurt," Naomi commented, reaching to pull Diana's coat away from her shoulder.

Diana flinched and pulled away to check on Hastings. She checked his pulse, made sure he wasn't injured in a way that required urgent care. There was blood under his head, but he was still breathing. Head wounds always bled a lot, so she wasn't overly concerned. His pulse was strong and steady, and if he woke he would have a hard time hurting either of them with his hands cuffed behind his back. Diana was almost relieved to find it had been his gun pressing against her; she pulled it free of his waistband. He'd been playing with fire; down the front of his jeans with the safety off.

Her own head was ringing with pain and her shoulder burned. She slid her hand under her coat and gently felt around the wound; her shirt was sticky and wet when she pulled it away from her skin.

"Do you want me to look at it?" Naomi asked. When Diana didn't protest, she slid gentle fingers under the edge of Diana's shirt, skirting around the wound carefully. When she retracted her fingers, they were bloodied. "He definitely got you. Should I take you to the hospital? I mean, he needs to go to the hospital for sure."

Diana pulled her phone out of her pocket with some difficulty. Still no bars. "Gas station. I'll stay and keep an eye on him. You call emergency services. We're going to need an ambulance for him, otherwise he can lodge a negligence case. I need to be looked over by the paramedics too, to be honest. While you're at it, mention that there is an officer in distress on the scene, badge number 872, and that the prisoner will need a guard. I'll keep an eye on him while you're gone, but the quicker the better." Diana eyed Naomi's headphones. "No, take me down with you. We can cuff him to something and leave him here; I can make the call."

"I can make the call. We can't leave him. Are you sure you're up to watching him? How's your shoulder?"

"I can deal with it." Diana moved her arm experimentally, grimacing. "Dealt with worse."

Naomi's fingers ghosted across Diana's cheek until she cupped it. She leaned her forehead against Diana's and closed her eyes.

"You deserved better," Naomi said, and Diana believed her. She'd told herself that over the years, but it had never rung true to her. She must have done something to deserve it—to deserve him. It wasn't until now that she truly believed it had nothing to do with her, and everything to do with how broken Andrew had been as a person. Naomi's hand traveled to the back of Diana's neck and her thumb rubbed gently at the column of her spine. Diana could live here, in the comfort and sympathy Naomi offered.

But she had a prisoner, and a bullet in her shoulder. Even so, she couldn't break away first. She waited until Naomi pulled back, her cheeks pink as though she'd said too much.

Diana dug in her coat pocket for her car keys and pressed them into Naomi's hand. "Off you go."

She took the man's gun and slid the safety on, then propped herself up in a chair with her service pistol, eyes on her prisoner.

Naomi slipped away almost silently, and Diana was relieved when the car started up a few minutes later. She didn't shift her gaze from the prone body on the floor.

CHAPTER THIRTEEN

Naomi pulled up at the hospital, breathing a sigh of relief as she helped Diana into triage to be assessed. The noise of the hospital was overwhelming, but it was an emergency. It would be worth the flare, to get Diana safe and attended to. The paramedics had gone ahead, using their radios to call ahead since the snow had knocked out telephone services in the area.

She was able to get Diana checked in with the information from her wallet, but the hospital needed more details than Naomi could find.

Call person? Naomi signed as someone helped Diana onto a stretcher.

Diana pulled her phone from her coat pocket and unlocked it. *Okay*, Diana signed, then scrolled through her phone and handed it over before she was wheeled to the back.

Naomi went outside, where it was slightly quieter, and called the contact Diana had selected.

"Hi, is this Kate?" she asked when someone answered the phone with a swear word.

"Mom? You're not Mom. Um, yeah, this is Kate. Sorry, I just got the kids down and forgot to turn the ringer off. Speaking?"

"This is Naomi Happleburn. I'm calling about your mother. She's okay but she was injured apprehending a criminal. She's at Montpelier General Hospital."

The woman on the other end of the call sighed as though she was used to these kinds of calls. "Not again. Wait, you're not a cop or a doctor. You don't sound like a receptionist."

"You take after your mother. She's fine. EMTs said it looks like just soft tissue damage, but they're taking her in to surgery now."

Kate chuckled. It was low and familiar, and it made Naomi look back toward the building which held Diana, wishing she was inside with her. She shivered again. It hadn't started snowing in the city yet, but it was cold enough to start at any moment.

"You're the woman she was protecting, aren't you? Look, I've just put both the kids down, and my husband is on call tonight—he's a doctor. You said she's okay, right? Should I wake the kids up and come in now?"

"No, the hospital just needs some details. I have her things, but I don't have all of her information. I mean, it's late, and she'll probably sleep after surgery. I've got nowhere else to go so I'll be here anyway."

"I don't mind coming in. I can get the kids up."

Naomi couldn't tell someone with small children to come out on a night like this to sit in a noisy waiting room. "I know you don't know me, but if you can't come tonight, I don't want her to be alone. Can you authorize me to stay with her? Just until you can get here."

"If you don't mind, that would be a huge relief. She's talked about you a little, and even though technically I think you're work, it sounded like she was having fun with you. Can you pass me over to the admission staff? I can tell them whatever they need. Not like it's the first time."

Naomi took a deep breath and went back inside, waiting until she could talk to the same nurse who'd admitted Diana. She handed over the phone and overheard the nurse confirm to Kate that Diana was stable.

Once she had Diana's phone back, she made a beeline for the exit, putting the phone back to her ear. "Thanks."

"Thank you for being there. I'll come in the morning, once the kids are up. If she wakes up and asks for me, call me back and I'll come in right away. Or if anything changes." There was a deep sigh. "I'll let Jake know, and I'm sure he'll come by if he can. Thanks again for staying with her. I wouldn't like to leave her alone, and she said she enjoys you."

"She did?" Naomi blinked, watching the snow start to fall. Right now, it was pure and white and clean, but in half an hour it would be gray slush coating the roads and parking lot.

Kate chuckled again. "Let me know if she needs anything and I can swing by the house before we come in."

"Do you want my number? This is her phone, and I don't think I should be using it unless it's another emergency."

"Sure."

Naomi rattled off her number, and they ended the call.

Diana looked so small in the hospital bed, her eyes dark and bruised. She was in a gown, and when Naomi touched her hand, it was cold.

"Could you please get her another blanket?" Naomi said as the nurse turned to leave. "How long will it take her to wake up? Do I need to call someone when she does?"

"Buzzer's here." The nurse showed Naomi the call button. "Maybe an hour. We'll drop in to keep an eye on her vitals."

When she left, Naomi leaned in close to Diana's sleeping face. "You're going to be okay. You have to be. I couldn't bear it if anything happened to you. I should have come down sooner. I shouldn't have let you face him alone."

The nurse came back with two blankets, handing the second one to Naomi before excusing herself. Naomi had her laptops, and more than enough work, but she sat still to watch Diana sleep, holding her hand.

When Diana woke, Naomi drew a deep breath.

"I'm sorry," she said, not looking at Diana's face.

"Not your fault," Diana said, blinking up at her. "His fault, not yours." Diana's eyes didn't focus immediately, and Naomi stroked the hand in hers gently, relieved when Diana squeezed her fingers. "Hell of a thing. You're a sight for sore eyes."

"They're definitely bruised," Naomi admitted, gently touching the cool pads of her fingers to the bruising. Diana closed her eyes. "Do you need anything? Oh, I should let someone know you're awake."

Naomi found the call button and pressed it, unable to tear her eyes away from Diana. When the nurse came in, Diana asked if the machines had to beep so loudly; to Naomi's astonishment, he turned off the audio feedback, reducing the noise in the room significantly. Diana's eyes kept drifting closed, but when they opened they were always focused on Naomi, a little smile on her lips.

"The doctor will see you in the morning, but you should be out of here tomorrow," the nurse told Diana. "They gave you a head scan, but since you're up and talking they're going to want the bed. Have you got anyone at home that can help you out?"

Diana looked over at Naomi and tried to shrug. She gasped when her shoulder moved. The nurse nodded and made a note in the chart.

"Worry about that tomorrow, huh?" With that, he left.

Once they were alone again, Naomi felt unexpectedly shy. She'd been running on fumes for the last few hours. The amount of noise that a hospital generated was not compatible with her personal comfort levels.

Diana looked over at Naomi's hand still in hers. "I'm glad you're here," she said, voice low.

Naomi smiled at her, running her thumb over Diana's knuckles. "I'm glad you're going to be okay," she admitted. "I can't help but feel like this is my fault. If I'd said something about the tunnel sooner, if I'd come downstairs earlier—"

"Honey, it's not your fault." As usual, Diana's pet term made her blush. "And if it hadn't happened the way it did, then you wouldn't be here."

"But neither would you."

"I mean, it could have gone either way. I keep thinking, what if I'd let you go home and they'd come again? What if you'd been asleep and they'd found you? I think I need to reassess my career because it came too close this time."

"It did," Naomi agreed, looking at the thick bandage on Diana's shoulder. The whole ordeal had been terrifying—David, her house, Diana. Naomi couldn't remember ever being as scared as she had been when she'd heard Diana's frightened voice tell the man to drop his weapon a second time, then the urgent, muffled scuffling from downstairs. When she'd heard the shot, she'd dashed out of her hiding place with her heart in her throat, hoping that Diana hadn't been hurt. It had taken too long to realize Diana had been shot—the man had been bleeding profusely, and Diana's blood hadn't shown up against her dark coat.

Diana blinked up at Naomi sleepily, as though she hadn't been worried for a moment.

* * *

Naomi hadn't been able to sleep; the hospital was too loud. But her eyes were closed when she heard footsteps approach the next morning. Medical staff had come in to look Diana over and check her vitals at varying times through the night, but these footsteps were different.

Naomi looked up when a woman peered into the room. Her arms held an infant, and she was followed by a little girl who was waist high to her mother. Naomi knew them by name; she'd seen photos, but the resemblance was even more striking in person.

Kate looked to be in her late twenties and had dark-brown hair. Her brow furrowed when she saw Naomi, whose hand was still in Diana's, where it had rested since she'd fallen asleep again. The fingers of Naomi's other hand had been absently stroking from Diana's wrist down to her knuckles. Since she was in the only chair in the room, she stood, moving closer to Diana without losing her hold on Diana's hand.

When Kate saw Naomi's headphones, she leaned down to speak to her daughter in a carefully soft voice. "Cousin Simon voices, okay, Violet?"

The girl nodded, looking over at Naomi with wide eyes. Kate straightened and walked over to the bed without disturbing the sleeping baby, which she adjusted into the crook of her arm.

"You must be Naomi. Thanks for the updates last night—I was up worrying anyway." Kate bent over her mother, checking the bandage, then gently brushing hair back from her face. "Oh God, she looks so much smaller like this."

"She saved my life," Naomi said.

Kate eyed her with wry bemusement. "She said you were in trouble. And that you like it quiet."

Naomi shrugged. It was true. She wondered how often Diana took work home with her like that. Kate looked around at the movement of beds and people in the hall outside.

"Do you need to go?" Kate asked, her voice still low. "I'll take care of her."

"I don't have anywhere to go," Naomi admitted. "My house is still a crime scene, I left my car at the cabin. All I have is in this bag. Do you want me to give you some privacy?"

Kate eyed her again and Naomi tried to make herself take up less space, tried to wrap the bubble of limited noise tighter around herself. She was down to her last set of earbuds; her hearing aids were charging yet again.

Kate was taller than her mother, and she had the same confidence. She was not quite as good-looking as Diana, but Naomi suspected she might be biased. Kate had a harder set to her jaw. Darker hair, darker eyes. The child in her arms made a little noise, and the little girl was fiddling with a machine. She too looked like Diana, or her mother, or both. Diana's legacy, her family.

"No, stay. If I know Mom, she'll be looking for you the moment she wakes up, and she'll be looking for a case update to boot. I keep telling her that she shouldn't be out in the field at her age." She gave Naomi a quick glance, gauging her age. "Not that she's old, she just shouldn't be out there wrestling criminals with her bare hands anymore." Kate sighed and sat in the chair Naomi had vacated and fussed over her baby. "Kate. Kate Rawley, and that's Violet, and this is Brian. We came as soon as we could."

"Thank you for coming."

"Of course."

Diana stirred then, her face pale, and Naomi poured her some water and helped her sit up to drink, holding the straw for her.

"Hey," she rasped, obviously trying to get her bearings.

Naomi pressed the nurse call button and stepped back as Diana greeted her family. Diana took stock quickly, not relaxing until her eyes caught on Naomi and stayed there, watching her. Naomi smiled, and Diana smiled too, turning to her daughter.

"Mom, you have to stop—"

"We had this discussion last time I was in here, and I told you to at least let me wake up before you start in on my career."

"It's too dangerous. Sure, it was your shoulder this time, and just a couple of bruises last time, but how many times do I have to come to the hospital because of your job? What if it's not the hospital calling next time? What if it's MPD telling me you got yourself killed in the line of duty?"

"She saved my life," Naomi said quietly.

Diana rolled her eyes, turning to Naomi. "You saved mine. He was looming over me, and the next thing I knew you were standing where he'd been, holding that wrench." Diana glanced over at Violet. "Either way, I was the target, not you. He followed me. He was looking for the cop who arrested his brothers and decided I'd do."

"I wasn't going to let him hurt you. I'm not—I've never been in a fight in my life. But I couldn't just hide."

"It's my job." Diana glared at Naomi. "You were supposed to stay hidden."

"I'm glad she didn't," Kate chimed in, watching the conversation with annoyance. "If she hadn't been there, what would have happened? I can't do this anymore, Mom. I can't worry about you like this. You won't always have someone to come save you."

"I don't often need to be saved."

"Once is too often."

Naomi glanced between the two, then at the little girl. "Hey, Violet? Do you want to come to the snack machine with me? They have gummy bears. We can leave these two to catch up with all their grown-up talk." Naomi looked at Kate for confirmation, wondering if she'd overstepped.

Kate's eyes flicked to Diana's, then over Naomi with the same level of scrutiny Diana had initially given her.

"I'd trust her with my life. And yours, and theirs," Diana reassured her.

"Hold her hand, Violet, and remember, use your Cousin Simon voice, please."

Kate held out Brian and Naomi drew back, completely at a loss as to why someone would willingly hand an infant to her.

"You saved her life, we're practically family." Kate rolled her eyes, still holding out her son.

"No, Kate, don't make her—if he wakes up, he'll be too loud." Diana sounded distressed, and Kate hesitated.

Naomi stepped forward, slowly raising her arms.

"He's asleep," Kate said, moving to hand him over.

"Not if you transfer him." Diana's voice was full of warning, but Naomi didn't back down. Once Diana was discharged, Naomi wanted to book a hotel room and sleep for days. She could deal with a few more hours if there was peace lurking on the horizon, her frayed nerves held together with the promise of respite.

Naomi carefully took the infant from Kate's arms. She settled him quickly with a little help from Kate and took Violet's hand. She took the kids out to the hall, letting Violet lead the way, knowing they would eventually come across a vending machine in the endless corridors. Violet chattered away, but quietly, remembering what her mother had said, and it started to make sense—she was telling Naomi about her day and how worried Kate had been. Violet had been given not one but two apple juices because mommy was distracted, and Brian had been smelly earlier and was no longer smelly. Naomi agreed with that, and paid for some candy at the machine, leading Violet to a hand-sanitizing station and making sure her hands were clean before opening the packet. Violet held it out politely for Naomi, who declined.

"I feel bad for Brian, because he's not allowed to have candy. All he does is eat and sleep and make smells and sometimes he laughs but he can't have candy, so I don't know what he's so happy about."

Naomi looked down at the child in her arms. He looked like Diana too, a little, in the nose, in the cheeks, in the smile on his sleeping face, the little dimple that matched Diana's. It made Naomi's chest ache.

Naomi paused in the doorway to Diana's room, making eye contact with both women before coming back in.

A doctor had joined them and stood reading the chart at the foot of the bed. "If this is your emergency contact, then you're cleared to go home with her; you'll need help for a few weeks. Surgery went well and your head scans came back nice and clear. We'll get the paperwork sorted out if you want to get dressed while you wait."

The doctor left, and Diana looked over at Naomi. "They said I'd need home help, and I know your insurance company hasn't replaced your carpet yet. I'm pretty sure your house is still a crime scene. If you don't mind, I have a spare room, and I could use an extra pair of hands for a few weeks."

"Oh, I can stay, Mom. We can sort something out—or you can stay with us if you want." Kate took Brian back from Naomi, and the little boy nuzzled back against the familiarity of his mother with no indication that he'd been upset about his little adventure through the hospital halls with a stranger.

"You have a family, my love," Diana told her daughter.

Naomi knew Diana was offering so Naomi would have somewhere to stay. She also knew Diana was going to be grumpy about accepting any help; the woman was fiercely independent.

"So? Will you stay? You'd be doing me a favor." Diana's voice was soft and low, the way it had been ever since they'd met at the gate to Naomi's property, when Diana had looked at her like she was something magical.

Naomi swallowed, nodding quickly.

"Good. We're both sorted, then. Help me on with my clothes?"

"They had to cut off most of them in surgery, and mine won't fit you. You might be stuck in the gown." Naomi dug through her backpack. She'd shoved everything in together, but she managed to dig out a navy-blue knit sweater she didn't recognize that must have been Diana's, as well as a pair of jeans. Diana's bloody bra, holster, and clothing had been left in a clear plastic bag, and her service weapon had been released to MPD when they'd dropped by earlier. Her belt, badge and boots were in another bag.

"Do you need a hand?" Kate asked, but Diana shook her head.

Kate took Violet and Brian out of the room and closed the door. Diana was still a little out of it, but Naomi managed to slip the sweater on over the gown before untying it to preserve Diana's modesty. The jeans were a little trickier, but using the chair, Naomi was able to get them up and fastened over Diana's hips. They were very tight, and Naomi's fingers brushed the soft skin of Diana's stomach as she fastened the button, pulling the gown out from under the sweater now she was dressed. Kneeling, Naomi slid Diana's feet into her boots.

"I don't think I thanked you," Naomi said. "I didn't really realize how much you were risking when you said you'd take care of me."

"Just doing my job," Diana said. Her right hand found Naomi's cheek and tilted her head back so their eyes met. "I'm not going to be able to fully sign for a while, only spell." Diana patted her injured arm, which Naomi had put back in the sling carefully. "I can try to get someone else that knows ASL assigned to the case, even if it's just an interpreter and not a detective. Once Hastings wakes up and starts talking, they're going to want you involved."

"I can manage."

"I can sit in, if you'd like?"

"I'd like that, yeah. Thanks."

Naomi helped Diana to her feet and gathered their things, headed for the door. Before she opened it, she braced herself for the noise, closing her eyes. She opened them and looked at Diana, who smiled at her, and Naomi found herself smiling back, despite everything.

CHAPTER FOURTEEN

Kate drove them all to Diana's in her SUV, Naomi in the back with the baby and Violet—who quietly babbled away like they were old friends. All Naomi wanted to do was go home and cocoon herself in silence, but that was impossible. She felt like a kid being picked up from soccer practice by someone else's parents.

"What do you need?" Naomi asked Diana when they pulled up at a large suburban house. The neighbors were close, the houses almost touching. The house was historic but newer than Naomi's, perhaps Edwardian.

"Help Kate with the kids. I'm fine," Diana said.

Naomi unbuckled Violet and lifted her down from the car. Kate took Brian into her arms while Violet stayed at Naomi's side like a shadow. Despite her words, Diana hadn't moved, so Naomi opened the car door and undid her seat belt, then put Diana's uninjured arm over her shoulder to help her to the front door. She dug in Diana's coat pocket for her keys and helped her inside before going back to help Kate and close the door behind them all.

She found the kitchen and started making hot drinks out of habit, letting herself get lost in the familiar noise of the kettle and the moment alone.

"What are you doing?" a little voice came from behind her. Violet had followed her. Naomi looked up, made sure Kate knew where her daughter was, then pushed the kettle a little further back. Violet's deep-brown eyes were wide and curious.

"I'm making a hot drink. Would you like tea or hot chocolate?"

"Hot chocolate!" Violet crowed, clinging to Naomi's leg as she tried to search cupboards.

"Kate?"

"Coffee, please."

It should have been more stressful. A strange house. Three strangers, new spaces, new noises. But Diana was okay, so Naomi was okay. It was quieter inside than it had looked from the street—Diana must have invested in double glazing. And Naomi's noise protection dulled most of the unfamiliar noises, along with the adrenaline that still pumped through her. Plus Violet was sweet, and she was someone Diana loved. Naomi let her fingers brush through Violet's hair as she made the hot drinks, the little girl still latched onto her leg and watching with interest.

Kate was brisk and efficient. She had Diana settled comfortably, even with a fussy baby in her arms. Kate took her coffee gratefully, and Diana took hers with a satisfied sigh.

"How do you always get it right?" Diana asked when she sipped, but the question didn't make sense to Naomi. The simple act of remembering how Diana liked her beverage wasn't something she considered difficult.

She saw the look Kate gave her, the way her eyes caught on the rainbow tape on her headphones, the way they narrowed in a facsimile of her mother's detecting face for a moment. Then she smiled and sipped her own coffee.

"It's pretty good," Kate agreed.

"Okay, where did you find her?" Kate asked, setting her mug down. Naomi was still in the kitchen while Kate and Diana had moved to the living room, but distance had never stopped her from hearing quieter conversations than this one.

"Crime scene," Diana joked.

"You have to stop bringing your work home with you." Kate's voice was lighter this time.

"Did you call Jake?"

"He'll be by later. He has to pick Ollie up from school, but Minnie will watch him when she gets home. They didn't want to overwhelm you." She hesitated. "Are we too much?"

"Never enough, my love," Diana said.

"You've got a gunshot wound."

"I'm happy to be with my family."

Naomi retreated further into the kitchen, Violet still shadowing her. She felt awkward. She would love to go find a hotel with soundproofing and lock herself in. But she'd been the cause of Diana getting hurt; she owed it to her to be here for her.

Kate moved like her mother. Careful steps, careful movements. Violet, not so much. Naomi appreciated that she'd grown up in a healthier environment, but it made her noisier. She slurped her hot chocolate, dug the marshmallow out with her spoon and sucked on it with relish.

"I'm four," Violet said suddenly. "I can spell my own name. In English and in American Simon Language." She demonstrated, moving her hands slowly with a lot of concentration, her tongue poking out as she moved her fingers. "But I like—" She made a "V" symbol and slapped it on her chest. "Cousin Simon gave me that name as a sign instead of spelling and that's what he calls me now. You can call me that too."

"That's very clever," Naomi said, unsure what age children learned to write, or how that translated to finger spelling.

"You're very quiet," Violet commented. "How old are you?"

"I'm older than you," Naomi said, a little uncomfortable in Diana's home, with her family, unsupervised with this child. She'd spent so long alone that she wasn't sure what to do with this family. Diana was fine; Diana was like being alone, but better, because Diana was there.

It was only temporary. Detective Busco had said that the crime scene investigators were supervising the insurance contractors as they finally replaced her carpet. Engineers were coming in to stabilize and secure the new tunnel. It would take a few weeks, at least, and Naomi didn't want to think about the bill.

Her insurance premiums would be a nightmare after this, especially since the unknown entrance to the home hadn't been secured. But they had approved the claim, and now she had contacts in the police department who might be able to make these kinds of calls for her.

"Mom!" Naomi heard Kate chastise and hurried to the living room to see Diana standing, a little unsteady on her feet. The hospital had prescribed some painkillers, which they'd picked up on the way home.

Kate's arms were full, so Naomi strode quickly across the room to push her back onto the couch, her hand on Diana's uninjured shoulder as she stared her down. "That's what I'm here for; to fetch anything you need so you don't hurt yourself. You only need to ask."

"Just wanted a book." Diana actually stuck out her lower lip, and Naomi laughed at her, letting go of her shoulder and reaching for the bookshelf behind her.

"Which one?"

"One of yours, with that hot detective."

Naomi rolled her eyes and dug through her bag, handing over the books she'd taken to the safe house with her. The others in the series probably hadn't survived the second house invasion, and she'd have to list the cost of replacing them too.

Diana smiled up at her, then pouted again as she tried to open a book with one hand.

Naomi sighed and dug through the bag again, pulling out her e-reader and quickly repurchasing the book in digital form. She would have to anyway; she was pretty sure the series was out of print now, and she hated having incomplete physical series of books. She'd salvage what she could, but she might have to digitize what remained of her library.

Diana smiled at her again the moment she figured out how to use the device with her one good hand.

"You stay there, or I'm getting the wrench," Naomi said, her tone light. It still resonated, the noise of metal against bone, still made her shudder. Diana just chuckled.

Kate watched with wide eyes, as though she'd never seen anyone treat her mother like that. As though she'd never seen her mother respond to a threat like it was a joke.

Naomi remembered, too late, that Diana's ex-husband had probably threatened her just like that. She could feel all her bravado crumble, anxiety finally hitting after all the noise and movement of her day.

"Sorry." She crouched next to Diana, touching her knee. "I wouldn't hurt you for the world. Don't make your poor shoulder worse if there's anything you need. That's what I'm here for. Just stay put, okay?"

"For you? Anything." Diana was already engrossed in her book, but she put it down to touch Naomi's hand where it hovered apologetically close to her, grasping it gently in acknowledgment.

Exonerated, Naomi retreated back to the kitchen.

"You mind that I'm here," Naomi said quietly when Kate came in with her empty mug, the baby nestled contentedly in her other arm. Kate looked surprised but not guilty, and Naomi quickly continued, "I wouldn't...I've never even hit anyone before, and I've been gay in Texas."

Kate took a moment to parse that sentence.

"It would have been in self-defense," Naomi clarified. "Still gay though. I saw you clock..." She pointed to the rainbow tape on her headphones. "It's not..."

"I don't mind. I don't even know you, other than what Mom's said about you. An extra pair of hands while she's injured can only help."

"She wouldn't be injured if it wasn't for me." Naomi could hear the guilt in her own voice.

Kate sighed. "If it wasn't for you, she might not be alive." She eyed Naomi again, assessing her. "And she seems to like you. I told her to sit back down, and she wouldn't. She's so independent it scares me sometimes. But she listened to you. I thought she was going to be a nightmare to take care of, but maybe it'll be different if it's you taking care of her. I think she might actually let you. I've never seen that before. She always does too much, doesn't trust anyone. Do you know how many of her friends I've ever met?"

Naomi shook her head.

"Four. I'm twenty-eight this year. Four people in three decades, and one of them is her partner, Ray, because he used to take Jake camping. So if she trusts you, if she let you meet me, if she took you up to the cabin, then I guess I have to trust you too. You must have done something—other than save her life—to earn it."

"You don't have to trust me, but I'm not going to hurt her. Had plenty of chances, if I was going to."

Kate shrugged and Brian fussed a little. Naomi waved at him and he smiled at her, waving chubby little fists in her direction. Naomi gave him a finger to hold and he cooed happily.

"Mom, can Naomi read me a book?" Naomi looked down to see Violet holding *The Velveteen Rabbit*.

"If she wants to," Kate said. She eyed Naomi again, shaking her head. "I don't know what it is about you, but I'm glad you're staying with her."

Naomi flushed deeply, taking the book from Violet and going back to the living room to read with her. Violet cuddled up against her on the couch so she could see the pictures, her fingers trailing over the pages as she quietly sounded out words to herself. Diana stretched out with her legs resting over Naomi's lap, where Naomi could rub them between turning pages. Kate nursed Brian in the recliner across the room. While Naomi liked to be alone, she could also see the appeal of an afternoon like this. Diana looked up at her and smiled, then her mouth turned down a little.

"You're awfully pale, Naomi. Did you sleep at all last night? Oh, of course not. I'll go make up a room for you now." She made to stand, but Naomi held on to her legs, keeping her firmly in place.

"The room will be fine, Mom. I know the beds are made. You're always telling us we can stop over whenever and stay the night. I'd almost think you were lonely." Kate gave Naomi what could have been a wink.

Now that Diana mentioned it, Naomi could feel the exhaustion settling in. There was an ache in her butt from the hospital chair, and an ache in her head that hadn't shifted with the aspirin she'd taken earlier.

She blinked a few times; no aura, so she wouldn't take her triptan medication. She'd been consistent with her beta blockers despite the changes to her schedule and lifestyle, so there wasn't much more she could do.

"I'll finish reading, but if you don't mind, I'll go lie down for a while afterward."

Violet squirmed happily as Naomi continued to read, aware of Kate's attentive gaze cataloguing the way she interacted with her daughter and mother.

When the book was done, Violet pouted and pleaded for another. Kate redirected her attention, and Naomi took her bag and followed Diana's directions down the hall. The room she'd been told to use was fully made up, and Naomi sank to the bed gratefully, putting her bag beside her and pulling out her headphone chargers. As much as she liked Diana and her family, the last two days and the night between had been far too much for her to cope with. She took off her headphones and checked the fit on the in-ear buds before she lay down, feeling her heartbeat pound at the base of her neck and the front of her skull.

She must have dozed because she started at the sound of the front door closing, then cautious, familiar footsteps through the hall.

Diana's head poked around the doorframe. "You could have closed the door."

"Here to help, not sleep."

Diana sat beside her on the bed and touched her face, brushing hair from her forehead with her right hand, the bulky sling restraining her left. Naomi had wished earlier that she'd had the energy to close the curtains, but the afternoon sunlight on Diana's concerned face was exquisite.

"Kate ordered takeout. I'm guessing you don't want to eat with us, but I thought I'd better check."

"Not hungry."

"Have you eaten today? Can I bring you one of your drinks?"

"It's fine."

"Naomi." Diana's voice was soft and disappointed. Her hand moved from Naomi's face down to her hip. "I know you're here to take care of me, but you need to take care of yourself too."

"I really can't." A little time to herself had softened the worst of the flare, but she could hear blood pumping in her ears. If she sat up, she would be nauseous. It was better to wait it out.

"Do you need anything? Any medication?"

There was movement in the doorway and Naomi turned her head. Kate stood there, holding Brian, her eyes on Diana's hand.

Diana didn't move it. She didn't look embarrassed or ashamed. She looked up at Kate and gave her a nod.

"Don't need anything," Naomi murmured.

"I'll get you an ice pack." Diana smoothed Naomi's shirt down and stood up.

Kate remained hovering awkwardly in the doorway. She cleared her throat softly and patted Brian's back. Naomi stifled the urge to insist that it wasn't what it looked like.

"Thank you for staying with her," Kate began, "but you don't look very well yourself. You've got my number. If she needs anything—or if you do—let me know, okay?" She smiled ruefully and moved out of the way as Diana came back in and offered Naomi the ice pack.

Naomi took it gratefully, sliding it behind her neck.

Diana didn't speak again, just offered Naomi one of the kindest smiles she'd ever seen, then slipped out of the room and closed the door behind her. Naomi, for the first time in a while, felt the absoluteness of being alone. Despite her pounding head, she already missed Diana.

CHAPTER FIFTEEN

When Kate came over later in the week, she handed Brian over to Naomi, tucking him into her arms carefully, even though she knew Naomi wasn't used to holding babies. Brian fit nicely in the curve of her arms, and he looked up at her with such a sweet, lovable smile that Naomi could forgive him anything. He had his grandmother's smile, and it was just as beautiful on his face.

When she looked back up, Kate was smiling, too. "I haven't seen Mom so cheerful for years, even though she's clearly still in pain."

"She's lovely," Naomi said without thinking, then blushed deeply. "I mean, she's been so kind to me."

Kate chuckled, and Naomi knew she hadn't fooled her.

"I'm glad she has you." Kate patted Naomi's shoulder before she walked off to do something for Diana, and Naomi stared after her, speechless.

Diana did have her. Naomi was fully gone on her.

Brian struggled in her arms for a moment before settling again, and Naomi hushed him, gently rocking him in her arms as she relished the moment alone with him. She tried not to flinch when Kate reentered the kitchen.

Kate glanced back at the living room, where Diana looked up from the book she was reading to Violet, her expression worried until she caught Naomi's eye. She signed, *okay?* and Naomi nodded.

Kate turned to Naomi. "Usually when she's on forced leave, she's all wound up like a spring. I've never seen her so relaxed, even if she is injured."

Naomi shrugged. It wasn't a question; it didn't need a response.

Kate watched her, then chuckled, her face dimpling in the same way Diana's did. "You always look so scared when I talk. Do you want me to sign? Am I too loud?"

"You're fine," Naomi said evasively.

"You don't flinch when she talks," Kate said smoothly, and Naomi focused very hard on rocking Brian.

"She's been good to me," Naomi said, aware that her stiff posture gave away her discomfort.

"You've been good to her too. Look, I know you said you were just protecting yourself when you took down the man who shot her, but it's her job to take care of people like you—victims of crime. She might not be here if you hadn't."

"I couldn't let him hurt her." Naomi's throat caught on the last word. "She told me to stay put, but I couldn't. Not once I heard—" Naomi looked to the living room, where Diana was happily absorbed in her granddaughter. She was gorgeous, confident, compassionate—and probably straight.

"Well, thank you anyway. For her sake. I've never seen her so…not happy, she's happy a lot. Relaxed. Content perhaps. I think she's counting on you sticking around," Kate said, her voice the same low tone that Diana used, too quiet to carry into the next room. "Once she's healed up, once your home is sorted out."

"We don't have anything in common," Naomi said nervously. She didn't want to think about what would happen when she could go home, when Diana no longer needed her or needed to take pity on her or whatever reason she had for keeping Naomi in her life so far. "I've been alone so long that I don't really know how to be a person anymore."

"She doesn't seem to mind. She clearly likes you."

Naomi looked away.

"Do you not like her?"

"Of course I do! She's the first person I've met since this happened to me that I can tolerate being around." Naomi realized how that sounded. "Not that you're—"

Kate held up a hand. "I get it. And I appreciate you helping out with Violet and Brian."

"There's enough of her in the three of you to make you tolerable too."

She hadn't expected Kate to understand, but she looked touched. "So you plan on keeping in touch?"

Naomi fidgeted. She'd wanted to return to her old life, but her old life felt cold and sterile now. It had been calm, sure, and contained and predictable. It was hard to think with the compressor fan of the fridge running right next to her.

"I see," Kate said when she didn't answer. "You tolerate her, but you don't like her."

"I do," Naomi blurted out, adamant and louder than usual. Diana's head snapped up, eyes locking with Naomi, who gave an *okay* sign.

Naomi had seen the way Kate looked between the two of them, her brow furrowed as she tried to decipher their relationship. Naomi had initially assumed she'd been trying to tell if Diana was being scammed. But Kate smiled at the soft way Diana looked at Naomi, and her questions sounded like she was asking Naomi's intentions toward her mother.

"I do like her. I like her more than I should." Naomi kept her gaze averted, but she could feel Kate's eyes on her.

Kate touched Naomi's forearm to get her attention. "Who's to say 'should'?"

"You, probably. That's your mother. She was married to your father."

"And she never once looked at him the way I've seen her look at you."

Naomi avoided Kate's eyes again, looking toward Diana in the living room. Diana caught the movement and looked up, smiling. Naomi's breath caught in her chest, and Kate chuckled beside her.

"I just want her to be happy. Well, and to be safe. She never listened to me when I told her I was worried about her, but a few days with you and she's finally getting out of the field and going for the promotion she should have gotten a decade ago. I already know you can keep her safe. I'd like to find out if you can make her happy."

Naomi blushed, her face burning. "She doesn't—"

"I have a lot of female friends. If one of them ever looked at me the way you look at her, I'd probably leave my husband like that." Kate snapped her fingers, the noise making Naomi flinch. "Sorry, but you know what I mean. And I really like my husband, so."

"We grew up in a different time," Naomi pointed out.

"You did. But things change. People change. It took her too long to leave my father, and it took me and my brother even longer to see that he wasn't there for any of us. You've done more for her this week than he did in their entire marriage. She's always been kind of—kind of sad. Self-contained and independent. It's nice to see her trust someone enough to let them help her. You tell her to sit down and bring her a drink and all the nervous energy in her fades away. I've never seen anything like it."

"She doesn't—this is all moot, because she doesn't—"

"You said you grew up in a different time. Things are better now. Easier. She can make her own choices. And she's obviously chosen you as someone she trusts."

"Even if—I can't give her the kind of life she wants. I can't take her anywhere."

"She doesn't need to go anywhere. She needs someone like you."

With that, Kate took Brian back, leaving Naomi speechless once again as she went to join Diana and Violet in the living room.

CHAPTER SIXTEEN

Naomi huddled in bed, unable to move without setting off more fireworks behind her eyes, behind her ears, in the sneaky small blood vessels of her brain. She'd seen the scans, and they matched where the pain originated, right above her right ear. She had taken her medication as soon as she'd noticed the line in her vision last night, but as always, it was too late.

She lay still. It was unbearable, even in the dark. And there was light outside the window, casting a pale shadow across the room with the curtains closed.

She could hear quiet footsteps muffled by thick socks. The door swung open nearly silently, but it was still too loud. Naomi thought she might vomit, feeling disoriented, worried she would fall off the bed even though she wasn't moving, hadn't moved for hours. It was only a little past the time Diana usually woke, and Naomi usually woke before her.

Diana was cautious when she entered and knelt next to the bed. There was a little click from one of the bones in her spine, below her ribcage. She didn't breathe out her words or even mouth them, just a tiny little noise of pain stifled in the dark. Naomi knew she must look pretty bad; Diana had been able to speak almost normally around her now that Naomi was used to her. She still primarily used low tones, but on occasion, when Naomi was a little louder, Diana would follow her example without seeming to notice or mind that Naomi led the volume level between them.

Naomi's eyes were open and leaking onto the pillow beneath her. She couldn't make eye contact. Diana's face was drawn close with concern in the half-light. Her hand reached out but stopped before it touched her and dropped back onto her own thigh.

Diana moved her hand slowly. *Help.* She spelled it out independently with her right hand; it was slower but silent.

Naomi lifted a fisted hand and shook it.

Doctor.

Again, Naomi shook her hand. *Loud.*

Diana nodded. *Doctor here?*

Naomi shook her hand, and Diana nodded again. She stood, then reached out and put her hand on Naomi's back in a gesture of comfort, careful not to exert any pressure. She left, and Naomi could hear her in another room, talking quietly, probably on the phone. More tears squeezed out.

Diana came back with an ice pack and rested it against Naomi's neck without moving her. The cold was soothing. Diana knelt again, making eye contact.

Doctor, she signed, and Naomi watched her lips as she mouthed the words with more care than required. "Coming soon. Favor."

Naomi lifted her hand to shake it again, but Diana took it and covered it with her own, slid her fingers between Naomi's and held it still. "Help," Diana mouthed, her lips not even making a sound on the "P."

Naomi was dimly aware that she was supposed to be helping Diana, not the other way around. When Diana let go of her hand, Naomi reached painfully for Diana's injured shoulder, trying to convey that she was letting Diana down. Diana didn't stop her or look upset. She just mouthed "okay," and let Naomi's fingers brush uselessly against her skin.

They stayed like that until Naomi heard a car stop in the street a few houses down. The car door closed quietly but the sound still managed to bounce around her skull, and Diana reached for her phone. Her face, lit by the screen in the dark room, was a vision of beauty to Naomi in her half-delirious state. All the little freckles stood out in stark relief on her pale skin.

Diana smiled and got to her feet again, and Naomi felt abandoned. Everyone always left her. People always thought she was too much when they saw how bad her life truly was, how much the pain crippled her.

The front door opened, and then there was a muffled argument downstairs.

Another woman's voice, pitched low to match Diana's. "You've never done this before."

"She trusts me."

"All the more reason for you not to! If it doesn't work, she'll blame you. She doesn't know me, so I don't care if she blames me. Besides, I want to get a look at this woman you think is worth getting shot for."

"It's not like that—look, can you be very, very quiet?"

"Sure. We hunting wabbits?" the woman asked flippantly, and Diana quietly laughed.

There was a pause, then the voices were even quieter, and careful footsteps approached the room.

Doctor, Diana signed as she came in, throwing a worried glance at the woman who followed her. Naomi had seen her before. She'd taken David's body out to the coroner's van.

The doctor held out a needle, then whispered in Diana's ear. Diana fingerspelled *sumatriptan*, and the other woman—large, dressed all in black, with a friendly face—reached for the blister pack of pills beside her bed. She whispered again to Diana, who nodded and lifted her right hand to sign, *When?*

Naomi held up four fingers, then made the circle to indicate hours. A moment later there was a stinging sensation in her arm as the needle dug in, followed by the noise of a Band-Aid being applied and cool plastic on her bare arm. When she looked up, the woman rubbed her fist against her substantial chest in apology, removing her gloves before taking Naomi's pulse.

Diana left and came back in with a bucket, not missing the relieved look in Naomi's eyes when she arranged it beside the bed, close to her face. Diana adjusted the ice pack so it felt fresh and cool against her skin. The injections weren't magic; she'd had them before. They did help, though. She might be able to move around by the evening if the doctor left another dose.

The doctor touched Naomi's face gently, moving her hair away from her eyes so she could look into them. Apparently satisfied with Naomi's pupils, she pulled her hand away slowly. She took both of Naomi's hands and squeezed them, and Naomi squeezed back. They went through a series of tests Naomi was very familiar with, pleased when the woman nodded.

"I need to check something else. It might hurt."

She removed Naomi's headphones carefully and felt gently along the line of her jaw, then up behind her ear. There was pressure and Naomi whimpered, feeling pathetic.

Diana's right hand shot out, gripping the doctor tightly around the wrist.

Naomi reached for Diana, trying to get her to let go. "She's your friend, she's not going to hurt me," she hissed through gritted teeth.

"Then why did you make that noise?" Diana hissed back, not relinquishing her grip on Daisy, who was watching their interchange with mild interest.

Naomi moved her jaw, wincing, then signed, *Okay. Didn't mean to.*

Diana let go of the doctor and pointed to the door.

* * *

In the kitchen, Diana leaned against the counter, watching Daisy rummage through her medical bag.

"Thank you for coming. I needed someone I knew would be careful with her."

"Someone you trusted? Yet you didn't trust me."

"You heard the noise she made," Diana said defensively. She crossed her arms as well as she could, the stitches in her shoulder reminding her not to push too far. The sling kept getting in her way; for the last week she'd been encouraging Naomi to go to bed earlier so she could take it off once she was alone. She was glad she was right-handed—she hated feeling so helpless. Naomi didn't make her feel helpless, though. It was all Diana. She was tempted to remove the sling now, but Daisy was even more likely to scold her.

She moved toward the cupboard. "Would you like a coffee?"

Daisy relaxed and nodded. "I think she has a temporomandibular joint disorder that's contributing to the hyperacusis. I'll give you a referral to someone who might be able to help. It won't be a cure, but it could make her more comfortable." Daisy looked at the liquid food on the kitchen counter and nodded as though she understood the significance. "Her poor jaw."

"She says chewing is too loud," Diana said sheepishly. "What's this terro—"

"Temporomandibular joint. It's where the jaw connects to the skull. Hers wasn't seated properly, which can interfere with hearing." Daisy eyed her with some interest, her mouth opening and then closing as though she'd decided against saying something.

Diana looked away, aware she'd overplayed her hand. When she looked back, Daisy licked her lips and tried again.

"Do you remember that case?"

Daisy didn't need to elaborate. Diana nodded, her jaw tight.

"You found that boy, Charlie, in the basement. They'd had him for two weeks. Ray came up out of the basement, distressed, when I got there. He pulled me aside and told me to brace myself and get a sedative. We had spoken a few times in the precinct and on crime scenes, but only professionally.

"He'd been right to tell me to brace myself. The stench alone—and then you. All wild-eyed and holding that stiff little body. Ray couldn't get through to you, and you wouldn't let either of us touch him. I didn't even know if you knew he'd slipped away, but he was cold when I had to sedate you so you'd let him go. We kept you out of the crime scene photos. Ray helped me smuggle you into my van and get you back to the morgue. I kept an eye on you while I did the autopsy. You threw up three times and cried once. When you finally let me touch you, I could feel your grief like a physical presence.

"If I were kidnapped, I'd want you to find me. If I were dying, I'd want you to be the one to be there holding me when it happened. You were on his side when he was helpless. You were the only kindness that poor kid knew in his last few weeks. You were on his side. But I'm on your side too. And Naomi isn't helpless. You don't need to rescue her, not from me. You asked for help, and I came because you asked for me. You've never asked for my help before. I wish you would have. I've seen how those cases hurt you, but you stay in the room while I work so you know everything. And, I hoped, so that I'm not alone when I have to work on someone so tragically disposed of."

"Bit of both," Diana admitted, shrugging. "I mean, I know it's your job. But you always meet my eyes when I look through the observation window. You're doing all the work. The least I can do is be there if it makes you feel better."

"Oh." Daisy took some time to digest that. "Well. Thank you."

She held out her thermos once the brew had finished and Diana filled it, smiling gratefully up at her. She hadn't realized, when she'd called, how deep their working relationship had been. She'd known about the boy, that she hadn't been in the photos, but she'd thought Ray had made sure of that, not Daisy. She poured herself a coffee and sipped it.

Daisy watched her for a moment. "Since I'm here, you look uncomfortable in that sling. You need me to take a look at anything?"

"Would you mind?"

Daisy rolled her eyes and set her thermos down. She washed her hands at the sink, then removed the dressings carefully. Diana felt a little exposed with her shirt unbuttoned and her shoulder out, but Daisy turned her attention to the wound without comment.

"Has she been helping you? Looks clean. Looks good, really. No pus, clean edges."

"I wouldn't let her." Diana blushed as Daisy's incredulous gaze met hers. Daisy clicked her tongue but held it as she applied a fresh dressing. "I'm used to being on my own, being able to take care of myself. The soft dressings I had Kate pick up have the border so it's just..." Diana made as if to cover the wound with her palm. "Easy."

"Girl." She trailed the word out as though it was a full sentence. "It won't hurt her to see your shoulder. Is there any particular reason you're so protective of her?" Daisy asked a little too casually as she slid Diana's sleeve back over her shoulder.

Diana sighed and put her arm back in the sling. "Jake and Minnie had just had Ollie. And I thought—what if it had been Jake? What if it had been Ollie? That poor little boy, all those broken bones, his lips blue. I couldn't leave him. But I couldn't save him. I was too late. And the people who hurt him were already gone." Diana took another deep breath, released it slowly. "My husband—my ex-husband—hurt someone defenseless in front of me. You saw how helpless she was when you came in. I swore I'd never let that happen again."

"Someone defenseless, or someone you cared about?"

"Both," Diana whispered, avoiding Daisy's expectant look.

After a beat of silence, Daisy closed her medical bag. She indicated some tablets and a loaded, capped syringe she'd left on the counter. "Those if she's not better this afternoon. If she's unresponsive or can't squeeze both of your hands with equal pressure, call an ambulance and let me know. I can meet you at the hospital, even if it's just for moral support."

"Thank you," Diana said earnestly. "Thank you for coming."

"Any time." Daisy reached out and touched Diana's good shoulder tentatively. "I can see why you like her."

Diana led her to the door, opening it carefully to keep the mechanism quiet.

Daisy turned to her. "I took photos. I never turned them in. I know you know you were holding him. But he was holding on to you as hard as he could. When you came to the morgue the next day like nothing had happened, like I hadn't had to sedate you and monitor you for most of the night, there was a bruise on your arm from where he'd been holding on to you. He knew you were there to help. He felt safe with you. It was the same way Naomi covered your hand when you touched me."

"I'm sorry. I didn't mean to hurt you."

"Oh, you didn't. You know that. You're very aware of your own strength. But even if you had, I'd have understood."

"I—" Diana sighed.

"I can see what you see in her," Daisy whispered. "Call me if you need me."

Diana nodded, bemused, and closed the door as gently as she could behind her colleague—no, her friend.

* * *

Naomi didn't quite sleep; the world was spinning a little too fast for that, the pain flat and dull as the bed lurched beneath her. Time passed. Diana came and went, sometimes offering water, sometimes bringing in an ice pack to replace one that had warmed against her neck.

Diana didn't seem upset or impatient, or even inconvenienced, even though she still had her arm nestled in the sling. Her friend had left soon after the injection, presumably giving Diana things to watch for since every so often she would check Naomi's pulse and make her squeeze with both hands.

Naomi managed to swallow some cold water from a silicone straw in the early afternoon, and Diana's relief was palpable. She awkwardly gave Naomi a second injection, her fingers gentle as she placed the Band-Aid over the new puncture.

Diana settled her hand on Naomi's back, rubbing carefully so her hand made no sound against the fabric. It was soothing enough that, along with the dose, Naomi finally felt herself starting to drift off. Diana's hand hovered over her head. Her headphones had lost charge hours ago, and for a moment Naomi hoped Diana would swap them out and recharge them. Instead she took Naomi's hand and held it again, and Naomi gripped weakly in thanks.

Naomi kept everything she needed next to the bed at home in deference to the unpredictability of her migraines, but it cemented how truly alone she was. Here there was more noise, no matter what Diana did to try to reduce it. There was more light, too. But there were also ice packs and cold water and injections that made existing a little more tolerable. And there was a warm hand in hers, someone who was trying to help her.

Naomi found her eyes leaking again, and then soft, warm, slightly calloused fingers brushed against her cheeks, too slow to make the sound of skin dragging against skin. It made the tears flow faster. She wanted to sob, but she'd be incapacitated with pain if she did, so she let the tears flood her cheeks, let herself take what comfort Diana offered.

When the tears stopped, Diana's hand returned to her back, turning the ice pack, fingers tracing over the hard knobs of Naomi's neck with tender ease that made her ache and cry again.

Why did she want more from Diana? Surely Diana had already given enough. She'd have driven anyone else away by now, but Diana's thumb rubbed soothingly over her knuckles, and her already quiet breathing was further subdued.

The screen of Naomi's phone lit up, and Diana dimmed it before signing *insurance*. Diana pointed to herself, and Naomi gave her a thumbs-up in agreement.

She left quickly, answering the call in a quiet voice. Naomi could hear her arguing, her voice sharp and low. She heard a frustrated growl, and then Diana making herself some food in the kitchen. She came back a while later with a popsicle for Naomi.

Naomi wanted to press it to her jaw, to her ears, to her forehead, but she resigned herself to sucking on it, watching as Diana took the phone from her pocket and set it gently on the bedside table. Naomi pointed to it, and Diana shook her head.

"You're stuck with me a little longer, honey," Diana said, her voice very low, her endearment the only welcome sound Naomi had heard all day. "Do you mind?"

"No," Naomi said, relieved.

"It's a relief to hear your voice again. You're feeling better?"

"Marginally." Even with a migraine, Naomi's brain still looked for the most accurate word in whichever language she was using. "Thank you."

"For what?"

"Doctor. Drugs. Staying."

"Naomi," Diana said, her voice cracking halfway through her name. "Of course."

Naomi didn't want to point out that there was no "of course" about it, that there were many people who'd just left her alone in a dark room. As terrible as she felt right now, she felt less awful because Diana was taking care of her.

"My friend—the doctor—"

"She was at a crime scene."

Diana paused, caught out on a technicality. "She's a medical doctor. You're just more alive than her usual patients. She wants you to book in with your GP. She wrote down a bunch of stuff to ask about when you go, and she's happy to talk to you if you'd like. She did a thesis on neuroscience."

"Good friend."

"Work friend. Well, I thought so. Shit. Sorry. I'm talking—" Diana made to get up, but Naomi reached out and held her wrist.

"No, keep going."

"Are you sure?" Diana settled back into a squat.

"You're a very nice distraction."

Diana blushed at the compliment. "I've been called better things, but not for a while. Okay. I thought we were kind of friends because she lets me hang out in the morgue when my team is bugging me. We both work with mostly men, and there's something nice about not being the only woman in the room."

"Sounds bleak."

"Crime scenes usually are. Anyway, I called her, and she said she could swing by with something over the counter that she could get but I couldn't and check that nothing was seriously wrong. I didn't think she'd go that far out of her way for me, and I didn't think you'd realize that she doctors people less alive than you."

Naomi wanted to say that Diana was worth going out of the way for, but she didn't. She didn't have the energy for the emotional toll it would take to admit something like that. She wasn't ready for that conversation, for Diana to reject her because she didn't like women, let alone Naomi. She just wanted to close her eyes and listen to Diana's voice drown out the rest of the world.

"She said to call if you got worse. There's not much she can do, but she'd be able to tell if you had a stroke better than I could." Diana breathed in. "She suspects you've had one before."

Naomi didn't confirm or deny the veiled accusation. "My health insurance only covered so much, and then I couldn't work so I lost it. Now that I'm freelance, I don't get the kind of access… your friend would know better than me what treatments I need to ask for."

Diana took the empty popsicle wrapper from Naomi and made as though she was going to stand. "Do you need anything?"

"Can you—can you stay? Until I fall asleep?" Naomi reached out, pausing before she touched Diana's face. Her thumb smoothed over one eyebrow, fingers ghosting over Diana's cheek. "You're the only thing I can bear to look at," she whispered, and Diana leaned closer to hear. Naomi's fingers ended up near Diana's ear, and she went with it, stroking the skin there the same way she had her cheek.

Aware of Diana's scrutiny, Naomi moved her hand forward again, and her thumb brushed Diana's lips for a moment, then settled under her chin, her eyes traveling Diana's face the same way her fingers had. "Thank you."

Naomi's fingers slid down to Diana's neck, found three freckles clustered together on the right side, and rubbed gently over the skin there. Diana didn't pull away. She just met Naomi's gaze. The way Diana looked at her felt like being cracked open, so slowly and gently that it made her ache.

Naomi's fingers moved back up, brushing away the tears on Diana's cheeks. Diana turned her face into Naomi's hand, a silent sob from her chest muffled against Naomi's palm.

"I don't like to see you in pain," Diana said when she could speak. "I'm supposed to be taking care of you."

"We can take care of each other."

Diana was silent for a moment, then nodded.

Naomi gave the bed one soft pat. "There's room for you."

Diana hesitated. "I don't want to hurt you."

"You never have, and I doubt you'd start now."

Diana stood and walked around the bed, gingerly lowering herself next to Naomi, taking her weight with her right arm. When she was settled, Naomi slid her head onto Diana's chest, her headphones sliding away so her ear rested on Diana's ribs over her heart. The sling was bulky enough that there was little other real estate available.

"Will it hurt if I touch your head?" Diana barely breathed the words. She was perfect.

"Please do."

Diana raised her hand, starting between Naomi's shoulder blades and working her way up, digging into the soft tissue, releasing some of the tension in her tight muscles.

Diana paused at the base of Naomi's neck, but Naomi didn't tense, didn't flinch. Diana dug her fingers in under her hairline.

Naomi moaned, and Diana froze completely, her body suddenly stiff against Naomi's where before it had been luxuriously slack.

Diana resumed after a moment, and Naomi shifted uncomfortably and carefully removed her headphones.

"Batteries are dead," she said, settling her head on Diana's chest again. Diana reached to take them, to charge them, but Naomi didn't let go. "Don't stop."

Diana obeyed, her fingers delving back into Naomi's hair. She felt so good. Her hands were so strong. Naomi moaned again, but didn't bother to be embarrassed this time, so floppy as to be almost boneless. It didn't take long before she fell asleep.

* * *

Diana didn't stop trying to rub away the dregs of pain from Naomi's head. The motions were as comforting to her as they seemed to be for Naomi.

Until now, she had found the loneliness of her life safe and comforting. Anyone she met would have to compete with the security she felt when she was alone, but Naomi wasn't competition; she enhanced Diana's life in so many ways that the sense of safety she sought in solitude paled in comparison to the ways Naomi made her feel safe and cherished. Being held as she cried. The way Naomi felt in her arms; so soft and warm and sweet. The way Diana felt like she melted every time Naomi nuzzled trustingly into her.

When they lay like this—and Diana was starting to admit to herself that maybe straight women didn't lie down with other women like this, especially not impossibly cute gay women—it felt like being held. But it was safer than being held. Naomi's hands didn't grip her or try to contain her, never tried to grope her, never closed around her wrists. Diana was free to leave at any time. There was no expectation or entitlement.

Diana had lived in this house for over thirty years, and it was the first time it had truly felt safe. It was the first time it felt like home.

She shifted uncomfortably; her shoulder bothered her. Naomi didn't wake. Her hair was so soft and gorgeous; it was such a deep, dark red, contrasting against her pale skin. Diana felt possessive over her for a moment; Naomi's partner hadn't had the patience or decency to lower her voice or change her life in any way after Naomi's had been so thoroughly uprooted. She'd made Naomi feel like an inconvenience. How could anyone consider Naomi an inconvenience?

Andrew wouldn't have left her if she'd had a sudden onset of hyperacusis. No, he'd have gloated over the opportunity to torture her, knowing public opinion would agree that she was just being too sensitive.

It was going to be so hard to say goodbye. Naomi had her own house, her own life. Diana just wanted to enjoy this time where their lives intersected. She didn't need to read into it. She could just hold Naomi and enjoy it.

So she did.

Until the front door opened suddenly, and Kate's voice came from downstairs. Naomi flinched, and Diana covered her ears as carefully as she could.

She'd forgotten Kate was going to swing by with fresh produce. If she'd remembered, she'd have canceled.

"Mom?" Kate was in the hall now, and Naomi had tensed up again, clearly awake now. A moment later her daughter was at the door, looking into the darkness of the room. "Oh. Sorry." Even though Kate had used the soft voice she'd adopted around Naomi, her volume dropped lower. "I'll, um. I'll go."

Naomi shifted as though she was going to try to move, but Diana gripped her.

"Don't hurt yourself for my sake," Diana whispered, but Naomi pulled away anyway. Diana extracted herself as gracefully as she could and went downstairs after Kate; she wasn't ashamed or worried about whatever Kate might think but she felt like she owed her an explanation. She found her daughter in the kitchen arranging fresh fruit in the bowl on the counter. Kate leaned back against the counter and eyed her.

"I didn't realize," Kate said finally. "I had hoped—"

"She has a migraine. I had a doctor come, and she's been really—"

"You don't have to explain anything to me. It's your house. I shouldn't have just walked in."

"I do need to explain, though. It's not how it might have looked."

Kate nodded, distracted. Diana wondered where the kids were before she looked at the clock. Noon on a Wednesday. Matt would be home with them.

"But you wish it was," Kate said. "Hell, I wish it was. You were holding her like the Titanic was sinking. Her headphones were off. And you're going to tell me it's not what it looks like?"

"Maybe it is what it looks like. Not yet, but maybe. It's too soon, isn't it?"

"It's been twenty years," Kate said, and Diana didn't know what she was talking about.

"We just met. At a crime scene, of all places. It's not professional."

"I was talking about how long it's been since you've dated. And I don't think it matters how you met, just that you did. I'm sorry I disturbed you. I was just checking in to see if you needed anything. But I think you've got everything you need."

The tears that had been surfacing all day rose again.

"Oh, Mom. Does she know?" Kate's face was drawn.

Diana swallowed, trying to coax her face into something more neutral, so Kate wouldn't worry. "How did you know?"

"She was holding your hand when we met. You look at her like you've won the lottery. You asked her to move in with you after a week."

"You don't mind? That I might like women?"

"Women, or a woman? I've never seen you like this around anyone else. You're so relaxed, so happy. I thought I knew what it was like when you were happy, but this is the happiest I've ever seen you."

"That's not an answer," Diana pointed out anxiously.

"Why would I mind? And what would it matter if I did? You raised me better than that, anyway." Kate shouldered her handbag. "I'll get going. I hope she feels better soon, and I'm sorry if I interrupted you, but I know you're in good hands."

"I'll pass it on."

"She won't be mad?"

"She's never mad." Diana paused and thought about Naomi, holding a wrench midswing. Even then she'd been more scared than angry—for Diana's sake, not her own. "Well, maybe once."

"But not at you?" Kate looked worried, and Diana wondered how much of those years with her father Kate remembered.

"Never at me, and never at you, I'm sure. And if she is, it's not the same—"

Kate nodded, then hugged Diana for a long time. She pulled back and touched Diana's shoulder over the sling. "Do you need anything while I'm here?"

"Just you. Just you being the way you are. And the fruit is nice, too."

"I'm serious, Mom. I know you'd never ask."

"The doctor already had a look at my shoulder. She says it's healing well."

"Can I load the dishwasher or something?"

"It's all been takeout, sweetheart."

"Then I'll take the trash out."

Diana sighed. "If you must."

Kate chuckled and took the bag from the trashcan under the sink. She looked up at Diana, considering her for a long moment. Her daughter always been astute. "I like her, and I like the way you are when you're with her. I'll text later. And I'll text before coming over tomorrow."

Kate closed the front door so carefully that Diana's heart was full again. She didn't know what she'd done to deserve such wonderful children.

She went back upstairs, selfishly hoping Naomi would still be awake, but she was asleep. Diana quietly gathered her various hearing appliances and set them to charge before fetching Naomi's e-reader and loading the book series she'd been reading since the safe house. She sat up on the bed next to Naomi and stroked Naomi's back as she finally slept peacefully.

CHAPTER SEVENTEEN

Naomi came downstairs late the next morning, still looking pale. Diana handed her a warm mug of her meal replacement and watched carefully as Naomi drank it all. She rubbed her neck; she'd taken off her sling and overdone it with her shoulder.

"Is your neck bothering you?" Naomi asked.

"It's from the sling, and from not using it."

"I could rub it for you?"

Diana uneasily sat in a chair at the kitchen table. She bent forward a little, granting access. Naomi's hands carefully landed on her bare skin, and Diana forgot to be wary. Naomi could snap her neck, and Diana would die happy at her hands. She heard a half-sigh eke out from her own lips, felt herself relax.

Naomi's fingers were surprisingly strong, probably from so many hours of video games and keyboards. She dug in at a knot and Diana had to stifle a moan. She'd paid for massages before, but the tenderness of the way Naomi cupped her skull reverently, the way her fingers rubbed away the tension at her neck were beyond anything Diana could put a price on. No one had ever been so gentle with her, so patient and caring.

"Not too hard, is it?" Naomi sounded concerned.

"No, it's perfect." She tilted her head back and felt the base of her skull cradled in Naomi's palm. She'd never trusted anyone this much, never enjoyed being touched this much.

She luxuriated in the rising want, ready and completely willing for whatever Naomi wanted to do to her—with her.

But Naomi's hands strayed only down her back, between her shoulder blades, digging in at any tension she found. It felt so good, and Naomi smelled so good.

"You have lovely hands," Diana said, aware of the silence and finding it, for once, awkward.

"You should see—" Naomi cut herself off, but her tone had been light, almost flirtatious.

"What?"

"Sorry," Naomi said. Her fingers found their way to Diana's scalp, curling slightly as she rubbed.

Diana had to stifle a moan. "What are you sorry for?"

"I was going to say something, but it's inappropriate."

Diana thought again about the hands touching her, about where else she'd like them to touch. A moment later, a fingertip deliberately trailed the shell of Diana's ear.

It was the single most intimate thing anyone had ever done to her. She felt herself flushing; not just her face, but all over, the blood under the skin rushing to the surface in response, every nerve ending coming alive. She was alert. Awake. Aware. Alive.

The finger, to her disappointment, drew away. She turned, the chair scraping against the floor in her hurry, and saw Naomi's face a moment before she flinched. It, too, was flushed and filled with wonder.

"I'm sorry," Naomi said again, her eyes not meeting Diana's.

"Don't be," Diana whispered, but Naomi still wouldn't meet her eyes.

"I mean, that you got hurt for me. Can I—can I see your shoulder?"

Diana could manage on her own, and she'd wanted to avoid Naomi feeling any form of guilt about her injury. However, now, she couldn't turn her down.

Diana unbuttoned her blouse, aware suddenly that she hadn't worn a bra since that last one had been cut off in surgery. She pulled the neck of the blouse over her shoulder to reveal the bandage. She heard Naomi's sharp inhale of breath. Naomi's fingers were gentle as she pulled the adhesive away from Diana's skin.

"Oh. That doesn't look so bad," Naomi said, possibly more to reassure herself than Diana. It certainly hurt badly enough. Diana's eyes closed as Naomi's fingers ghosted over her skin, careful not to hurt her or apply any pressure. "Did I ever thank you?"

"I put you in danger. I never once thought it was following me to find you."

"He still would have found me. He would have blamed me for his brothers' arrests too." Naomi's fingers were heavenly; she was so considerate with her touch. She found Diana's collarbone and traced it for a moment, then retreated to the wound on Diana's shoulder. "I'm so glad it wasn't worse. I was so scared for you."

"You didn't look scared. You looked angry."

"He was hurting you." Naomi swallowed as her fingers rounded the wound. Her fingers brushed so gently over Diana's skin that she shivered.

"Thank you," Naomi said finally. "For protecting me. But no one is coming after me anymore, and I came here to help you. Please let me." Her voice was swollen and hoarse.

Diana typically changed her own dressings after a shower. It was awkward, sure, but it was preferable to figuring out some kind of modesty to allow Naomi access to her shoulder without revealing too much. Naomi's touch was so nice that maybe it would be worth the extra effort. Naomi's eyes slid from hers for a moment, and Diana glanced down.

Without the pressure of Naomi holding the blouse away from her shoulder, the neckline was indecent, and Diana's nipples were hard, her cleavage deep, an expanse of breast exposed. She'd been too late for the burning bra movement, and too early for the breastfeeding in public movement. Now they'd been ravaged by time and two kids and yet Naomi seemed to find them interesting. Her breath had quickened, and she swallowed audibly.

Diana felt gratified. She had no compulsion to cover herself further, felt no violation from Naomi's perusal of her exposed chest. She checked again; no areola was visible, but her nipples were so hard and obvious against her blouse.

"Oh. Um. Unless you're uncomfortable. I didn't mean to…"

"I'm not uncomfortable if you're not," Diana said honestly. "I just don't want you to feel guilty."

"Too late," Naomi said wryly. She swallowed again and deliberately stepped away. Diana took the hint, buttoning her blouse again.

Diana had never been so aware of her own body, a lingering pulse beneath her heartbeat, lower. She wanted something more, and it felt like she was being unfair to Naomi by not telling her.

But they were just breasts. Given the chance, anyone who liked them would take the opportunity to look. Even Diana had found herself lost in cleavage more than once. It didn't mean that Naomi felt anything for her. She just felt guilty.

It was still too new to be sure. It had been only a few weeks, far too soon to make any kind of firm decision. She was attracted to Naomi, but they might not be compatible.

Naomi had a good life without anyone else in it. She'd seemed perfectly happy with her setup before her home had been broken into. Diana was noise and mess. She had nothing to offer Naomi in terms of a relationship. Just stress that she didn't need, guilt over Diana's injury, and a reminder of one of the worst things that had ever happened to her.

It was better to wait. If Naomi wanted her, Naomi would let her know somehow.

Naomi gave her a tight smile, her eyes worried. "Your neck?" Her voice quavered.

"Oh." Diana bent her head side to side with a satisfying crack. "Much better. Thank you."

* * *

"You never looked at Dad like that."

Diana glanced up; Jake had appeared in the kitchen. It was Sunday, and he and Minnie had brought Ollie over for family dinner, which they'd also brought. Matt and Ollie were now out in the yard with some sort of sports equipment Matt had brought with him. The others were in the living room; close, but not close enough to overhear. Kate and Minnie were watching Naomi read to Violet, letting her sound out words before they spelled them together in ASL and made the sign for the word as well. Despite the activity being mostly educational, she could tell that both Naomi and Violet were having fun. Violet clearly adored the attention; her giggles made Diana's heart swell.

Naomi had been too distracted to prevent Diana from getting her own coffee. She poured one for Jake while she was at it. She was getting better at using just one hand.

"You're doing it again," Jake pointed out as he accepted the mug. "You look at her like she's Pandora's Box."

"What do you mean?" Diana tore her gaze away from Naomi.

"Like she's full of hope. Or you are, I can't tell. You're as bad as each other."

Diana stared at her son, trying to process. "And where does your father come into it?"

"He doesn't anymore. That's kind of the point. You're divorced. You're single."

"How is that relevant?"

"Oh, Mom." Jake looked at her with such pity that she felt flustered. She wanted to defend herself. She was a detective; she had deduced what Jake had been implying.

But defend herself against what? Hope?

"We get taught in the academy that crisis bonding isn't permanent," Diana said shortly. "Trauma and—"

"I've never seen you like this. You're not working, and you're not champing at the bit to get back to work." Jake sighed. "Look, I know we don't talk about it, but what happened with Dad… therapy wasn't really available back then, was it? But it is now. I know the precinct is really pushing for psychological support, and even if the stigma is still there, you've more than earned your position. No one can fault your career. You deserve…" Jake trailed off. "You still look scared, sometimes. Of a man who hasn't been in our lives longer than he was. You deserve to be happy, Mom. You've got time, now."

Diana pointed to her shoulder.

"That's what I mean. You know you'd be agitated being on leave by now if she wasn't here. I hope you keep her around. I like what she does to you. You've always loved your job. Not more than us, but sometimes it felt like it, growing up. Now I understand that it wasn't me and Kate you were running away from. But you don't have anything left to run from, and you haven't for years. She brought you to a standstill single-handedly. Maybe it's time to let yourself love something else."

Diana looked over at Naomi, who looked up, feeling Diana's eyes on her. She smiled shyly, as though she'd overheard the conversation and agreed.

"Mom. No judgment. I just want you to be happy, and this is the happiest I've ever seen you. If you're worried about what Kate and I are going to think, don't be. You're the one who raised us. You know we're not going to care who you date as long as they take care of you, and from what I've seen she does that very well."

"What could she possibly see in me—"

"She asked me and Matt to use sign language to talk to her because our voices are too deep to filter out well. But when you talk, she looks at you like you hung the moon for her. I don't know what she sees in you, but she likes whatever it is."

Diana shook her head. It was ridiculous. They hadn't known each other very long—too short, surely, for Diana to trust her so much. Naomi would be relieved to return to her world of solitude. She'd just been grateful that Diana hadn't been louder, that was all there was to it.

"I came to get her when her house was broken into. I took a bullet when the same people followed her to where she should have been safe. It's just something people do when they think you saved their life."

"You did, though, didn't you? If you hadn't stepped in, would anyone have come for her in time?"

"She was well-hidden."

"And she kept you from getting your skull smashed in by smashing someone else's. I think it's more than that. I can't see her being violent unless something really important to her was under threat." Jake leaned in and kissed her forehead. "You go back out there with your coffee. I'll serve dessert. And remember, you can always call me if you need anything."

Diana looked over at Naomi. She had everything she needed for the first time in her life.

* * *

"Do you...has it been okay, staying here?" Diana looked up from her book. Naomi had been staying with her for a few weeks now—well over a month, surely—and Diana had heard no complaints. There had been no other migraines, although Naomi retreated to her room when she was overwhelmed.

Naomi didn't look up from her gaming handheld. "I like hearing you. It's like hearing the boiler kick in when it's cold. I might be able to survive without it, but it certainly makes things more comfortable. I'm happy here. I am. It's noisier than I'm used to, but it's worth it."

"What's worth it?" Diana asked, expecting to hear something else about feeling safe.

"Being with you." Naomi's face flushed red. "I mean, the inconvenience of noise is canceled by the pleasure of your company."

"Net sum zero, huh?"

"More than that," Naomi said softly, looking back at her screen. "We're friends, aren't we? I'm not just another victim to you? You don't let just anyone come home with you from a crime scene and meet your family, do you?"

"No, but—"

Naomi smiled up at her, a more common sight as she grew more comfortable with Diana. She shrugged as though Diana had given her the answer she'd wanted to hear. "The insurance company will be through with the repairs soon. And your shoulder is healing really well. I'll be out of your hair soon enough."

"I like having you here," Diana said, surprised it was true. Naomi was a good house guest; clean and—obviously—quiet. But she was also gentle and considerate.

It was nothing like living with Andrew. Naomi more than pulled her own weight. She was cheerful mostly, sometimes withdrawn but not oppressively so. It was just that Diana was so sensitive, so used to reading moods that she noticed. She gave Naomi space then.

The kids liked her, too. She might be biased, but she was so careful about who she brought around her family. She trusted Naomi, not just with herself, but with the people she treasured most.

And Diana had barely had to use her shoulder at all, with Naomi monitoring her closely enough to step in and lift anything Diana tried to reach for before the tug of pain could even remind her. Naomi's other hand would trail over Diana's back to let her know where she was, and Diana found herself reaching for more things than she really needed just to feel that reassuring touch. There was usually a smile too, when Naomi handed over whatever Diana had wanted.

It was ridiculous. Someone showed her a little kindness, some basic human decency, and Diana was half in love with her. She'd accepted her captain's offer for psychological services following the shooting; Jake was right. She'd been through the service before, but only when mandatory. She hadn't realized how tight and restricted her life still was until she met someone who made her want to be open and affectionate.

When Diana spoke, Naomi listened. She valued every word against the effort of hearing it, and found it worthwhile, her mouth twitching with mirth. She didn't wander Diana's house all night the way she had the safe house; she was using more of the gummies than she had back then and apparently sleeping better.

Diana had forgone closing doors. If she dozed off while reading, Naomi would look in on her and remove her glasses. She always whispered a good night, and Diana always had a good night's sleep since she knew Naomi was close.

After more than twenty years of sleeping alone, her bed suddenly felt too big. Too empty. Like there was room for someone else, in her bed and in her life. She'd thought having Naomi in her house would be enough, but at night she felt the distance between their bedrooms sharply, wondering if Naomi could hear her breathing from so far away. If Naomi was scared, would she come to Diana? Surely she would. Diana should feel proud rather than hurt that Naomi felt safe.

Naomi's gaze dropped, her cheeks still pink.

Diana had never felt lonely before she'd met Naomi. Now she felt lonely every time she looked away.

* * *

Later that week, Diana had an appointment to remove her stitches—and she felt like a bra was warranted, since she was leaving the house. She called out softly and soon heard the soft footfalls of Naomi's feet approaching the bedroom door.

The door opened, and Naomi came in, eyes averted.

"I need some help," Diana said, embarrassed. She'd managed to get the straps of the bra over her shoulders, but there was no way she could fasten it without help. Her shoulder wasn't going to let her move it that way. Naomi looked up, her eyes catching on Diana's chest and widening. Her breath caught.

Even with the ugly, healing wound in her shoulder, Naomi was looking at her like she was something beautiful. She caught herself and looked up, not quite meeting Diana's eyes. Her tongue made a nervous appearance, brushing against her lower lip before tucking that same lip under her teeth. Diana was stunned that she'd elicited this kind of reaction, even though it was what she'd been hoping for.

"I don't think I should. I could get you a button-down instead."

Diana wanted to ask why Naomi couldn't help her, but the flush on her cheeks was answer enough.

Diana had never really felt attractive. She'd been set up on a few blind dates after the divorce, but no one had been so adorably flustered by the sight of her covered breasts. She turned her back, and a moment later, Naomi's fingers brushed against her shoulder blades, straightening the straps and gliding across Diana's back. They didn't linger after she'd managed to join the clasps, but Diana could hear how Naomi's breathing had changed. She turned again.

"That wasn't so hard, was it?" Diana asked, her tone light.

Naomi's hands were shaking, and her eyes were averted again. It gave Diana confidence. Naomi was rattled by her body. It was a good portent.

"Shirt?" Naomi eyed the T-shirt Diana had picked out. She shook her head and left, leaving the door open only a crack behind her.

Naomi came back with one of her own hoodies, holding the sleeve out carefully, not jostling Diana's sore shoulder at all. She held out the other sleeve too, then stepped in front of Diana to fiddle with the zip, her face down, her cheeks still flushed. She pulled the zip up, stopping short when it became obvious her fingers would brush Diana's covered breasts if she continued.

"Keep going," Diana prompted. "I don't mind."

"I do," Naomi said, finally looking up and meeting Diana's eyes. "I mean, I want to help you, but I don't want to touch you. Not like this."

Oh. It wasn't attraction making her act like this. She was embarrassed, probably for Diana. She didn't want to touch her. Not her breasts, at least. She was just being polite because Diana had asked for something, and Naomi felt indebted to her.

Her chest hurt worse than the bullet wound in her shoulder when she tugged the last few inches of zipper up herself. She flinched and saw the self-recrimination on Naomi's face.

"You understand, don't you?" Naomi asked, her eyes searching Diana's, but Diana looked away first this time. She felt so foolish. She'd thought—just because Naomi was gay, Diana had assumed the attraction she'd been trying to deny was mutual.

Naomi deflated and turned away. Her shoulders were hunched. Diana hadn't seen Naomi physically close in like that since the loud noises of the hospital.

"I don't mind," Diana said quickly, wanting to do anything to take the slump out of Naomi's posture. "It's okay."

She almost didn't hear Naomi say, "It's not," as she excused herself from the bedroom.

* * *

The insurance company called the next day. Diana answered Naomi's phone, already irate that they had once again ignored Naomi's communication preferences. The construction team had been sending emails of their progress, often with photos of what they'd been working on or anything unusual they'd found. Diana had been impressed; construction had clearly come a long way.

When the insurance representative Diana had been arguing with for weeks said that the repairs had been completed on Naomi's home, Diana's heart dropped. Naomi looked concerned, and Diana had to smile.

"They say you can go home now. Do you want me to check before you go over, just in case?"

"I'm sure it's fine." Naomi hesitated, looking at Diana's shoulder.

It was healing well, and while Diana couldn't carry anything particularly heavy with that arm, she didn't really need Naomi to stay any longer. Naomi had given her statement a month ago. The Hastings case was closed, with one confession and enough evidence in their home to tie them to the string of burglaries across the city. She had no more excuses.

Naomi probably wanted her own life back.

"I'll come and check the property. If they missed anything, or if it doesn't seem secure you can come back here any time."

But her home, this time, was pristine, and Diana had to let Naomi slip through her fingers.

CHAPTER EIGHTEEN

Diana had physical therapy downtown, so while she was out, she stopped at the precinct to check on her paperwork. Her promotion had gone through, and once she passed her physical, she would come back to desk duty in the upcoming weeks as a lieutenant. That would keep the kids happy. She no longer needed the sling, but she still struggled with her own bras.

She stopped by Daisy's office off the morgue, holding two envelopes, feeling stupid and exposed in the open hallway. She was relieved when the office was empty and went to leave her meager offering of appreciation on the desk.

"Don't tell me you're already back at work," Daisy said, her tone an accusation as she came into the room behind Diana.

"No. Naomi asked me to thank you."

"I already got the flowers." Daisy pointed at her desk. A beautiful arrangement was in pride of place, and Diana felt a little flare of jealousy, even though she'd received an almost identical bouquet. It was strange being here with a visitor's tag. She could see into the morgue from here. No bodies on the tables today.

"Well, I appreciated you coming around to help out. I didn't know who else to call who'd understand."

"You're lucky I like you," Daisy said, giving Diana a cheeky grin.

"I am," Diana admitted.

"You'd have done the same for me. I know you reported Lee and Josh."

Diana froze. She'd hoped she'd shut it down so efficiently that Daisy would never hear of it. "They were revolting." Diana didn't want to remember exactly what they'd said about the coroner, but it hadn't been flattering or appropriate for the workplace.

"And they lost their jobs because of you. Because you stood up for me. You never told me."

"What they said would have hurt you. And I was just doing my job."

"That's not part of your job. God, you think once you hit a certain weight or a certain age those kinds of comments would stop. But they never do. You've kind of been my hero ever since."

Diana hadn't had any idea that Daisy held her in such high regard. She handed over the gift card and the thank-you card self-consciously.

"She's a lucky girl, despite those migraines," Daisy mused, tucking the cards into her bag.

"How so?"

"She's got you, doesn't she?"

"Why does everyone keep saying that?"

"It's the way you look at her."

Diana hadn't been expecting a real answer. "How do I look at her?"

"Like she's a mystery you're trying to solve. Or a Christmas present, all wrapped up. I don't know, I just know I'd be very lucky if anyone looked at me like that."

"I've never—"

"People can be gay now, even you," Daisy said reassuringly, and Diana laughed.

"No, I was going to say that I've never met anyone like her before."

"Some people never meet someone like her. I said she was pretty lucky, but perhaps you are too." Daisy moved past her and went back into the lab, leaving Diana standing speechless in her office.

*   *   *

Diana knew Violet had asked Naomi to her birthday party; the little girl had been gloating over it for days now. She'd been upset that Naomi had moved out, and it had been hard to explain why she'd had to. That Naomi had her own home that was better suited to her requirements meant nothing to Violet. She'd pouted that first afternoon, and Diana was too much in complete agreement with her assessment of the situation to tell her to stop before they both burst into tears.

She'd have kept Naomi, if she could have. Not as a hostage, not forever. But she would have asked her to stay a few more weeks at least.

Not that Diana needed help anymore. She could manage on her own, and having Kate or Jake drop by every afternoon was starting to feel a little insulting. She'd healed well. She'd been seeing the physical therapist the department had recommended, and she felt strong again. She could drive and cook and read, and she'd return to work in a few weeks.

She'd followed up those appointments with the employee assistance program, and she had started to talk about Charlie and all the other people she'd been too late to save. She'd been talking about Andrew too, and Naomi. She felt better than she had in years. She could see now that she'd been unable to trust anyone with her family, let alone herself, but she'd let her daughter hand her infant to Naomi with only the concern that he might hurt Naomi.

She'd just seen Naomi make a man comatose, and she'd let her take her grandson and granddaughter out of sight.

She still wasn't sure what it meant. She wasn't sure if she was gay or just relieved to be treated like a person by a potential suitor.

Either way, she was learning how to let go of some of the habits she'd learned to survive Andrew.

Diana looked at herself in the mirror. Years had passed without her noticing. Her hair was graying, and there were lines around her eyes and mouth. She looked washed-out and tired, faded somehow. She did her best with a little makeup, and she picked out a nice dress from her wardrobe. She'd been meaning to wear it to her next work event, but it would do for a birthday party too. She was nervous. She'd be seeing Naomi again, if she came. Maybe Diana should text her and make sure? They'd parted as friends, but Diana hadn't wanted to bother her, and Naomi had kept up the radio silence from her end as well.

The dark-blue dress looked nice against Diana's skin, and she shook out her hair, examining herself carefully. Maybe she should give in to her hairdresser and have the grays colored. If she wanted to start darting again, she'd need to get confidence from somewhere, especially after the deep dejection she'd felt since Naomi left. She hadn't realized how much richer her life could be from sharing it with someone who thought she mattered. She paired the dress with heels to give her a little height, and she chose her peacock scarf and midnight-blue coat for the inclement weather, leather gloves already in the pocket.

Diana knew she was stalling; knew she was anxious. What if Naomi hated her? She had every right to. Diana had failed to protect her, put her in danger, and then hit on her while she was in a position of power. Anxiety made her look only more drawn, and she rubbed at the line it made above her eyes before sighing and heading out.

Diana scanned the room. She took the cake she'd baked for Violet through to the kitchen, nodded to Kate, then looked around, relaxing once her eyes found Naomi.

Naomi looked nice. She was wearing wool slacks and a shirt that made Diana want to run her fingers over it and under it and all over her. Maybe it wasn't the shirt. Maybe it was Naomi that looked so touchable.

One of the mothers from Violet's daycare was talking to her in a voice a little bit too loud. Diana could see Naomi flinch, and then Kate lifted her head and started to head over.

Diana was closer. She stepped in front of Naomi.

"You need to lower your voice," Diana said, her tone not quite a threat.

When the mother didn't lower her volume, Diana tapped her lip. "Alberti. You're the one with, what, three unpaid speeding tickets and two parking infringements, correct?"

The woman shut up. Diana reached behind her, and Naomi took her hand.

"Thought so," Diana said, leading Naomi away.

"You don't have to blackmail people into being nice to me," Naomi hissed. She sounded annoyed, and Diana's heart sank even as she held Naomi's hand tighter, leading her through the house and into the nursery.

"I shouldn't have to, but if I do have to, I will."

"I'm not some damsel in distress," Naomi objected. "Not anymore. No one here is going to try to kill me, are they? I don't need your protection. You protect yourself too much. Me, too. That woman out there was harmless."

"And yet, she was harming you."

Naomi couldn't exactly argue with that. She chewed on her lip. She seemed annoyed, specifically at Diana. The house was quiet, but still louder than her usual tolerance would allow. There was tension in her face and jaw that didn't go away when Diana closed the door behind them to block some of the noise.

"I'm okay," Naomi insisted.

"And speeding through a school zone isn't a victimless crime."

"It is a shitty thing to do. But it's not about her. You're infantilizing me. I can fight my own battles."

"As long as you have a wrench on hand," Diana said.

Naomi rolled her eyes. "I've been taking care of myself for longer than you've known me. Just because I'm disabled doesn't mean I need you to step in for me. I'm capable."

"I know you are. That's why I mentioned the wrench. I intervened for her sake."

Diana's face was impassive, but she couldn't stop the smile from reaching her lips, betraying her serious tone. In spite of herself, Naomi chuckled.

"I'm sorry," Diana added. Her kids had said the same thing when they'd been growing up. Overprotective, they'd called her. They didn't know what she dealt with, what she'd been trying to prevent from happening to them. They didn't know how cold poor Charlie had been.

"I know," Naomi said. "But you understand, don't you? That I can advocate for myself."

Diana turned to face her. "I'm sorry. I don't like it when people don't treat you well, in case you haven't noticed. I know you can stand up for yourself. Thanks for coming, by the way. Violet's thrilled you're here. So am I."

Naomi was silent, watching Diana carefully. Her face only softened at the mention of Violet. Her hand remained in Diana's, and her thumb was rubbing over the back of Diana's knuckles, seemingly out of habit. Diana had missed her touch. She was so gentle, so careful. Her thumb slid up to touch Diana's wrist before she pulled away, looking guilty.

"I shouldn't have come."

"You're welcome here, more welcome than the parents from Violet's daycare, and the least I can do is keep you safe from them."

"You…"

"I'm so happy to see you," Diana continued. "Now come on, there's someone I want you to meet." She was slower this time when she reached out, and Naomi met her hand halfway.

* * *

Simon had a whole world built in a video game, and he deigned to let Naomi join him once she showed him the panda headphones she'd brought for him, his eyes lighting up when he saw that they matched Naomi's.

Diana smiled and slipped away to catch up with some of the extended family. When she came back, Naomi and Simon were playing a racing game, gently trash-talking each other.

"I didn't expect you to get along quite so well," Diana admitted, sitting on the couch next to Naomi, who smiled and then let out a string of not-quite swear words. "Or for him to listen to you say all that out loud."

"It's okay when she talks. Her voice has a nice…a nice… temperature." Simon looked up at Diana. "Yours is better too now. She's a good influence on you. You should keep her."

Apparently satisfied with this advice, he turned his attention back to the game and thrashed Naomi in the next race.

Kate propped herself in the doorway, watching for a moment.

"Naomi might want some personal space," Kate suggested.

Naomi turned her head to look at Diana, meeting her eyes with a smile that Diana returned. Naomi sighed and turned back to the game, leaning against Diana.

"I'm fine if you are," Naomi said, and Diana leaned in as well. Simon, too, had clustered in, almost on Naomi's lap, and Diana wondered what she'd done to be lucky enough to have found someone her whole family loved almost as much as she did.

"We're about to get the cake. Would you like to join us?" Kate was good with Simon; always a yes or no question for him to answer, and never any offense taken either way.

Simon shook his head, but Naomi reluctantly pulled away, ready for the birthday rituals.

Kate ambushed Naomi while she was washing her hands in the kitchen.

"I've wanted to apologize for a while about walking in on you with Mom. It was your room, and if Mom wasn't anywhere else then she must have been with you. I would have expected her to look scared or ashamed of being caught, but she only looked comfortable. I want that for her. I want her to be happy, and I think I only know what it looks like when she's happy since she met you."

"It's not that simple," Naomi said weakly. She didn't want to have to explain that she'd let Diana know that she wanted more, and Diana hadn't understood or hadn't wanted more or hadn't wanted Naomi.

It was true that they enjoyed each other, but Naomi didn't think she could just be friends with Diana. Her chest had clenched painfully on seeing her this afternoon, and it was the hope that made it hurt worse. Even after being turned down, Naomi was hoping it had been a mistake.

"Your mom—she's an incredibly kind, generous woman. But I'm—I'm not what she wants. I'm a freelancer. I don't have a steady income or a career trajectory. I'm not often able to come to events like this, and she loves you guys so much it would hurt her to stay away. She deserves—"

"She deserves to be happy, and you make her happy."

"I don't think I can, that's the thing." Naomi swallowed. "She deserves better." Naomi had had lots of time to get used to being disabled, but she still felt it like an open wound. Diana could do better. Diana could get someone healthy who could treat her right. Naomi was in the way, with all of her confused feelings. She touched her headphones self-consciously and Kate's eyes softened the same way Diana's did.

"Can you forget about that for a minute and just listen? She let us meet you, even the grandkids. Simon too. I don't think you know how big that is. Since Dad she's been incredibly paranoid about who she introduces into our lives. I don't think she's trusted anyone since. She doesn't talk about work, but I know she sees all of us as potential victims, and she always says it's an acquaintance or a family member that's the biggest risk. It's been, what, two months?"

Naomi nodded, and Kate nodded too, as though that proved something.

"She's a good judge of character. She has to be, in her line of work. She hasn't always been, but I trust her judgment these days."

"You're giving me your blessing?" Naomi asked, still confused.

"You don't need it. I'm just saying…" Kate chuckled. "I don't know what I'm saying. But if it's me or Jake or the kids that's keeping you from asking her out or whatever people your age do when you want to date, then you need to know that it's not an issue for any of us. I like the way you treat her. I don't think she'd let anyone else treat her like that, man or woman. She's soft for you. She listens to you. She finally went for the promotion after years of us nagging at her just because you asked her to consider her personal safety. I don't think she would have let anyone else take care of her. She's so independent. And I don't know if it's that you're not a man and she's been gay all this time or if it's just that she likes you more than she cares about people thinking she's gay. I don't really care, it's not my business. But you're the gay one. I mean, you've been gay for longer. You're more experienced, I guess, in what a relationship like this would look like. I think she's just scared."

"She doesn't like me," Naomi said, her voice impossibly small as she confessed the thing that broke her heart. "Not the way I would like her to."

Kate squinted at her. She looked so much like Diana as she assessed Naomi that it was almost physically painful. "She thinks you're not interested in her because she's not your type or something. She didn't elaborate, but she thought you were the one who wasn't interested."

"She's only the most interesting person I think I've ever met. But I said something, and she shut me down."

"That's not what she said." Kate's eyes narrowed further, trying to compare what she was hearing now to what her mother had told her.

"It doesn't matter. I can be—I can be her friend." Naomi's voice cracked on the last word.

"Oh, Naomi," Kate said, her eyebrows scrunching in sympathy.

"Thanks for inviting me." Naomi knew her smile was stilted, and she pushed away from the counter. "It was as quiet as you promised it would be."

"Violet insisted. Look, even if it doesn't work out between you, we'd still like to see you."

"Thanks," Naomi said, gathering her coat and sliding out the door she quietly closed after herself.

* * *

Diana caught Naomi on the way to her car, still struggling with her coat against the cold night air, in such a hurry that she only had one arm in. She slid the other in awkwardly once Naomi deliberately turned to wait for her.

"I'm glad you came. Simon adored you, and he doesn't take to new people. Hell, he doesn't even like half the people here. And Violet was talking about you all week. And I have to say—I'm sorry. I put too much pressure on you. I made it awkward, and I should have just been happy with how it was."

"No, I'm sorry. I didn't know what I could say."

"I shouldn't have put you in that kind of position."

"Well. I'm glad I came, then."

"Don't be a stranger, okay?" Diana held her arms out and let Naomi choose.

Naomi stepped forward without hesitation, sliding her arms around Diana to complete the hug, nuzzling in against Diana's uninjured shoulder, even though the other one was mostly healed.

"I wish things had been different."

"Me too," Naomi said, looking at Diana like her heart was breaking.

Diana pulled away slowly, then leaned in. In the crisp winter air, her breath huffed in a cloud that Naomi inhaled, holding her breath and Diana's as Diana moved in closer. Her lips grazed Naomi's cheek, her bottom lip brushing against Naomi's upper lip in the corner of her mouth. She was so soft. She swallowed and Diana felt it, along with the ever-present rush of blood to her cheeks whenever she thought about Naomi's mouth. Diana pulled away, shoving her hands in her coat pockets and drawing her shoulders in. Naomi stood frozen, processing. A smile crept unwittingly across her face, and she nodded.

Naomi moved forward again, her hand sliding under Diana's coat to pull herself as close to Diana's chest as she could as she hugged her goodbye. Diana hadn't been prepared, and her hands ended up over Naomi's coat, holding her even closer. It felt okay. It felt right. It felt like Naomi hadn't minded that Diana had kissed her, just a little bit. It felt like Naomi had maybe liked it, like maybe Naomi still liked her. Not in the way Diana wanted Naomi to like her, but it was a relief to know that Naomi didn't hate her. The soft press of Naomi's breasts against Diana's own chest warmed her, and it was a struggle not to press up flush against her.

Naomi pulled away easily, resettling her beanie over her headphones. She stepped back, her breath filling the space between them.

Thank you, Naomi signed. It had been a long day, a long evening. *Nice family*, she added, and Diana nodded.

Welcome, Diana signed, then realized it might be taken as a "you're welcome" to Naomi's thanks. *Always welcome*, she added quickly.

Diana walked Naomi to her car and opened the door when Naomi clicked the fob in her pocket. She waited as Naomi got in and buckled her seat belt, then nodded.

"Drive safe," Diana said gently, closing the door with the softest push so that the latch barely clicked. Naomi smiled up at her, then drove off into the night, leaving Diana wondering if she would ever see her again.

Kate was waiting for Diana at the front door, shivering even in her thick coat.

"Mom, what the hell?"

"I thought you liked her?" Diana said mildly.

"I do, but you said you weren't dating."

"We're not. I don't know if we're even really friends."

"Mom, you kissed her."

"On the cheek. To thank her for being here for Simon."

"She didn't come here for Simon."

"Well then, Violet."

"Mom! She was here for you!" Kate's exasperation was one of the delights of Diana's life, but it didn't lighten her spirits. Not tonight.

"She doesn't want me." Diana spoke quickly, to get it over with, to rip the Band-Aid of rejection off. It was awkward having this conversation with her adult daughter.

Kate's face softened out of the expression she wore when she was ready for an argument. "You've never really had friends. None that I ever met. I was worried about moving out, the thought of you all alone in that big house. It's nice that you have a friend. It's just a shame that she isn't more. If you let her go, it'll be the biggest mistake you'll make in your life."

"I thought marrying your father was the biggest mistake I ever made."

"Yeah, but you got us out of it, so you're ahead on that score."

Diana laughed and jostled Kate's shoulder. "You're right, you know. You were both worth it. There used to be only two people in the world I cared about, and now there's seven of you."

"I think there's eight," Kate said quietly, in the tone she used for Naomi.

Diana took the point, nodding.

Kate's husband, Matt, had spoken to Naomi confidently and easily with his hands, translating some words into other English-based sign languages for her, which Naomi seemed to find fascinating. Diana didn't know why she'd worried. It was Jake's wife who sometimes forgot her volume, whom Naomi retreated from with a tight but polite smile.

And Simon—watching Naomi with Simon had been almost magical. His face had lit up when she signed to him. He'd settled himself snug against her side to play a game with her, and Diana had been struck again by how quickly the people in her family were drawn to Naomi. Violet clearly adored her, Kate kept giving Diana knowing smiles and looking between the two of them, and Ollie always ran to show Naomi his latest drawings. Jake had been won over the first time he'd seen Naomi bring Diana a coffee, the way Naomi's hand pressed Diana down against the chair so she wouldn't get up while she was supposed to be resting. Even Brian cooed quietly when she held him.

And Diana was gone on her too. All the way gone on her.

"It doesn't matter," Diana said, her voice sounding hollow to her own ears. "We don't want the same things."

"Mom. Have you seen the way she looks at you?"

"I know. I thought so too. But we talked about it, and she's not—she doesn't have to be into me just because she likes women."

"I just think you'd be good together. I'd never seen you so happy. I've never seen you look at someone like that. I just want the best for you, and I don't think you're going to do better. The whole family likes her."

"I know, but maybe it's time I try."

"You're going to hit the gay bars? Pride parade?"

"I don't know, baby, but thank you for understanding."

"I do love you, Mom. And it's freezing out here. Come back inside and warm up before you go home. Or you can stay, if you'd like? Violet would love birthday pancakes."

Diana looked at Kate, then pulled her into a hug. "How'd I get so lucky, to get a kid like you?"

"You raised me. C'mon, inside."

CHAPTER NINETEEN

Although Naomi hadn't pushed her away or told her off, Diana felt like she'd asked too much, presumed too much. She needed to apologize. Not for almost but not quite kissing her—it was the closest she'd ever come—but for not asking first, for not getting consent. She knew what it was like to be kissed by someone she wasn't interested in, and she was horrified that she might have subjected Naomi to that.

Of course, showing up unannounced at her house wasn't great either, which was why she'd texted Naomi earlier, asking which gummies she wanted. She hadn't answered, but Diana had checked both websites, and the online store that delivered was sold out of the ratio Naomi preferred.

She looked at the brown paper bag on the passenger seat and wiped her hands on her jeans, looking at Naomi's front garden. Worst case scenario, she left the container in the mailbox, and Naomi would either forgive her or she wouldn't. Best case scenario, Naomi would let Diana in and show her what the house looked like when criminals hadn't trashed it. And maybe Naomi would understand.

Diana hadn't felt this way about a woman—about anyone— before. But she knew what it felt like now, and she wanted to feel it again. If Naomi didn't want her, and if she really was interested in women, she could see how that went. Maybe get a girlfriend. Naomi probably thought Diana was too old to be experimenting. She probably wanted someone out and sure, someone proud and active in the community, the way she had been, not someone who'd been in the closet for close to five decades. Not someone who hadn't even realized she hadn't been attracted to anyone before Naomi.

Naomi would want someone who could please her. Pleasure her. Whatever. It was in those books, the kind of things Naomi probably liked, and they sounded wholly unappealing if the other person involved wasn't Naomi. It made her upset to think about someone else touching Naomi. Would they know how loudly their nails sounded on Naomi's skin? Would they keep their voice low and modulated so as not to hurt her? Would they appreciate Naomi's sweet smile and soft hands? Would they see her for who she was, not just a disabled woman? Would they love her because of everything she was, or would they just use her for her lovely body?

Naomi deserved better. She deserved better than Diana, but she deserved better than that too. Even if Diana didn't know what she was doing, she'd read the books. She could figure it out. That wasn't important. She could learn.

What was important was that Naomi was treated like an entire person, that her boundaries were respected. Diana hadn't done so well at that lately. Hell, even showing up barely announced might be considered pushy, but she knew the difference the medication made to Naomi's quality of life. She wanted to make amends. She wanted Naomi in her life because Naomi had drastically increased the quality of her own.

She wiped her hands on her jeans again before she got out of the car and into the field of view of Naomi's cameras. She went to the gate, breathing in heavily. She tucked her chin into her scarf, wishing she'd worn a beanie too. She didn't expect to be outside long; either Naomi wouldn't answer, or she would let Diana in.

She took a deep breath and tried to hype herself up to press the button that would let Naomi know she was there.

* * *

Naomi had been used to being alone. Since her hearing had changed, it had been necessary to give herself a lot of downtime to recover from being outside. It was hard to make or keep friendships, let alone relationships with a reduced window of socializing. In the last few months, she'd spent more time with Diana than she had with anyone over the past several years.

She hadn't hated it. There had been hard parts, and when her migraines flared, the gunshot from the cabin reverberated through her skull in live-action replay.

It was a shame that it didn't look like things would work out between them. Diana was lovely—not just to look at or hold, but to listen to and laugh with. She was compassionate and caring. She had a smile that made Naomi's own mouth twitch upward. Being flung abruptly into the other woman's world had been easier to adjust to somehow than her return to her own home.

The large house felt empty. Naomi felt alone in a way she hadn't noticed before. She'd moved her home office so she could sleep in the room with the safe room attached. She found herself testing the gate and checking the cameras more often than she used to. It was quiet enough here that she didn't need constant hearing protection, and she realized what a strain it had been to live with Diana. Still, she missed her.

She'd managed to hand over all her finished work and pick up some new contracts. She'd had to stretch some deadlines, but despite her efforts to keep her involvement with the brutal murder of her neighbor and the subsequent repeated attempts on her own life quiet, the case had made the news, and she'd gained leniency and sympathy, as well as more clients. She had enough work to keep her busy, but not enough to keep her mind off Diana. There would never be enough work to get Diana off her mind.

Diana hadn't known, probably, what she'd been offering when she'd asked Naomi to help her dress. She'd known Naomi was gay, but she hadn't known that Naomi was attracted to her. Naomi couldn't touch her like that without letting her know, but Diana hadn't understood. And when she had, she'd withdrawn into herself, pulling away to protect herself.

Naomi finished another email, finalizing her last bill for a project. It would be nice to have some money coming in; despite the property insurance, her rates had risen as a direct retaliation. Diana had recommended a different insurance company for her, but it was too much effort as they preferred phone calls, like every other business. She especially missed Diana making and taking calls for her.

She still felt such a fool. She'd been hoping—desperately—that Diana had invited her to stay because she felt the same attraction Naomi felt. She'd seen her in that bra—it had been nothing special, not lingerie, just a practical black cotton bra, unclasped, the cups falling forward, almost offering their contents to Naomi, the expanse of soft, creamy skin bared to her eyes. Her brain had completely stopped. She'd forgotten how to breathe. The slightly darker areola barely visible, the brief puckering of skin leading to her nipple. And then Diana's curious gaze, the shy little smile on her face; she'd looked pleased by how flustered Naomi had been.

Naomi had thought Diana had been shy because it had been some sort of flirtation. She hadn't considered that Diana might merely be embarrassed at not being able to complete a simple task on her own. That moment still lived in her brain, rent free. The soft, pale cleavage. Naomi knew Diana's breasts were soft; she'd slept on one of them.

Diana had insisted, and Naomi had complied, fastening the bra easily, trying not to take advantage of the situation. Naomi hadn't wanted the first time she touched Diana to be while dressing her after she got shot. Naomi had wanted to touch her—God, she'd wanted to touch her—but she wanted to touch Diana because Diana wanted Naomi to touch her, because she wanted to touch Naomi as well. Not because she was reliant on Naomi to help her dress, not because it was required for her modesty. Because she wanted it, because she wanted Naomi.

And she hadn't.

She'd said as much, had shut down, flinching as she took over the task of dressing herself, and Naomi hated that she'd made Diana feel so unsafe that she'd hurt herself to hide her breasts from Naomi's prying eyes. It hadn't been as awkward as it could have been, afterward, but the lighthearted mood was gone. Diana no longer joked with her, clearly hurt that Naomi had been envisioning their relationship as more than she'd wanted.

There was movement on the monitor that housed the camera feed of the gate and Naomi glanced over.

Strawberry-blond hair. Skinny jeans, no badge on the belt. Thick coat, a sprinkling of snow on the shoulders. Naomi pressed the intercom button, then released it. Diana jumped, then looked up at the camera.

She held a paper bag up with a wry smile and signed *peace offering*.

Naomi unlocked the gate, watching Diana approach the door. She pulled on her headphones and brushed off her sweatpants as she got up to meet her at the door. Diana stood on the threshold and held out the paper bag.

"Delivery," she said quietly, gauging Naomi's tolerance for noise

Naomi took the bag and stood back, gesturing for Diana to enter. Her cheeks were pink with cold, and when she removed her coat, her scent wafted out. The muscles in Naomi's chest tightened at the familiar perfume—something soft and old fashioned that suited her completely. She'd missed this woman so much it hurt.

Naomi peered into the bag. The strawberry gummies she favored, in the right ratio. Her throat tightened.

"Can I come in?" Diana asked, even though her boots were already off, her gloves tucked in the pockets of her coat, already hanging on the coat rack. Her scarf—the same peacock one Naomi had admired so long ago—looked cozy around her neck.

Naomi nodded and retreated to the kitchen, Diana following her.

"You're mothering me."

"Trust me, the last thing I have for you is any motherly sentiment."

"Then what? You're always hovering, trying to protect me."

"I'm trying—I suppose I'm trying to show I can provide for you. Protect you. But not as a child—you're what, two years younger than me? I want to take care of you the way someone wants to take care of their wife."

Naomi stopped, speechless. "W-wife?"

"I know, it's too soon for any of that. I guess I thought I was flirting. Trying to show you I was strong, a good provider. A good choice in—in partner. I've been seeing someone. Not—not like that. A therapist. Like you said, Andrew was a long time ago. I don't need the same coping methods I used to. I don't need to protect everyone in my life; not when they don't want me to."

"Oh." Naomi looked down at the gummies she'd set on the table, then back up at Diana. "Oh."

"And I know you don't want me, you made that clear, so this is an apology for making you so uncomfortable. You don't need to avoid my family just because I made a mistake. I can stay out of your way."

"Wait—you think I don't want you?"

Diana sighed and sat at the kitchen table, lifting the chair so the legs didn't drag on the tiles, the way she had so long ago. Naomi watched her fingers trace the grain of the wood. "I came over because Kate said I'd spent long enough being miserable. She said you make me happy, and even if it's not the way I want you to make me happy, I should keep you in my life because she misses me being happy. I miss being happy. I miss you, and I want you in my life in whatever capacity you can bear to be in it."

"Wait. How did you want me to make you happy?"

"I don't know. It seems stupid now. I know it was just work, and you were just trying to stay alive and sane, and you must have been scared and stressed out the whole time. But I realize now I'd been hoping that you'd—I did need help getting dressed, but I'd been hoping you'd—I don't know what I was thinking or what I wanted but you didn't want whatever it was, so it doesn't matter. It was presumptuous of me, to assume you wanted me, and probably homophobic too. I don't have a lot of friends. I'd like you as a friend."

"Wait, you thought I wanted you?"

Diana's eyes dropped to her hands, her thumb running over the tips of her fingers then along the inside of her ring finger. The wedding band she usually wore wasn't there.

Naomi felt a surge of hope.

"I know. I said it was presumptive."

"I mean, I wouldn't put it that crudely. But the reason I didn't want to touch you then was because I was supposed to be taking care of you, not enjoying myself, and I wouldn't be able to do one without the other."

"You'd have enjoyed it?"

"Look at you! How could I not?" Naomi let out an exasperated laugh, incredulous that anyone could resist Diana's charms.

"Oh." Diana's brow furrowed the way it did when she was deducing. "But you wouldn't touch me. I know I've had kids, that you've probably seen better-looking women wearing much less, and I shouldn't have thrown myself at you like that, not while you were under my roof."

"I thought you understood that I didn't want to—to touch you until you were healed. So I wouldn't have to worry about hurting you. Then I thought I must have been wrong, when I thought you might have been offering. I mean, you were married to a man, and maybe I was just hoping too hard. You'd been so kind and gentle with me that I'd hoped—wait, you wanted me to touch you?"

"I wanted you to." Diana's voice was husky. "And when you didn't, I thought I was wrong. I came here to apologize for assuming you were attracted to me, just because you're attracted to women."

"You weren't—you weren't wrong."

"Oh."

Naomi's cheeks flushed. She looked down at the bag Diana had brought, retrieved the package within and stared at it as though she was absorbed in the nutritional details. She could feel Diana watching her.

"Then I don't need to apologize?"

Naomi barely glanced up. "I might have to. I didn't—I wasn't thinking very well at the time. I can see how I didn't express myself well."

"You can make it up to me," Diana said, resting her chin in her hand, elbow on the table. The fingers of her other hand tapped gently on the surface, too quiet to make a noise. She came to a decision and took her scarf off slowly, feeding the tail through the loop and straightening it out, then folding it carefully and placing it on the table. She wore a brown leather jacket, which she began to unzip. Naomi's breath caught, her eyes fixed on the zipper.

"Too loud?" Diana asked, concerned.

"Too…too…" Naomi wet her suddenly dry lips, unable to look away. "Just give me a second to—to…" Naomi watched as Diana finished unzipping her jacket. "Oh my God," Naomi said, when she realized Diana's intent.

Diana chuckled softly and pulled off the jacket, flinching as it came over her left shoulder.

"Uh, how am I making this up to you?" Naomi asked, once her brain had come to terms with the situation.

"Just keep looking at me like that, honey." Diana reached for the buttons of her forest-green blouse, starting from the top. She paused two buttons in. "I can do it myself, but I would like some assistance with my shirt."

Naomi didn't answer. She couldn't process the words, transfixed as she was with the skin Diana had exposed. When she was able to raise her eyes back to Diana's face, all she saw was fond amusement in those hazel eyes.

"Do you still want to touch me?" Diana asked, and Naomi nodded immediately.

"More than anything," Naomi breathed. "Yes, please."

"Then come over here."

Naomi bit her lip as she got to her feet, Diana rising to join her. She hadn't done this for a long time, and she was pretty sure Diana had never done this with a woman before.

"Do you mind if I—can I kiss you first? Take it from there?"

"I think I'd mind if you didn't." Diana's eyes dropped to Naomi's lips, a little furrow between her eyebrows. "Is this going to be too loud? Kissing, I mean. Given you have trouble chewing."

"I think I can manage a kiss or two."

"You think, or you know?"

"I think," Naomi said, letting her hands slide under Diana's blouse at her waist. Diana's skin was so soft and warm and welcoming under her fingers.

Diana hummed with pleasure at the simple touch and came closer. "So you haven't been with anyone since your hearing changed?"

"And you haven't been with anyone but your husband?"

"We're a pair, aren't we?" Diana chuckled, but she shifted closer still. "I'm game, if you are. What do you want to do with me?"

"Whatever you're comfortable with. And if you're not comfortable, we can stop."

Diana looked uncertain and suspicious, as though this wasn't an option that had ever been presented to her before. It about broke Naomi's heart to see her process the words, the way she breathed in as she met Naomi's eyes with all the trust she had in her. Naomi had always trusted Diana; to have it so obviously returned made her chest ache.

"But what do you want to do with me?" Diana bit her lip, her confidence slipping a little.

Naomi let her eyes drift down to Diana's cleavage, then further down, to where Diana's belt rested above her hips. She let her hands follow her eyes, sliding her fingers under the waistband a little. She untucked Diana's blouse; the sensation of Diana's bare skin against her fingers made her tremble.

She leaned forward and pressed her mouth to Diana's jaw, letting her lips slide up under Diana's ear, her teeth closing softly around the lobe. She felt the little twitch from Diana's hips, the rippling of her stomach muscles as Naomi nibbled lightly. She spoke directly into the beautifully curved shell of Diana's ear. "Everything. I want to do everything with you. And when we're too worn out to move, I want to fall asleep with you, and wake up with you. I want to touch you, I want to taste you, I want to hear you."

Naomi ran her hand through Diana's hair like she'd always wanted to. Diana closed her eyes and leaned into her, and Naomi kissed her. Diana's lips parted for her, slow and sweet, no hesitation. Her breath caught and she moved closer to Naomi, pressing them together. She drew away to look at Naomi, her thumb rubbing over Naomi's lips as she cupped her face.

"I knew you'd be soft, but I still…you're so much softer than I thought…" Diana closed the distance between them, kissing Naomi more gently than she'd ever been kissed. Naomi's chest ached from the sweetness of it, the soft restraint of the press of Diana's hips against her, the way Diana's breath caught as Naomi finally touched her.

Slowly Naomi let her fingers run over Diana's scalp, then down her shoulders to the dip of her back, the bones of her hips. Diana kissed like she was savoring it, like she wasn't quite sure this was real yet, and Naomi wanted Diana to feel secure and safe with her. She pulled away slowly, but Diana drew her back in, her hands grasping Naomi a little more firmly, sliding up under her shirt, letting out a tiny moan as she found Naomi's bare skin beneath. She whimpered softly when she felt the fabric of Naomi's bra.

Naomi pulled away and was momentarily distracted by that cleavage again. "You don't mind if I leave the headphones on?"

"They're part of you. Why would I mind?"

"Other people might, but you wouldn't even notice unless I mentioned it. That's why I like you." Naomi let her hands rest on Diana's hips again, moving closer.

Diana leaned forward, as quiet and gentle as she always had been with Naomi. Her lips were soft and sweet and not at all hesitant. She was slow, aware of any noise she made. Her hands found Naomi's waist, then slid up under Naomi's shirt again, smoothing over her skin. Naomi pulled back, her breath all caught in her chest, her eyes caught on Diana's chest again.

Naomi leaned back against the table and pulled Diana closer again. She unbuttoned the lower buttons of Diana's shirt and saw the soft peach fuzz line that led down from Diana's navel. Diana shuddered when Naomi ran her finger along the little trail of nearly invisible hair, and Naomi looked up at her face anxiously, checking in with Diana, who looked just as anxious.

"I should have gotten rid of it. I didn't think you'd actually—"

"Don't you dare. It's gorgeous. You're gorgeous. Did I really go all this time without telling you?"

Diana didn't look as though she believed Naomi, but she didn't pull away or try to cover herself. Naomi worked on the rest of Diana's buttons, slow and careful.

"When I was driving up to the cabin, I was so worried about you. I realized it was more than I should be, for someone who was just a witness." Diana closed her eyes when the last button came undone, then quickly looked at Naomi's face with anxiety written over her own.

Diana wasn't wearing the standard black bra Naomi had been expecting. This one was a deep-green lace that matched her blouse and scarf, and it took Naomi some time to drag her eyes away. When her eyes finally met Diana's, Diana looked shyly pleased again, flattered by Naomi's response.

Naomi had to swallow before she could speak. "For me?" she asked, wondering what she'd done to be so fortunate.

Diana looked amused. "You've seen them before. They're nothing special."

"Not like this. Not knowing you want me to touch you the way I want to touch you. That's what makes this so special. That, and it's you. It's perfect. You're perfect." A needy, breathy noise escaped her own throat when Diana's hands rested on her back, sliding down.

"I do. I do want you to touch me. What are you waiting for?"

Naomi licked her lips, seeing Diana watch the movement hungrily. She ran her hands over Diana's bare back, learning the dips and curves of her spine. Naomi lifted her mouth to Diana's throat and Diana let her head drop back, exposing more of her skin. Naomi slid her tongue up Diana's jaw, back toward her ear, letting her lips close around the lobe this time.

Diana's hands tightened on Naomi's waist. There was a little whimper that Diana managed to half swallow that made Naomi dig her teeth into the flesh beneath them. Diana's pelvis pressed against her, incredibly warm against Naomi's hip. The whimper came again, and Diana pulled away.

"I can't—I've never had any problems being quiet. I didn't think it would be a problem."

"It's not a problem. That's what the headphones are for. But do you mind if I switch out to the hearing aids as well?"

"No, of course not."

Naomi disentangled herself and left the room on silent feet. She fetched her hearing aids and came back, leaning against the table as she took her headphones off and inner-ear protection out.

You trust me too much, Diana said with her hands.

Naomi looked away and replaced her ear protection, putting the headphones back on over her hearing aids. "You've proven yourself over and over to be worthy of it. But I do have to ask. Why me? You have every woman in the world to choose from. Why me?"

"I doubt that." Diana scoffed, as though she doubted her own ability to draw the eyes of every woman in the room.

"Excuse me, but you're pretty much a lesbian wet dream. If you walked into a gay bar, you'd leave with a lot of numbers and more handcuffs than you went in with."

Diana blushed. It was adorable and a little sad how unaware she was of her own beauty.

"So?"

"So why me?"

"Okay, but why me? I'm a divorced workaholic."

"Really? You don't know? It's not only that you're gorgeous and incredibly sexy." Naomi found her hands on Diana's ass, found herself distracted, squeezing it absentmindedly. "You've been so kind to me in a way most people aren't."

"I was doing my job."

"You were kind when you didn't need to be."

"And no one else is?"

"You've only dated men, haven't you?" Naomi asked.

Diana nodded.

"Were they kind to you?"

"Not—not for long."

"I never got the sense you were kind because you wanted something from me. I got the sense it was because it's who you are fundamentally." Naomi looked back up. "I mean it. You could be with any woman you wanted, not someone who can barely stand to hear your voice, not someone who can't kiss you without hearing protection."

"Maybe you're right. Maybe I could have any woman I wanted." Diana looked at Naomi with that intangible expression. "But the only woman I've ever wanted is you."

"Oh." Naomi felt a weight lift. She didn't need to be anything; Diana accepted her as she was. Diana knew everything about her and liked her anyway. Diana didn't like women. She liked Naomi.

"Make that the only *person*. I don't know if that makes me gay, and frankly I'm too old to care about labels. I just feel something for you that I've never felt, and I want to see where it goes."

With that, Naomi nodded and let her hands drift up behind Diana to find the clasp of her bra.

The breasts beneath were even more magnificent than Naomi had expected them to be. They filled Naomi's hands when she cupped them, more than filled her hands. Diana's nipples were pink and hard against Naomi's tongue when she leaned down to lap at them. She ran her fingers down the plane of Diana's stomach and felt the muscles tense with anticipation under her gentle touch. She reached the waistband of Diana's tight jeans, finding the belt buckle and unhitching it. She wanted her hand inside those tight jeans, to see her knuckles move against the fabric.

Diana was new to this. Naomi didn't want to overwhelm her, and right now Diana had all but stopped breathing.

Naomi pulled away, looking up. Diana's face was flushed, as was her chest. Her eyes were wide and a little unfocused. She swallowed and pulled Naomi up to kiss her again, her fingers grasping for Naomi's clothes, pulling Naomi tight against her where she stood.

Naomi had imagined Diana as a slow and reticent lover, as someone Naomi would have to teach and guide. But she was passionate and generous. They were only making out. Once reality hit, once the clothes came off, she might lose her nerve or be repulsed by Naomi's body. She might not want to reciprocate once she'd been sated, once Naomi had fulfilled whatever purpose Diana had come here for.

"What are you doing to me?" Diana panted, close to Naomi's headphones. She sounded almost desperate, sliding her hands up and over Naomi's bra, pulling it up so she could palm Naomi's breasts. Diana moaned into Naomi's mouth, then stifled herself.

"I like the noises you make when I'm the one making you make them." Naomi wasn't sure if that made sense, but Diana moaned again, not loudly but without holding back this time.

Resting one hand on Diana's chest, Naomi gently pushed her back. Diana looked disappointed, then confused as Naomi took off her shirt. Her bra was askew from where Diana had tugged at it, so she undid it, hearing Diana's little gasp as her breasts came into view, the nipples hard even though the kitchen was warm. Diana pulled Naomi against her.

* * *

"Take me," Diana said, and Naomi obeyed immediately. Her hand slid into Diana's jeans, making the fly bulge against the back of her knuckles. Diana's breath caught; she hadn't expected this, hadn't known she was ready and waiting for Naomi's fingers moving smoothly over her.

"How long have you been waiting for this?" Naomi asked, her voice a long moan as she felt Diana's need, her fingers gliding easily over the deep well of want within her.

Diana froze, and Naomi edged away slowly, looking to her face with concern. Diana had things she wanted to say, things she needed to say, but Naomi brushed a very wet finger against her and she had no words left, no language but a low moan dragged from somewhere so deep that she had never heard it spilled from her own lips before, overflowing, pulsing against Naomi's palm as her other arm wrapped around her, keeping her upright, keeping her grounded, keeping her stable. Diana's fingers dug into Naomi's forearm when she tried to remove her hand, and she understood, moving her fingers in such a delicious way that she had no choice but to follow their movement. Diana pressed herself against the gentle pressure as Naomi held her close.

It was the first time Diana had felt like an active participant, wanting just as much if not more than her partner did. She found her hips tilting against Naomi's questing fingers, found her mouth seeking Naomi's, breathing her name into her lungs, trying to brand her, to claim her, to be as physically close to her as two people could possibly get. The curve of her breast and her hip met Diana's hands perfectly, and Naomi's hips moved as well, seeking out Diana and finding her, moving against her with the softest, sweetest noises coming from those warm, generous lips.

It had been worth waiting for, Diana tried to convince herself. All these years, never knowing. All those years spent lying next to a man who resented her existence, punishing her for being stupid enough to marry someone who hated her. All those years of being handled roughly or not at all were worth it because somehow she'd ended up here, being treated as though she was precious, being handled like something delicate.

She pulled away and met Naomi's eyes. Naomi's fingers were tight against the swell of her, Diana's impossibly wet heat drenching Naomi's talented fingers. Naomi's expressive brown eyes were unusually dark, her hand not stilling inside Diana's jeans, pressing, caressing knowingly, like she'd done this before, and she probably had, but Diana hadn't and the climax that struck her had the impact of decades pent up behind it, a sobbing crescendo even as she felt the answering catch and release from Naomi, the throbbing heat of Naomi against her hip.

On shaky legs Diana tried to remain upright, failing and leaning against Naomi, who happily took her weight. Naomi laved tiny kisses against Diana's cheek and throat. When Diana opened her eyes again, Naomi was watching her, a smile on her face like she knew what Diana was thinking.

They were both a mess. They had been careless in their desire to touch each other, and Diana could finally see the breasts she'd been touching with reckless abandon, pale and soft, the hard nipples already familiar to her fingers. Diana had to hold back from kissing her again, trying to focus, trying to figure out what was happening.

Even better than that was Naomi's lips, swollen from kissing, her eyes dark as she assessed Diana—who was in a similar state, one of her arms still caught in a sleeve, the rest of the shirt mostly discarded, her bra undone, the straps pushed down so it drifted high on her chest. Naomi's hand pressed against her again, drawing out a low moan from Diana, which Naomi stole with another kiss.

Diana wondered why she didn't feel ashamed. She was being taken—albeit skillfully—in the kitchen by a woman in broad daylight. Usually she felt self-conscious during and after sex, but there was no room for shame with Naomi looking at her like she was made of gold or something more fragile and wonderful, something desirable. And Diana planned to return the favor. She would be Naomi's equal even though everything they'd done had been foreign to her. She wanted Naomi. She had for a long time now. She'd never wanted anyone like this before.

Naomi surrendered to her, melted at her touch. She was like one of those expensive chocolates that dissolved as soon as they met the mouth; warm and delicious and the most luxurious thing Diana had ever let herself indulge in.

Perhaps that was why she wasn't ashamed. Naomi respected her, and she respected Naomi. There was no room for shame, just as there had been no room for fear between them. Diana understood, now, the concept and purpose of Pride. She was proud to have reduced this eloquent woman to wordless wonder, proud to have been taken by her, too desperate to wait long enough to leave the kitchen. She understood, now, why Naomi had told her she deserved better.

"I was going to say, 'take me to the bedroom,' but this works too. I mean it worked. It definitely worked for me," Diana panted, once she could speak.

Naomi laughed. A genuine, room-temperature laugh. She didn't flinch or stop herself, and a moment later she was kissing Diana again, her teeth catching Diana's bottom lip and pulling deliciously at the edge of pleasure. Diana nudged herself against where Naomi's fingers were still wedged against the zipper of her jeans.

"Worked for me too. Damn. That was the most beautiful thing I've ever seen." Naomi pulled away and looked up at Diana, a soft smile on her face, all the softer for having been pressed against Diana's own smile only moments ago. "If my sweatpants even touch me, I'm done for."

Diana didn't want—Naomi had been so generous and giving—Diana didn't want to leave sweatpants to do the work she so longed to do.

Naomi's nipples were pebble-hard, and Diana assisted her onto the kitchen table, sliding one of those nipples into her mouth, hard and perfect against her tongue. Naomi gasped and pushed against her, a stilted thrust that Diana arrested.

"Please," Naomi begged. "You won't even have to touch me. Just let me…" Naomi's hips canted into Diana again, but Diana pulled away.

"I want to touch you," Diana said around a taut, pink nipple, her voice sounding husky, even to her own ears.

"I'm not going to—ah—last long enough. I'm sorry."

"Don't be sorry for that. But can I? Do you want me to? Can you wait long enough for me to at least try to see if…"

Naomi nodded and bit her lip as Diana's hand slid down the waistband of her sweatpants, straight into slick warmth, Naomi already tilting herself into Diana with a high-pitched little noise that Diana wanted engraved in a sound wave on her tombstone.

"Diana," she breathed out, suspended for one long moment before Diana felt it, the tremor, the pulse of Naomi against her fingers, and then Naomi was kissing her again, her hips still moving, dragging out the pulsing heat of her, nearly dripping down Diana's fingers.

No one had ever wanted Diana this much; Diana had never wanted anyone this much. It felt like a huge compliment, to have a woman so aroused that she only lasted a moment before coming so hard as Diana touched her for the first time. She smelled so good that Diana growled, low and deep, some foreign awakening.

Naomi had been so turned on that Diana hadn't even had time to find any landmarks, disoriented in this foreign land. Diana shifted her fingers and Naomi gasped, tilting her hips, enticing Diana inside. Already aching again, Diana complied, the soft velvet heat of Naomi welcoming her, Naomi's warm breath in her ear with no rhythm to it, just a primitive urge to force oxygen into her respiratory system while Diana took her on the table.

Diana had never even done this to herself. She'd never had an orgasm, she knew now. She'd thought she'd had one or two, but the memory of them paled in comparison to the pulsing heat still throbbing between her legs, the want inside her building higher the further she slid into Naomi.

No wonder men were obsessed with sex. Naomi was so frictionless, so liquid around her, so eager and willing, and her hand had woken up where it was still lodged in Diana's jeans, finding her need with such accuracy that Diana beat her to the precipice. Eyes fixed on Diana's face, Naomi joined her moments later, biting her lip as Diana bottomed out, knuckle-deep in her, palm pressed against the throbbing hub of her.

Naomi trembled when Diana withdrew, and Diana brought her damp hand up to brush some hair from Naomi's face.

Reluctant to smudge Naomi's pretty face, Diana brought her fingers to her mouth to clean them off. She'd wondered about this, read about it, and she hesitantly licked the tip of a finger. Naomi tasted—Diana moaned, and Naomi kissed her, and their breasts met, pressing softly together, making Diana moan again.

Diana helped Naomi to the bedroom on unsteady legs, kicking off her jeans in the doorway, tugging off Naomi's sweatpants when she lay down. She was learning a language she intended to be fluent in by the end of the night.

Diana hadn't known what to expect. She'd read those books, sure. But she still hadn't known what was expected from her, what she'd expected from Naomi.

She hadn't expected it to be so loving. She hadn't expected it to be nice—although she had always enjoyed whatever time she spent with Naomi. She was so smooth. Even her sweat smelled good to Diana, and it tasted even better, fresh off her skin. It was like Diana had wandered into a sunlit clearing in the middle of winter.

Diana certainly hadn't expected to enjoy it so much. She ran her fingers over Naomi's bare shoulder, hearing Naomi sigh as she snuggled in closer. She'd enjoyed not only being touched by someone who knew what they were doing and was excited about touching Diana, but she'd also enjoyed the rest of it—Naomi's body and all it had to offer, the little noises Naomi made when Diana was so close to getting it right, the way Naomi had guided her, the soft velvet warmth of her.

She'd loved it all, every moment. Even when she'd been uncomfortable, because Naomi had not only noticed, she'd also cared about Diana's comfort, and without needing to be asked or told she'd adjusted so she could put a pillow under Diana's back for support, withdrawn enough to check in with Diana, and been so gentle and loving that Diana had caught herself crying twice. Naomi held her, comforted her, kissed her with such tenderness that Diana's entire body ached for her, not minding that they'd paused what they were doing, not minding when Diana needed a break.

Diana stroked her palm down Naomi's side, hearing her sigh again. Diana hadn't even known what she'd needed, what she'd been missing out on, and Naomi had shown her anyway.

Naomi was so soft, so beautiful, so gentle and patient.

"I think you cast a spell on me," Diana said finally, when they'd worn each other out. Her fingers gently stroked the bare, freckled skin of Naomi's shoulder. "That first night, when you came out of the mist with your hair glowing. Like Red Riding Hood. Like a fairy tale."

"I didn't," Naomi said. "But when I met you, I felt like I'd found something I'd lost a long time ago. Part of myself I thought I'd left behind. You understood without needing to be told." Naomi yawned and turned her face into Diana's shoulder, her lips pressing against the bare skin of the healing wound so gently and tenderly that Diana ached from the intimacy. Naomi was kissing it better, and Diana had never had anything better happen to her than Naomi. "I was so resigned to what I'd become that I didn't see that I could still have something I wanted."

"And you wanted me?"

"Still do," Naomi said, matter-of-factly. She looked nervous again. "If you'll have me, I mean. If you want me."

"Of course I do." Diana wondered how there could be any question about it, how Naomi could doubt how torn up Diana had been from wanting her. "Didn't I prove it to you yet?"

Naomi's smile was shy but delighted. "You could stand to prove yourself a little more," she said, letting her lips brush against Diana's throat.

They weren't quite done with each other yet, after all.

"How did I not know?" Diana asked a little later. She was lying on her side, letting her fingers brush over Naomi's bare body. "How could I not know?"

Naomi leaned over and kissed her. "You weren't raised to expect to be anything except what people expected from you. You were raised to accept what you expected."

"But I mean..." Diana ran her hand over herself. She heard Naomi's breath catch and saw her eyes widen even though she must surely be sated by now; then again, Diana felt like she had only scraped the tip of the surface of want. Once Diana's shoulder was fully healed, she had plans for Naomi's future that involved a lot of inventive ways to use walls in ways that hadn't been intended by the architect. Mostly taking her against all of them. "Surely some of that I could have figured out by myself. I'm a detective."

"You never gave it a shot on your own?"

"Never saw what the fuss was about. Damn."

"It feels kind of criminal, considering how easy it was."

"If it was easy, it would have happened before."

"Maybe, maybe not. Depends on a lot of factors. Mood, anticipation, ovulation, attraction."

"So you're not worried about doing—whatever we're doing— with a straight woman?"

Naomi chuckled. "You're not straight, Detective. Straight women aren't that into me. Not knuckle-deep into me. Where did you even..."

"Well, I mean, I hadn't been with a woman before. I didn't know if I'd be that into—into what we did. But I figured I enjoyed you a lot more than anyone else. It was you taking all the risks. I might not have been any good."

"Yeah, actually, how did you—"

"I, uh, I read a lot of those books. They were quite—uh—informative. And you did most of the work."

Naomi's smile was shy when she lay back beside her, especially considering what Diana had seen that mouth do.

Diana kissed her again, rolling over and pinning Naomi beneath her. "Oh, and I know you're fond of calling me 'Detective,' but you're legally incorrect as of two days ago."

"What should I call you then?"

"You're talking to Lieutenant Stapleton. But you can call me Diana."

"You'd better make it up to captain soon."

"Why?"

"Well, I won't go down on your ship, but I will go down on you."

Diana chuckled, feeling Naomi's own laughter against her chin, then her lips again. "I think we proved I don't need to be a captain for you to do that."

"I know, but 'aye, aye, Lieutenant' just isn't as sexy."

"You don't think I'm sexy?"

"I think I disproved that theory quite some time ago." Naomi pulled away so she could look at Diana again—all of her—hungrily. Diana felt herself stirring, although she had been sure she'd been completely sated only a few minutes ago. Naomi had done more for her in an afternoon than Andrew had done during their entire marriage. And she felt more for Naomi—more affection, more desire, more of everything she hadn't realized her marriage had been missing—than she'd ever felt for anyone.

She let a finger trace over Naomi's lips, watching as Naomi's mouth fell open for her. Naomi trusted her with everything she was. She leaned down to kiss her, dragging her lips slowly over Naomi's to show her esteem, her affection, her gratitude. Naomi smiled against her lips.

"Throw the book at me, Lieutenant, because I am going to break the federal Lawrence vs Texas laws on you."

"I already told you. I'm not a federal agent," Diana reminded her.

Diana couldn't get enough of the feel of Naomi's skin under her fingers, or against her own skin. It was like after a lifetime of strawberry flavoring, she'd finally tried a real strawberry, and it was better than she'd ever expected.

Naomi had been fastidious about rectifying Diana's lack of orgasms.

But Naomi had also spent the time making Diana feel safe and coveted. A lot of things made sense now.

Diana hadn't expected to be able to please Naomi. She'd thought she'd be too inexperienced, not even able to figure out her own body. But Naomi had been so easy to read, such a good guide, and Diana had actually wanted to do—everything. Everything with her.

She'd never liked her own body, never lingered in nudity, knowing it to be an invitation. She didn't mind extending that sort of invitation to Naomi; Naomi was more than welcome to Diana.

There was no hurry or shame here. If she were to dress, so too would Naomi, and Diana couldn't bear to lose sight of her now that she'd seen all of her.

Daisy had called Diana possessive; she knew this now to be true. She thought of Naomi as hers, almost since they'd met. She knew Naomi was her own person, but she wanted Naomi to be hers in some way. In this way.

Naomi, oblivious, stretched out beside her with a little yawn. "Would you like dinner? With what you brought me, I should be able to eat something."

"I want you," Diana said, her voice hoarse.

"You did already prove that," Naomi conceded. "But you can have me again after dinner if you'd like. I'm hungry, and it seems like I was never hungry until I met you."

"Good," Diana said. She'd been overbearing, she knew that now. But she could already see the difference in Naomi's body from when they met. The knobs of her spine weren't as sharp and obvious, and there was a softness to her that hadn't been there before. "I'm sure it's just all the weed you had to take to put up with living with me."

"I liked living with you. I hadn't been lonely before, but now that I'm not with you I notice." Naomi yawned and Diana watched. "Dinner?"

"If you're sure."

Naomi looked down at Diana, partially covered with the sheet, and her face was very serious. Her hand slid over Diana's chest, cupping her chin as she leaned down to kiss her tenderly.

"I'm so sure."

And then, after dinner, cuddled up on the couch, Naomi asked, "Would you like to stay the night?"

Diana closed her eyes and kissed Naomi's temple, holding her close in front of the muted television, missing the plot as subtitles flashed past. "More than anything," Diana whispered.

Naomi hummed with pleasure and let herself nestle truly against Diana, like she'd been holding back all this time. Their bodies welcomed the proximity and adjusted automatically to make each other comfortable.

Diana enjoyed everything Naomi's body had to offer, and it had all been amazing, but she loved the way they fit together like this almost as much. The way they melted against each other, the intimacy of holding and being held. The comfort of existing with someone who not only enjoyed but delighted in her company. Diana felt safe and welcome and she hoped she made Naomi feel the same way.

"Since we're talking," Diana said seriously. "I know you've already been invited, and you turned Kate down when she asked. But I was hoping it might change your mind if it was me…asking you to be my date for Christmas dinner with my family."

Naomi's eyes misted up and Diana held her, concerned.

"I'm sorry. I shouldn't have asked. You told Kate no, and no means no, I keep screwing this up. You're right; it's going to be too noisy, and we won't make up for your own family. I'm sorry I asked."

"I'm not. I'd love to come, if I'm coming as your…date."

"It's too soon for anything else, isn't it?"

"Date sounds perfect." Naomi kissed her like she was something wonderful.

"You'll tell me, won't you? If I'm asking too much? Expecting too much? If it's going to set off a migraine flare, then of course I don't want you to come. I want you to take care of yourself. It was just…" Diana exhaled, watching her fingers dance along Naomi's flank, grasping her hip at the end of their journey. "Just me making sure you know I like you. I haven't done this since I was a teenager, and it never felt like it mattered back then. You matter. That's why I'm so nervous."

"I'd love to come."

"I thought you already did," Diana joked with relief, gratified when Naomi chuckled.

"And I will again. But I mean it. I'd go anywhere with you, for you, as long as I'm with you. As long as I'm your date. As long as—as long as I'm yours."

They hadn't spoken yet about how serious this thing between them was. Diana took Naomi's hand and held it, sliding her fingers over skin so soft and lovely, over a hand that fit perfectly in hers. Diana brought Naomi's hand to her mouth and kissed her knuckles.

"I'm yours," Diana said quietly, meaning it. "If you want me. I mean, I want you. As my date. I want you to come with me. I want you to come for me, but only if and when you want to."

Naomi gave her a look so soft and loving that Diana's anxiety faded away, and she held Naomi close, kissing her temple. It might be new, it might not last forever, but for right now it was what Naomi had said—perfect.

EPILOGUE

Diana opened the door, kissing Naomi's cheek and taking her coat. Naomi turned back to her shyly; she was in a forest-green blouse and a pair of corduroy slacks. She was wearing a little makeup, and her headphones matched her blouse.

"Oh. Oh, wow. You look gorgeous. I mean, you always look gorgeous, but I wish it wasn't Christmas dinner right now even though I feel like all my Christmases have come at once and hopefully we will later too, but, um. You look gorgeous. You always do, because you're gorgeous, but you're especially gorgeous tonight."

Naomi chuckled and kissed Diana's cheek. "Thank you."

Diana looked behind her, into the house, then dragged Naomi into the room that once had been the parlor. She kissed Naomi thoroughly, unable to help herself.

"Who is it?" Jake called from further in the house. Naomi flinched and Diana pulled away.

"We're working on it. Sorry."

"It's Christmas. I didn't drive, and I hope you have a spare bed for me." Naomi smiled her mellowed grin, which Diana understood.

"That can be arranged." Diana rested her forehead against Naomi's for a moment, then took a deep breath. "Are you ready?"

"As I can be," Naomi said honestly.

* * *

After dinner, Naomi took Brian to the back room to give him a bottle so she could have a break from all the noise of the Stapleton family, and so Kate and Matt could have a break from Brian. She looked up, unsurprised, when Diana joined her a few minutes later.

Diana looked nervous. "Daisy said if we got married, I could get you on my health insurance. I have really good health insurance. She said there are some more things she can look into, to make sure you're more comfortable when you do have to be at events like these."

"I bet your insurance is really good. You've been shot and stabbed and you still have a house and a cabin all your own." Naomi looked down at Brian. "You know no insurance or medical intervention will actually fix me, don't you? You don't expect me to be cured? You know that's never going to happen, no matter how good your health insurance is?"

"This is how you are, and I love how you are. I don't like that it hurts you to exist, but I'm happy to change my life to make yours more comfortable."

There was silence between them for a moment.

"You're one in a million, Diana, but I'm very independent," Naomi said carefully. They'd spent almost every night together since Thanksgiving, shortly after Violet's birthday. Almost every day, too.

Naomi had never pictured herself dating again, but it hadn't felt like dating with Diana. It had felt like coming home after an especially long and lonely day. It had felt like having a family, sharing Diana's. Brian nuzzled into her, and she watched him closely. He was such a lovely, happy baby. He was sitting up on his own now, and Naomi had loved watching him grow. Violet too was growing up, her reading voice so much more confident.

Kate had always welcomed Naomi, and Matt was more than happy to sign all night. He had a wicked sense of humor, and he'd convinced the rest of the extended family to learn ASL so they could find out for themselves what he and Naomi were laughing over. Jake always made a concentrated effort to soften his voice, understanding that his register rather than the volume was the issue and not taking it personally.

It was the best Christmas Naomi had been part of since she was a kid and still believed in made up things like Santa and unconditional love from her family. She felt accepted and loved, and while efforts had been made to accommodate her, they felt effortless, natural, like they didn't mind the inconvenience as long as Naomi felt comfortable and welcome. She'd offered to feed Brian for some peace and quiet, but also because she inexplicably wanted to cry.

"And so am I."

"I don't really need your health insurance. But I do need you."

"If it sweetens the deal any, I, um. I do actually love you. Sorry. I probably should have started with that. Not health insurance. It's not very romantic. But I would like to marry you because I love you, not just so you'd be able to access my health insurance."

"You're very practical," Naomi teased, then grew serious. "In fact, it's one of the things that I love about you."

However, something had been bugging Naomi. Diana rarely initiated sex. She seemed pleased that she'd figured it out, and she was affectionate as well as passionate when Naomi offered it to her, but she seldom asked for it. She had even turned it down a few times. She was enthusiastic in the moment, but it made Naomi insecure. It made her wonder if she'd coerced Diana into something she didn't want.

"Are we okay? You are attracted to me, aren't you?" she asked finally.

"Of course I am. More than anyone else I've ever known. What's brought this on?"

"You never initiate, and sometimes you turn me down. I'm probably just feeling insecure, but it makes me wonder."

"Oh, honey." Diana kissed Naomi's temple and Naomi leaned into her, closing her eyes as Diana's arm slid over her shoulders. "It's the luxury of saying no without consequences. I always want you. But sometimes I still panic at the thought of sex, even with you. Sometimes I just want to be held, and if I say no, you hold me without pressuring me for more. And that's—if I have to be honest, that's almost better than sex. To be respected when I make a choice and not have you withdraw affection or become violent or even give me the silent treatment. You don't resent me for it. I still get to touch you all over, I still get to kiss you while I figure everything out. You make me feel valued and loved no matter what we do, and sometimes I just want to curl up with you and feel your heart beat against my chest with nothing in the way. I hadn't realized it was hurting you. I'm sorry for being so selfish. My therapist said that you can't take the measure of someone until you tell them no, and you are the only person I feel safe enough to say it to."

"Oh. It's not—I just, you know. You were straight before me. It just made me wonder if you were attracted to women. Or me." Naomi shifted Brian in her arms and settled in closer against Diana, who kissed her temple again.

"I was never straight. I don't think so, at least. I just wasn't sure enough of what I wanted until it became so obvious that I could no longer ignore it. With Andrew, I didn't care enough to turn him down when he asked me to marry him. With you, I feel like a stupid teenager. If you wanted to rob a bank with me, I totally would. I'd do anything for you. This is the first time in my life— the first relationship in my life—where I can say no and know with complete certainty that nothing bad will happen to me. It's the first time I've felt truly safe with someone."

"Yet your thoughts immediately turn to felony. Interesting." Naomi chuckled.

Diana shook her head, rolling her eyes. "I'd give up my job if you asked. I already took a promotion I'd been putting off because you were worried."

"I'm not going to—I don't want you to make life choices around me."

"You're the only life choice I've ever made on my own. My marriage, my career—my parents pushed me into both. It's ridiculous. I'm in my fifties and I've barely made any choices for myself. My parents bought the house. I inherited it and the cabin simply because my brother already had property. I'm always going to choose you. I know it's too soon for a lifetime commitment, but I've wasted too much of my life without having you in it. So if you're worried I'm not attracted to you, I can prove it to you later. If you're worried I'm not serious about you, then you need to come up to my bedroom right now."

"There are people here, Diana!"

"Not for—not for that," Diana said, blushing. "Come on. It'll just take a minute."

Naomi passed Brian to a smirking Kate, who raised her eyebrows suggestively as she followed Diana upstairs. There was a jewelry box on Diana's bedside table, and Diana picked it up.

"I took it out of my safe deposit box a few weeks ago. I thought it was too much, too soon, but if you have doubts then I need to prove I'm serious about you." She handed the box to Naomi. "It was my mother's," she added nervously when Naomi didn't respond, staring into the box. "I know it's an old-fashioned wedding ring and it's not modern and you deserve one that you like…"

"No, it's perfect. It means something to you."

"You mean everything to me," Diana said, her voice cracking.

"You said something earlier, and I didn't really—I mean, I love you too."

"Then that's enough of an answer. For now. I'll ask again in a couple of months, but it's not just health insurance for me. I've never been able to picture spending the rest of my life with someone, and now I'm mad because the rest of my life doesn't feel long enough when it's you I get to spend it with."

Naomi had found herself melting a lot over the last few months. When Diana used sign language, when she tailored her voice to comfortable levels, when she smiled with that dimple. But now Naomi was melting all over again.

"I'll be counting the days," Naomi said breathlessly. If she accepted tonight, with all of Diana's family here, she couldn't have her way with Diana as her brand-new fiancée. But knowing that Diana knew all of her and saw all of her and wanted to marry her anyway was enough for now. She wanted nothing more than to marry this woman with her infuriatingly tight jeans and nurturing nature, a woman who accommodated her effortlessly, who had never been annoyed by Naomi's aversion to noise, who had selflessly let herself get shot to protect Naomi. "In fact…" Naomi dug in her pocket for a moment, pulling out a little velvet jewelry pouch of her own and turning it over in her hand before handing it to Diana.

Diana opened the pouch and took out the emerald ring Naomi had chosen so carefully, matching it against the color Diana most often wore. She watched as Diana examined it, then slid it onto the finger that had remained unadorned since Diana had come over to apologize. She saw Diana's tongue wet her lips as though she was about to speak, but she swallowed instead, her eyes shining gold behind welling tears.

"I'm just annoyed you beat me to it," Naomi said nervously as Diana's arms opened for her. She hadn't expected to be rejected, but it felt too soon. But as Diana had said, they'd wasted so much of their lives without each other that waiting seemed senseless.

She stepped forward into Diana's strong arms and felt them close around her. She nuzzled closer against Diana, warm and comfortable. Diana kissed her forehead, and they wondered how, of all things, it had started with shutters.